Thistle AND Twigg

ALSO BY MARY SAUMS

Midnight Hour
The Valley of Jewels
When the Last Magnolia Weeps

Thistle
AND
Twigg

MARY SAUMS

ST. MARTIN'S MINOTAUR
New York

THISTLE AND TWIGG. Copyright © 2007 by Mary Saums.
All rights reserved. Printed in the United States of America.
No part of this book may be used or reproduced in any manner whatsoever
without written permission except in the case of brief quotations
embodied in critical articles or reviews. For information,
address St. Martin's Press,
175 Fifth Avenue, New York, N.Y. 10010.

www.minotaurbooks.com

Book design by Mary A. Wirth

LIBRARY OF CONGRESS CATALOGING-IN-PUBLICATION DATA

Saums, Mary.
  Thistle and Twigg / Mary Saums.—1st ed.
    p. cm.
  ISBN-13: 978-0-312-36063-4
  ISBN-10: 0-312-36063-0
  1. Widows—Fiction. 2. Alabama—Fiction. I. Title.

PS3569.A78875T47 2007
813'.6—dc22

                                        2006048684

First Edition: April 2007

10 9 8 7 6 5 4 3 2 1

Thistle AND *Twigg*

one

Jane Thistle Arrives

I knew from the first there was something odd about Tullulah, knew it even before I saw the town itself. The feeling struck and traveled deeply into memories I'd not thought of in years, something vague and hard to discern, like an overgrown path found at last with a little searching. Oh, yes, I felt it immediately, as soon as I entered the forest that surrounds it, guards it like a secret treasure, and it was this, you see, that drew me in.

My first day as an official citizen of Tullulah began with a spectacular omen of things to come. A monstrous brown snake, at least eight feet long and several inches thick, slithered across the threshold of my front door. Naturally, the men from the moving company had left the door open all morning as they moved furniture and boxes inside. It didn't occur to any of us this might be seen as an open invitation to the local wildlife.

The snake zigzagged across the wood parquet and down the hall, then turned right into the living room as if he'd dropped by for tea. He meant us no harm and came to none himself, although I must say I'm not at all squeamish and would certainly have shot the trespassing beast if necessary.

One of the men screamed. The others laughed at the poor fellow, but if the truth were told, we all had a good scare. The snake sidled with frightening quickness, its sideways movement making it difficult for us to predict the direction of its intended course. One of the movers grabbed a wide push broom then scooted the snake, a nonpoisonous one I was assured, out the door and off the porch.

The incident, though surprising, was also strangely calming, I thought, as I watched the snake swish across my yard into the tall grass that bordered Anisidi Wildlife Refuge next door. The snake's ancestors, as well as those of the other animals here, had survived on this piece of land for centuries, longer actually. As the newcomer, I intended to live peacefully with my neighbors, even those of the reptilian persuasion. Within reason, of course.

This, after all, was why I came to this place of special beauty after discovering it completely by accident. Do you believe in chance? I'm not altogether sure I do anymore. For now, let us say that it was, in fact, chance that brought me here.

Almost twenty years ago, I was driving from Florida where my late husband, Colonel John Bradford Thistle, and I lived. In the fall of that year, he'd received a transfer to a facility in the Midwest and had already flown there to begin his new assignment. It fell to me to stay behind, pack our belongings, and arrange for the moving company, just as I had done many times since our marriage years earlier when he was a dapper young officer and I was his English bride.

My leisurely drive northwest from Florida was, for the most part, uneventful until an hour or so past Birmingham where, on a whim, I decided to take an alternate route, away from the interstate, for a more scenic drive.

And scenic it was. I had not seen such beautiful valleys and farmlands since I'd left England, perhaps earlier when as a child I'd visited my grandparents in Wales. The thought of their home, the surrounding countryside, the mysterious look of the land, the play of light and color all came back to me, stirring memories.

That's when it began, the odd sensation. At first, it was only that, just a hint of something fresh and new in the air, like the scent of pine that blew in my open windows. A large highway sign indicated I could enter Bankhead National Forest at the next exit, and I could see a great expanse of green ahead as I topped hills.

Trees grew thicker on either side of the road as the car traveled steadily upward. The air was heavy with the sound of birds' wings rustling in and out of branches. I had the sense of going back in time, as if I were returning rather than arriving, something I couldn't define.

I crested a small hill and slowed as I passed a little clearing with a neatly painted white board sign that bore three lines of text in pretty script: "Welcome to Tullulah, Population 9,523, or Thereabouts." A lattice trellis framed it, twined with ivy and a beautiful yellow climbing rose. Below me, perhaps a quarter of a mile away, I could see a quaint town square that echoed the neatness of the welcome sign. Beyond the buildings, a vast green backdrop of forest stretched to the horizon, with occasional rock-face cliffs jutting out of tree-covered mountains in the distance.

While I waited at the first stoplight just outside of town, I had a lovely personal welcome. A mockingbird lit on my car door's rearview mirror and cocked an eye, studying me, then sang a melodious greeting. He trilled through quite a repertoire, looking at me all the while. One gray wing was a bit damaged on its white stripe, yet the bird was able to hop into the air and fly for a short distance as it sang a three-note farewell.

I drove around the square to look for a place to eat and parked near the City Grill. And there, as I walked down the quiet sidewalk, was where I first saw the girl.

She waved coyly to me, smiling as if she had a secret, then ran quickly around the side of a building. I'd say she was about seven years old and had long dark hair in ringlets falling past the shoulders of her white lace dress.

I looked down the alleyway as I walked by it, but she was nowhere in sight. I wondered at the time if perhaps she wasn't being naughty, playing outside in her fancy dress when I was sure her mother would have forbidden it.

I thought no more of it, had my meal, and drove slowly about the little town before leaving, trying to put my finger on why the area brought back memories of my childhood. Not even memories really; there was no certain place that reminded me of another specific location from that time. Yet there was a connection, I was certain of it.

And then a strange thing happened. As I drove out of town, I glanced at the welcome sign again, this time at its reverse side. To my eyes, the sign said, "Come Back, Jane," as I passed it. I would have sworn it.

I braked instantly. Fortunately, there was no one behind me. At the next opportunity, I turned the car around and drove past the sign once more. It clearly said, "Come Back Again." I attributed misreading it the first time to being distracted, perhaps a little disoriented by driving in a new place, or to driver's fatigue. However, deep down, something disturbed me. I didn't know why.

It would be another year before I figured it out. Tullulah haunted me all that time. I took to studying the area and its history, searching for books of which there were precious few. That scarcity may have been the great attraction to studying it. It was a new and exotic place of which I had no knowledge.

So, when I had to drive through Alabama to Florida again a

year later, I made a point of visiting Tullulah. I rolled down my windows, breathed in the pine scent, and drove past the welcome sign toward the town square to park near the City Grill, just as before. And just as before, there was the little girl, waving coyly, standing in her white lace dress, running shyly away and disappearing behind the same building. She hadn't aged a day.

I must say I was a bit shocked. After I thought about it awhile, everything fell into place. I understood the connection to my past, why I'd experienced the déjà vu. My childhood had been filled with such images, ones dismissed by my parents and siblings, so much so that I pushed them all away and had forgotten them. But now, after years of denial, they'd come back to me. I could see ghosts.

Something about Tullulah must have made them visible once again. I had no such visions elsewhere. After my return home, I began more intense study of the national park and the other woodland areas of northern Alabama. I dreamed of it, of the deep tranquility I'd felt while in the midst of the forest, and of returning one day. Not for the ghosts, certainly, but for the serenity and the indefinable quality in the air that, once breathed in, possessed me with a great longing for its peace. Years later, when my husband passed away, there was no question what I would do. When his estate was settled, I packed a bag and spent a week in Tullulah looking at property.

There was really only one choice. One place had a strong sense of connection, and of peace. The old house beside the wildlife refuge, far outside the town limits, seemed to call to me and welcome me in.

It's just what I've always wanted, to live in a beautiful place where I can relax and never have to move again. The Colonel and I had a deal, you see. Traveling from base to base had been necessary for his work. I knew that when I married him. Since his job required constant travel, he promised our retirement years would be spent wherever I wished. After so many years of having no roots, I realized my home was wherever he was happy. He liked Florida, so I told him that's where I wanted to retire. We were content there, but when his health began to fail, I knew I would not stay after he was gone.

Through the years, Tullulah had been my secret, the one thing I didn't share with my husband. I knew he wouldn't be happy in a small town, this one in particular. It was much too quiet and sleepy of a place. His personality craved movement, excitement, lots of goings-on around him. He was a city man, accustomed to the bases filled with likeminded men who had also seen the world and conquered it.

No, I knew he wouldn't care for Tullulah, not at all. For me, it represented everything I'd missed. Beautiful countryside, a slow pace of living. But most of all, a different sort of community from those we were used to. No flat utilitarian, ugly buildings of blocks painted white, or worse, service gray or green. Here the houses and even the businesses surrounding the courthouse square all had personalities to match the people—open, friendly, and beautifully devoid of the harsh, sarcastic atmosphere of cramped city life.

After that second visit to Tullulah, I became restless, obsessed even. I'd always been a student of history and of the natural world; those things fascinated me and led me to the love of archaeology and ancient civilizations. Learning about the first inhabitants of the area, several native tribes and all new to me, and the array of wild species and their habitats sparked my mind as it had not been stimulated in many years. And so, when the Colonel was gone, I sold our house in Florida, hired a moving company, and set off for my new life.

After the snake incident that first day, I thought it wise to have a pistol handy. My new house was, after all, bordered by the wildlife refuge on one side and a privately owned forest on another, both of which surely harbored many a wild animal. I found a pistol easily in my old antique trunk, but had no luck in locating the proper bullets among the packing boxes. With the thought that it could be days, weeks even, before I had everything unpacked, I determined to get a box of bullets when I stepped out to pick up lunch for the movers and myself.

That was how I came to meet Phoebe Twigg, a lifetime resident of Tullulah, who has become my closest friend. I'm sixty-seven and she is sixty-five, although she looks much younger. Her most prominent feature is her flaming red hair, of which she is understandably quite proud. Her clothes reflect her flair for the dramatic with wild color combinations. She makes me feel quite pale and small in comparison.

Phoebe is a perfect dear. She makes me laugh. There's nothing she loves more than to entertain with a good story. Facts are of minimal importance and serve only as a springboard for great leaps of imagination and elongated stretches of the truth.

Unfortunately, someone unfamiliar with Phoebe's tendency to embroider reality overheard one such fantasy and came to believe Phoebe knew more than she actually did. Although she didn't mean to, Phoebe put us both in great danger. I have absolutely no doubt, however, she'd tell a much different story.

two

Phoebe Twigg
Sets Things Straight

*D*on't you believe a single word Jane Thistle tells you. She means well, bless her heart, and she's sweet as can be. She just doesn't always understand what's going on down here like I do.

It's not her fault. Jane is about the smartest person, man or woman, I've ever known. She can tell one Shakespeare play from another. Operas and symphonies, too. All that hard stuff. I want you to know she can tell which modern psycho artist painted what, even with nothing but dots and splatters to go on.

And those artsy things aren't even her strongest subjects. History and archaeology are what she loves because she has worked on dig sites ever since she was a teenager. And trees, Lord have mercy, how she loves plain old ugly trees and plants. Knows their

Latin names and everything. Anything green, old, or dead and gone for centuries, Jane knows about it.

I bet she didn't tell you any of that, did she? That's because Thistle is a real lady and she don't go around tooting her own horn like a brazen heifer. She's a bona fide proper Englishwoman, even though she says she's completely American now after living in the States for nearly fifty years.

Yes, ma'am, I tell you what, Jane Thistle is sharp as a hound's tooth and is a saint on top of that. She'd have to be to put up with that Colonel Board-Up-His-Backside husband of hers for so many years. I never actually met him, you understand, but I've seen his pictures. From the way she carries on about him, you'd think he hung the moon or invented chewing gum or something.

She really is so naive about people. Her husband probably made her that way, always barking orders at her, I bet you. Now, she wouldn't say that in so many words. But I can tell he must have been an ornery old cuss from the way he's glowering out of every single one of them pictures in her house like a mean bulldog.

Oh, I know he was a colonel, but titles don't mean zip to me. And I'm not saying he didn't have one or two redeeming qualities. He had at least one I know of: He taught Jane to shoot. Now that I think about it, if it hadn't been for that, I wouldn't have met her that first day she moved to town.

She was standing in line at the back counter of Harvel Wriggle's Sporting Goods Store. My brother Eugene was having a birthday, and I had gone into Wriggle's to buy him a new tackle box since fishing takes up the better part of his mind.

"Pardon me, sir," Jane said, and I knew right away she was English. I grabbed the closest tackle box, a plastic lime green see-through number, and hustled over to stand in line behind her. I just love British accents and I didn't want to miss a single word.

Harvel Wriggle noticed her accent, too, which only confirmed what I've always known about him—he's not as dumb as he looks.

He slicked his hair back with one hand, flattening his cowlick down.

"Yes, ma'am. What can I do for you?" he said, with the cowlick springing up at the end of his sentence like a question mark on top of his head. I couldn't help but laugh which, from the look he gave me, Harvel did not appreciate one bit.

He turned his attention back to Jane, all cute and silver-haired and hardly big as a minute. I wondered if she fixed her own hair. It waved and curled just perfect around her ears. Very classy. Jane has what I call a high-class face, with her little turned-up nose and high cheekbones. She's got real black eyes that sparkle, and she's always smiling. The beige and camel outfit she wore that day also showed what good taste she has and how subdued and genteel she is. I wouldn't be caught dead in beige myself, way too drab, but it looked good on her.

"Yes, thank you," she said to Harvel. "I'd like to purchase a small box of 9-millimeter bullets and another of 12-gauge shotgun shells, if I may please."

Well, let me tell you what. You could have knocked me and Harvel both over with a chicken feather. I knew right then Jane and I were going to be close friends.

Harvel just stood there, staring at her with his mouth hanging open.

"What's the matter?" I asked him. "You look like you never heard a lady ask for bullets before."

"Well," he said and cleared his throat. "It is mighty unusual. I believe it's a first, around here anyway." Some old retired guys, who hang out there at the store because their wives can't stand them in the house all day, chuckled like it was the funniest thing in the world.

Believe me, I've been around here a long time, and I know exactly how these men think. I could read Harvel's mind like his forehead was made out of Cling Wrap. He might be laughing but inside he was scared. Men around here like their women docile as old cows, and don't want to face the fact that one might get trigger-happy. I tell you, it was a real treat to see old Harvel squirm.

I tapped Jane on the shoulder. "Thank goodness 'unusual' ain't the same thing as 'illegal,' right, hon?"

I winked at her and nodded at Harvel, who hadn't moved an inch and still had his hands flat on the counter. I said, "Harvel." I said, "Women are citizens just like you men. We've got the right to bear arms just like y'all, don't we? Unless you boys have gone and changed the Constitution of the United States of America when I wasn't paying attention. It *is* legal for a woman to buy bullets, isn't it?" I jerked my head toward the boxes behind him.

"Yes, oh yes," he said, finally turning around to the shelves behind him to pick out the two boxes Jane had asked for.

Meanwhile, I introduced myself. Jane and I had a nice little chat. She told me she had picked up some lunch for herself and the men from the moving company. After she got her bullets, she had one more stop, to buy an electric blanket. Jane had seen the weather forecast for chilly nights later in the week and realized the little thin blankets she'd used in Florida weren't going to be enough in Tullulah, especially with fall coming on.

She told me she'd only been for a couple of short visits before deciding to buy a house here. It struck me as being a strange thing, to move someplace where you don't have any relatives or friends. Don't you think that's strange? I mean, especially at Jane's age. But that was really none of my business, so I didn't pry.

I told her I already knew where she lived. Everybody knew. The old Hardwick place out Anisidi Road had been empty and on the market for at least a year due to its remote location and high price.

Jane told us about a big snake coming in her house that morning; that's why she thought she better come get some bullets. One of the old geezers in the corner said, "I reckon that ain't gonna be much help against some other things in that house." His buddies all giggled and shook like a bunch of little girls.

"Don't pay them any mind, Jane. They're only here because the mental hospital ain't got room for all of them right now."

The Hardwick place is kind of famous around here. It sits on the edge of the refuge, way out there by itself in the sticks, and is over a hundred and fifty years old. The Daughters of Historical Southern Heritage got it designated as an official historic site some time back. This was because the house was used as a hospital for Civil War soldiers wounded at the Battle of Cokers Branch, which happened not too far away. Bullet holes are still all over the old brick fireplaces. So, naturally, that made the house's asking price pretty steep, too high for most folks in town.

Jane said she liked it being out by itself and planned to take long walks everyday on the refuge trails that are right close to her property. Since I like to get out and walk, too, I told her I might go with her someday.

"Let's get together sometime soon," I said.

"I'd enjoy that very much," she said as she turned to go. "Please stop by anytime. So nice to meet you, Phoebe."

I told you she was a lady. "Hey, listen. Hang on just a minute, Jane. Let me pay for this and then let's walk out together."

While Harvel was ringing up the tackle box, I said to him, "Before you total that up, I'd also like to purchase a box of bullets, if I may please." I smiled at him. Mind you, I had no need of bullets myself and had never even touched a gun in all my sixty-five years. But when Jane stood up to the regime like she did, even if she didn't know she was doing it, it was a star-spangled moment for me.

Not long before, I'd seen that home-decorating show *DiDi Moody's House of Beauty*, which comes out of Florence on Wednesday mornings. DiDi said that the best room accessories are ones that have special meaning to you personally.

It was like a light went on. I went straight upstairs and got in my cedar chest where I kept such things, stuff that represented important days in my life. I took a small tablecloth that had been a wedding gift and covered a little table my granddaddy made. On top, I set my most special treasures. So see, I wanted those bullets for my table, so I'd remember Jane standing up to the Man for her rights, right here in Tullulah, Alabama, where I was an eyewitness. I had no intention to actually use the bullets. Although, when Harvel piped up, I admit a good use for them did cross my mind.

"Aw, Phoebe, come on now," he said, snickering. "That's ridiculous. You don't have a gun. And wouldn't know what to do with one if you did. *Snick snick snick.*"

"Harvel Wriggle." I blew out some steam and bit my tongue rather than give him a piece of my mind. "Just give me a box of bullets like I asked you, please." Sometimes a lady has to get a little mean before a man will listen, although I pride myself in having a soft voice and kind manner at least ninety-five percent of the time.

"Well, you have to tell me what kind," he said and winked at the old geezers. "Do you want .45 caliber? .357? How about some .44 Magnums so you and Dirty Harry can go out and blow away some street punks?" More guffaws from the eejit corner.

"Ha. Ha. You're just as funny as you were in junior high."

I looked around on the shelves. "Right there," I said pointing. "The blue box with the little picture on it. I like that one." I looked closer when he handed it to me to see what the picture was on top. "A sword and an olive branch?"

Harvel plopped his hands on the counter. "Yep. Made in Israel."

"Oo-wee. Now that's what I'm talking about," I said. "Serious high quality."

He gave the old guys another look but I didn't care. I left thinking about more important things, like a little gift for Jane and where on my memento table I'd display my pretty new box of Israeli bullets.

three

Jane Goes to Phoebe's House

"Now then," Phoebe said, as she gripped her brown paper sack and adjusted the purse on her shoulder. We walked outside the sporting goods store onto the town square's sidewalk. It was a glorious day with a hint of autumn in the air. Only a few high clouds dotted the sky that was a deep cerulean blue. How nice it was to breathe air heavily scented with the maples, oaks, and evergreen trees that were so prevalent, even in the middle of town.

When I turned my head toward Phoebe, I looked in the direction of the City Grill. Just beyond it in the alleyway between the café and Lloyd's Drugs, a small head peeped around the corner. It was the little girl with ringlets. She grinned and waved to me. I smiled and waved back without thinking, then dropped my hand self-consciously.

Phoebe glanced in her direction. I assume she saw nothing, for when she turned again to me, she had a most curious look on her face, one that questioned my sanity.

"What I'm thinking, Jane," Phoebe said, politely ignoring the incident, "is, rather than you going and buying an electric blanket, let me just give you one."

I was taken aback. I tried to protest but she insisted.

"No, see, here's the thing. My sister Geraldine gave me one for Christmas two years ago. I tried it one night and nearly burnt up, even on the lowest setting. I'm just naturally hot-natured. I only used it that once, and it was with the sheets and comforter straight out of the dryer, so the blanket is clean and like brand-new. I put it right back in the box, so it doesn't even have any dust on it."

"My goodness," I said. "That's very generous. I'll be happy to pay you for it."

"Heavens, no. You'll be doing me a favor, getting it out of my way. Here's my car. Where are you parked? Come on and follow me over to my house, why don't you? That'll take care of that, and you won't have to go buy one. Save your money. You might need you some more bullets," she said with a wink.

We drove to a quiet, older neighborhood only a few streets away from the square. The houses looked as if they were built in the twenties or thirties, most in a bungalow style. Phoebe's house, painted a cheery lemon yellow, had a screened porch in front trimmed in white. A variety of mums and pansies filled her flower-beds with a beautiful display of color. Ivy grew beneath dark green window boxes and shutters. An American flag attached next to the porch's entrance moved gently in the breeze. Leaves from large maple trees made a beautiful sound in the wind as shade and sun-light dappled the front lawn.

"What a beautiful place," I said as we walked into the backyard and up the steps to her back door.

"Why, thank you. Come on in. Don't mind the mess."

There was no mess. We stepped into the kitchen that was tidy as could be. The aroma of baked fruit pies filled the room, which was shining and spotless.

Phoebe led me through to the living room and said, "Make yourself at home." She reached into her brown bag from Wriggle's, came out with the box of bullets she'd just purchased, and set it down on a table by her couch. She eyed its position a moment, then moved one end of the box about a quarter of an inch. "Now then," she said, and with a satisfied smile, she disappeared up the staircase.

Light flooded the living room through four paned windows where pastel coral curtains had been drawn aside. The hardwood floor shone as if freshly waxed and polished. Several large beige rugs highlighted in oranges and browns lay scattered about the floor. They had a Native American look, as did the entire room. On each wall hung paintings of Indians on horseback or in family settings. Several dream catchers of twine and feathers decorated one of the windows.

I walked to her television set. Video boxes, all lined neatly and in alphabetical order, filled a shelf underneath a video player. The first were how-to titles: *Appliqués for Every Occasion, Country Cooking with Carlene, Gardening for Four Seasons, Make Your Own Slipcovers, Martha Stewart's Simple Springtime Entertaining.* Next came movies: *Cobra, Delta Force, Dirty Harry, Missing in Action, Rambo: First Blood, Rambo: First Blood Part II, Rambo III, Red Heat, The Trouble with Angels.*

The table where Phoebe had placed the bullets held other objects of interest. I walked over to see them more closely. A lamp took up most of the space, its shade an Indian pattern in turquoise and deep brown. A white satin rectangle with a picture of a waterfall and the words "Ruby Falls" covered the table. Royal blue tassels hung off the corners over a red underskirt. Figurines of a black bear and two cubs huddled close to the lamp. On the wall above it, a novelty clock in the shape of Elvis Presley clicked the time, his dancing, splayed legs rocking left, right, left, right as a pendulum.

When Phoebe returned, she caught me staring too long at a flat, furry object lying outstretched on the tabletop like a miniature bear rug. Instead of a roaring bear head, however, this one had the head of a chipmunk.

"Oh, that's Petey," Phoebe said. "I ran over him when I was taking my driver's test. Flattened him like a little pancake. I got so upset that the instructor giving me the test put his arm around me and asked me out on a date. That was Ronald. His daddy was a taxidermist, so Ronald knew how to stuff animals himself. He fixed Petey up and that was his first present to me. We got married four months later."

I searched for words. "Love at first sight, eh?"

Phoebe sighed. "Yeah. He was a good one. Now then, I hope this will be all right," she said. She handed me a box and lifted the top so I could inspect it. The blanket was in pristine condition, just as she had described it.

"I don't know what to say. Please, let me pay you."

Phoebe's head shook adamantly. "No way. It's a gift. Like a housewarming present, okay?" She patted my arm. "I'm so happy you're here. I hope you won't get bored in Tullulah. We don't have much in the way of fancy entertainment or anything."

"I'm not looking for that. I know I shall be very happy here. Especially if everyone is as kind as you have been. I see you have quite a movie collection to keep yourself entertained."

"Oh! Goodness, you must think I'm terrible with all those shoot-'em-ups. I keep a couple of little boys down the street overnight sometimes. Their mama died about a year back, so me and a couple of other folks take care of them every now and then, you know, to give their daddy a break. Lord knows he needs it with those two. Those movies keep them occupied. I sure don't like the blood and guts parts, though, so when they come on, we go fix us a treat in the kitchen. But I have to say I like ones with a little action because they've got some good stories and some good heroes. And it doesn't hurt that the actors are mighty fine-looking young men. That reminds me, those boys asked me if I'd get them another Chuck Norris movie. Don't you just love him? He is the cutest thing. He's the best-looking one of the whole bunch and the best fighter, too."

Phoebe slipped the blanket box inside a canvas bag with handles. "Here, take this bag. I've made about two dozen of them in art classes. You might be able to use it." Fabric transfers of little children in Native American dress decorated one side of the orange bag. In the background, a deer and an eagle watched the children play. I gratefully accepted both bag and blanket and thanked her again.

On the way to my car, I reflected on the not-so-very-subtle comment made by the man at Wriggle's store concerning my house and its possible spirit inhabitants. I tried to remember what Vince Murphy, my real estate agent, said when he first showed me the house. Although it was much roomier than the one I'd moved from in Florida, I didn't feel lost in it. Quite the contrary. I told Vince it felt as if I weren't alone at all, to which he gave me a sheepish look and said something along the lines of, "No, you'd never have to worry about that here."

It wouldn't have mattered if he'd told me straight out that the house was haunted for, from the moment I saw the Hardwick place, I was entranced. This was it, I thought to myself. I knew it in my bones. The yard, the house itself, the surrounding wooded areas of the Anisidi Wildlife Refuge all drew me in immediately. This was home. I wouldn't have cared a whit if I'd learned there might be others likely to inhabit it along with me.

The house is a two-story farmhouse with an open porch that stretches across its entire width. The two large rockers there when I first viewed the house came free with purchase. Maple, dogwood, sweet gum, oak, pecan, apple, and peach trees shade the large lawn that slopes gently to the borders of the refuge. Inside, the rooms are spacious and cozy at the same time.

Renovations some twenty years earlier modernized the kitchen, and the bathroom fixtures and their black-and-white tile floors were from the forties. Though very well maintained, little else that I could see had been changed since the house was built in the mid-1800s. Before I moved in, I had a local carpenter repair a few minor things and also had him build in floor-to-ceiling bookcases in the largest room, which I planned to use as my den.

I had only one neighbor. Cal Prewitt owned all the land across from me on Anisidi Road. His was a one-hundred-plus-acre plot that ended at the wildlife refuge, which also served as my own property's right boundary. To the north, the Prewitt land extended from the road to a range of cliffs overlooking the Tennessee River and below to the flatland on the river's banks, next to the refuge-duck sanctuary.

I learned these things and a few stories that did not speak well of my new neighbor from Vince, as well as that Cal was getting on in years and was not in the best of health. When I told Vince I would be interested in making an offer on Cal's property as well as the Hardwick place, he laughed.

"I doubt Cal would sell," he said. "People have been trying to get him out of there for years."

"Could we ask? He may have changed his mind since receiving his last offer."

He laughed again but on seeing I was completely serious stopped smiling and began to look worried.

"No, ma'am. I don't see how we could ask. He doesn't have a phone, and I ... that is, everyone knows it's not safe to go down that road."

He pointed to a gap in the hog-wire fence overgrown with tall grasses. There, a one-lane road disappeared into the brush. An old weathered piece of board with hand-painted lettering was tacked to a rusted gatepost, minus a gate. It read, "Stay Out—This Means YOU," in uneven characters.

"Could we please try? Surely he wouldn't mind discussing business that might profit him?"

Vince Murphy weighed the options. Sweat poured down his forehead as we stood in the heat. He ran a finger under the tight collar of his white short-sleeved shirt and then under his light blue tie to loosen it. While he patted a handkerchief around his hairline, his face wrinkled as he considered whether to heed the sign and his better judgment, or take a chance on increasing his commission. The money won.

"Okay," he said, "Let's give it a try. We can drive through one time and look around, even if we don't find Cal." He sounded as if this was his hope—that we wouldn't encounter him. Unfortunately, this had not been the case.

Once past the entrance, the road changed abruptly from asphalt to red dirt with a shallow overlay of rock. On either side of us, fields and woods looked as if no human had ever set foot in them.

We came upon a small, wood-frame house that had once been painted white. A sagging carport jutted out from one side, and an old barn sat farther back in the lot. The only vehicle we saw was parked on the grass, an older model truck with faded green paint.

Just as Vince slowed to a stop, we heard the crack of a shot being fired. Both of us jumped in our seats as the hood ornament of Vince's Chrysler broke off and whirled through the air.

A loud voice yelled at us. "Didn't you see that no trespassing sign?"

From my position scooted down low in my seat, I peeked up through the windows but could not see the speaker.

"This here ain't the refuge," the gravelly voice said. "This is private property. No visitors allowed."

Vince moved up from his slouched position just enough to yell out, "Cal, it's Vince Murphy here. Tuck and Louise's boy. We don't mean no harm. This nice lady with me is your new neighbor. She's buying the Hardwick place and thought you might want to sell off a little piece..."

"I ain't a'selling nothing! And don't you come here no more, you hear me?"

Before Vince could answer, another shot rang out over the car. Vince quickly put the Chrysler into reverse and jerked us backward over the bumpy road.

We never mentioned the additional land parcel again.

I had another glimpse of my new neighbor before I moved in, when I came to town to close the real estate deal. While walking in the shade of a little dogwood grove on the west side of my front yard, I happened to glance across the road. An older man in a cap stood watching me, but quickly turned and disappeared behind a thick hedge that blocked my view.

"Hello!" I called out but no one answered. I couldn't let the opportunity pass. Now would be a good time to introduce myself, I thought, and also remind him I might be interested if he ever decided to sell. Who knows when I might have another chance, if indeed he was as reclusive as I'd been told? But after another hello with no response, I assumed my neighbor was indeed not the talkative type and gave up.

It was only when I turned to go inside that a little shiver of apprehension went up my spine. The hedge could hide a gun as well as a man. Though I knew this particular man probably only shot at intruders who ventured on his land, I couldn't help feeling a slight tingle in my back as I walked, perhaps more quickly than necessary, the last few steps from yard to porch.

four

Phoebe Confides

I watched Jane get into her car and drive away. I hadn't
known how to tell her the truth. If I had, she might've
packed up and left the same day she moved in, and for no reason.
The truth is, rumors around town have it that the Hardwick house
is infested with spooks, just like that old geezer down at Wriggle's
implied. Talk about rude. There was poor little Jane, all happy and
new in town, and he couldn't help himself from bringing up the
ghost thing right off. Thank goodness I have more self-control. I
don't tell everything I know to whoever passes by.

The old maid that had lived in Jane's house for ninety-two
years until she passed away was a little wacky. When people visited,
she'd stop right in the middle of a conversation and start talking to
the air, like somebody invisible was in the room. You know, like
Jimmy Stewart and that giant rabbit. Only, in the movie, the rabbit

turned out to be real. Miss Hardwick's special friends were straight out of her own loopy mind. And even though everybody knew that, somehow the stories got twisted and blown up until people started saying she saw ghosts and the house was haunted. Which is so immature. I don't know how some people call themselves adults but play like ghosts are for real, and then they make up stories and spread them around and around for fun. None of them really believe in ghosts, either, I'd bet you, they just like to jaw. I reckon it's like Santa Claus. You know he's not real but you still talk about him. And UFOs. Have you noticed you never hear little children claiming aliens captured them and experimented on them? Only grownups. What makes that, I wonder? Seems like ghost stories appeal to all ages though, and everybody around here, young or old, loves to talk about the local ghosts.

Just because Jane's house is old and isolated, and because Civil War soldiers camped out and slept in it, the storytellers around here can't help themselves from talking about the Hardwick place. It's like a lie magnet. It's got all the other classic scary movie clichés going for it, too, like strange sightings in and around the house, a big graveyard in the back, a long history of crazy Southerners in the family. The whole thing is like a cross between *Poltergeist* and *Hush, Hush Sweet Charlotte*. To some uneducated people. Even I've had what those nuts would say was a supernatural experience there, but since I have more intelligence and common sense, I know better.

It happened when I was a kid. I went to the Hardwick place with my mama when I was six years old. She'd been invited to a tea party and took me along since there wasn't anybody else to keep me that day. One of the other ladies, Lorene Clark, brought her daughter, too. Donna, who was a year younger than me, had real short brown hair done in a bowl cut.

Miss Ina Hardwick, the loopy one and last of the family, brought little plates and cups for us to play with while the ladies visited at the big table. I'll say this, now, she was a sweet lady. Not a bit stuck up. It was something to get an invitation to the Big House, which is what everybody called it. Back then, nobody had any money or nice things in their houses, so going to the Hardwick place, all grand and full of pretty china and expensive furniture, was like going to Buckingham Palace. I'd just stand there and stare at the glass chandelier and that beautiful mahogany staircase because nobody had anything like that.

Donna and I were sitting by a bay window, one that went all the way to the floor and had lots of small panes. We sat our dolls next to us at the child-sized table Miss Ina brought out for us. Like I said, Donna had short hair and I had mine tied back into a ponytail with a yellow ribbon. Miss Ina came over to check on us, and when she did, she touched the top of my head. She ran her fingers through my ponytail and said, "Where'd you get such pretty red hair?" I smiled and shrugged my shoulders. Everybody always said that.

Donna and I kept playing with our dolls and teacups, and Miss Ina went on back to the ladies. I picked up our little teapot and was about to tip it into a cup when I felt something rub over my head. I turned around but nobody was there. I started to pour Donna some tea and it happened again. I put my hand on my head, nothing was there, but all of a sudden I felt something pushing my hand down the length of my hair, like it was in front of a brush and somebody was brushing my ponytail.

I hollered "Mama" but she told me to not interrupt Mrs. Smartt, who was talking about her homemade ointment for poison ivy. I probably huffed a little bit but let it go. It kept happening, the whole time we were there, and when I told Mama on the way home she laughed at me.

She told Daddy when he came in from the fields and he had a good laugh, too. I got mad and crossed my arms. He scooped me up and said, "It's nothing to worry about, hon. It was just one of them Hardwick ghosts a'playing with you. They was probably lonesome and liked having you there." He tweaked my nose and told me to go wash up for supper.

They never let me forget that story, let me tell you, not none of my brothers or sisters, and would trot it out when they wanted to make fun of me. Of course, I don't believe any of that foolishness now. You exaggerate when you're a kid. It was probably nothing but a draft in the old house that happened to blow right where I sat.

five

Jane Meets Her Neighbor

After I left Phoebe's house with my new blanket, I drove down the street and saw the Piggly Wiggly grocery there at the corner of Meadowlark and Main. I tried to think if I had all I needed for the moving men's lunch and slowly made my way into the parking lot. Although I'd bought two jugs of tea in addition to our barbecue and side dishes, it occurred to me that the movers might prefer colas. A nice cake or pie might also be in order for them. I'd never known hungry young men to turn down dessert.

It is my habit to always check my surroundings when out and about, walking or shopping alone. Before getting out of the car, I automatically made a circular sweep of the immediate area, as I say, out of habit rather than sensing any sort of danger. To my left, a young woman pushed a baby stroller out the store's automatic door and down the small ramp into the lot. No cars were parked in the rows of spaces directly in front of mine. Two women who looked like mother and daughter stood at the nearest car to my right, several spaces over, unloading grocery sacks into the trunk of a white sedan. I used the rearview and side mirrors to check behind me, and there I saw an odd thing.

Several rows back at the far edge of the lot, an older model Jeep Cherokee reversed into a space next to an old van that had seen much better days. The man from the Jeep wore a wide-brimmed black cowboy hat, a brown knit shirt, jeans, and dark boots. He had a moustache and his skin had the look of a lifetime of outside work. I guessed his age at mid-fifties to early sixties, and the age of the man who came out of the van to meet him at early to mid-thirties. The younger man's bearing and buzz cut marked him as former military, of that I had no doubt. He wore a black T-shirt that stretched across a tight chest and large arm muscles. His boots and BDU pants, with their many pockets, were army surplus. A faint white scar, untanned like the rest of his skin, trailed from below his right ear and disappeared under the neck of his shirt.

The two didn't shake hands, nor did they waste any time in idle chitchat. Immediately on emerging from the Jeep, the man in the black hat opened his rear door on the driver's side and took out two things, a fishing rod and a large tan duffel. The younger man slid the side door of his van open, inspected the rod, and placed it inside his vehicle. The older man then unzipped the duffel and held it out for his ex-military friend who had a quick look inside, moving things about in it with his hand. He nodded his head curtly, rezipped the duffel and put it in the van as well, then slid the door shut. Less than two minutes went by from the time the Jeep parked to the departure of the van.

It's true, the incident didn't indicate criminal activity, only roused a mild curiosity. I made another quick scan around the parking lot and carried on into the grocery.

I returned to the house and stayed home the rest of the day. A few hours more of directing the men as they brought in heavy furniture and then the quiet hours of unpacking once the movers were gone left me bone weary and ready for bed.

I found my aspirin bottle and was about to pour myself a glass of water when I heard a commotion outside. It sounded as if someone were yelling, as if in pain. But as the voice drew nearer, I realized the person approaching in the darkness was not hurting. He was singing.

I peeped out the front window's blind. As the figure came into view under the security light at the edge of my property, I could see for certain it was a man, a very thin one. He wore a plaid flannel shirt and wrinkled pants a size or two too large. Several days of stubble darkened his cheeks and chin. He continued singing while staggering from the middle of the road to the side, getting ever closer to my front yard.

He saw me behind the blind. With an open-mouthed grin, he exposed several dark gaps where teeth had been and began singing louder. To my astonishment, he waved to me and proceeded to walk toward my porch steps.

He leaned on the railing and slid up to the porch, braving the perilous steps with only a couple of slips. His hands reached out and down to the rocker nearest the window where I stood. With a look of victory and relief, his body fell limp as he flopped into the chair seat and made himself at home.

With a wave of his hand, he seemed to be letting me know he was all right. He rocked back and resumed his serenade, thankfully in a less boisterous voice. His eyes closed as the rocker creaked a fervent accompaniment, keeping time with his song.

I studied him a moment, then looked blankly about my living room. What was I to do with an unexpected and undoubtedly inebriated man, so late in the evening? At first I considered calling the police. As odd as it may seem, I was afraid that would seem unneighborly, if indeed this was, as I suspected, my only close neighbor, the notorious Cal Prewitt, local hermit. How odd, this sudden reversal in his attitude. What might have caused it, other than an indulgence in too much drink, I couldn't guess.

My instinct was that he meant no harm. I didn't think I would need a pistol but, half-ashamed of myself, I dropped a small one, hardly bigger than my hand, in my sweater pocket, just in case. I must learn to adjust to the isolation of the house. And I would. Later.

As I opened the door, Cal was ending his rendition with great emotion. I closed the screen quietly behind me as I stepped onto the porch.

When I felt a respectable time had passed at the end of his number, I stepped in front of the rocker and waited for his eyes to open fully.

He looked me over top to bottom and put both feet down flat to stop the creaking rocker. He moved yellow-stained fingernails slowly to an inside pocket, never taking his eyes off me. As he did so, I let my hand drop casually to my pocket as well.

"Mind if I smoke?" he said lifting out a crumpled pack of cigarettes.

A small sigh escaped my lips. "Not at all. That's what porches are made for, eh?"

The lines across his forehead relaxed. "Yes, ma'am. That and dogs. A porch seems empty without a big old hound dog."

I nodded. "I was just about to have a cup of tea. Would you care for one ... Mister Prewitt, is it?"

"Yes, ma'am. Cal Prewitt," he said. "Tea would be very nice, thank you kindly, Miz ... uh ...?"

"Thistle. Please call me Jane," I said as I put out my right hand. His grip surprised me. From the smell of things, cheap bourbon, I'd say, and a lot of it, I'd expected a much more feeble shake.

He rose slightly from his seat. His attempt at a bow put him off balance a tick and sent him quickly back into the rocker seat with a plop.

"I'll just be a minute then." I hesitated, watching to be sure he was well settled.

"Yes, ma'am," he said, "this porch here definitely calls for a dog."

He put a cigarette to his lips and squinted as if smoke already clouded his vision. He struck a match, drew in the first puff and said, almost to himself, "You'll do fine," as he relaxed and set the chair to rock again.

I let the screen tap quietly closed behind me and left the front door open, wondering if he meant I'll do fine in making our tea, or if I would make an adequate substitute for a porch dog.

When I returned, I had another visitor on the porch. A large, black, smooth-coated dog, mostly Labrador with perhaps also a little spaniel, lay next to Cal's rocking chair. He raised a big square head and greeted me with a friendly blink of his eyes.

"I told Homer to stay at home but he don't listen." Cal said. "I hope you don't mind."

"Not at all. Nice to meet you, Homer." He yawned before resting his head on the porch's wood planks and settling in for a nap.

As it turned out, Cal and I had a very pleasant conversation. He thanked me over and over for the tray of sandwiches and cake I brought out with our tea. They were no trouble at all since the makings were left over from the lunch I'd bought for the movers. He was rail thin. I wondered how long it had been since he'd had a good meal.

We talked of my husband's military service and of Cal's own experiences in Italy in the forties after World War II. We spoke of places in London he'd visited during that time and of my family in England. Mostly, we talked about Tullulah, northern Alabama, and how they had changed over Cal's lifetime.

"But my place has never changed. Same as it was for thousands of years."

His words made me sit stock-still. I hardly breathed. "You mean, so few people have lived and built and worked in the area."

"No," he said. "I mean nobody has ever done any of those things here. Nobody white, anyway, besides my family. They used the flatlands down below the bluffs for farming and building their own houses. No, the woods have been kept just like they were ten thousand years ago. Longer than that. Only a handful of us, son to son, lived on the bluffs. The big house burned down in 1958. I'm the only one who has lived up here since . . ." His voice trailed away. "Since the seventies. Nobody ever cut into the woods, just used these close fields for the house. A few acres for fruit trees, a little for keeping horses and chickens and pigs and cows. All the rest is the same."

An uncorrupted wood. The thought ran through me like fire in my veins. It was a nature- and history-lover's dream, to be so close, to have a chance at even a short time of study. My skin tingled in the cool air. I was here, at the threshold of an untouched forest, one that might be made available to study at my leisure by only asking.

The conversation continued and, though interesting, Cal bordered on incomprehension most of the time. The drink, I imagined. It was actually all quite amusing, though I didn't laugh, only listened and enjoyed the performance as his words fell and rose and ambled like the slow flow of a creek. He made many references to heaven and angels, to punishment of the wicked, and was particularly fervent in denouncing all traitors and warmongers. He spoke in a voice reminiscent of Native American chiefs concerning the Great Spirit, and even spoke Cherokee at times in his more poetic recitations. When his ramblings took a turn toward the spiritual and supernatural, I didn't take the opportunity to mention the little girl I'd seen downtown, nor did Cal did say anything about my house and its possible otherworldly occupants. Perhaps I'd feel more comfortable talking about it when I got to know him better. And when he was a little more sober.

He was attentive when I spoke of my love of wildlife, and how I'd studied every book I could find on the nearby counties. I asked if he had a favorite story, something to tell me about the history or people of the area.

"Let's see. There's the one about when the white men first came. The valley here was a hunting ground shared by several tribes. The Chickasaw controlled it through most of that time, but there were Cherokee villages here, too.

"A Scottish trader named Charlie came through with an expedition. This was in the mid seventeen hundreds. Charlie got here and didn't want to leave, so he asked the chief of the small Cherokee town nearby if he could live and work with them. The chief agreed since Charlie was a skilled hunter and fisherman, and understood the Indian ways better than the other white men he'd been traveling with. So, Charlie stayed on.

"The chief had one daughter, *Usti Tseni*. Little Wren. She and Charlie fell in love, had children, and were happy together. Then, a few years later, another band of whites came through, only they weren't respectful of the tribe and had no interest in passing through peacefully.

"First, they took all the food they could find. They burned the village's outer wood defense and some of the huts inside. Then they started killing. Charlie and his father-in-law stood together and fought them off. They and the other men of the tribe managed to kill all the attackers, but Charlie was shot in the chest at the end and didn't survive. The chief found Little Wren at the door of her hut, stabbed to death while trying to defend her children."

"How terrible," I said and shuddered. "That's not a very happy story for right before bed."

"It's the way it was," Cal said. "It happened all over, not just here." We sat a while without speaking before Cal finished the story. "The chief dug their graves himself. He laid his daughter and Charlie in the ground next to each other. In Little Wren's palm, he placed an acorn and closed her fingers around it. He put a maple seed in Charlie's hand and did the same. A year later, the chief and what was left of the tribe had a special ceremony of thanks when they saw the shoots of new saplings coming out of the graves. They celebrated because, to them, Charlie and Little Wren and their love for each other were still alive."

I brushed a tear off my cheek and the night slipped quietly away as we sat. We sipped the rest of our tea, looking out over my yard and across to Cal's land. His thoughts became increasingly disjointed and slower as he tired, and he began to mumble strange things again. I could hear and remember only one such soliloquy, which sounded like another of his Cherokee poems. He translated for me: "In a dark moon, when the stars touch the earth, the Old Ones come down, to help the People." We sat in the quiet as golden lights of fireflies blinked on and off in the dark as they hovered over my yard and the meadow across the road.

Cal sighed and rose slowly from his chair. "I reckon Homer and I need to get on home. I do thank you for the tea and the kind hospitality. Been a long time since I've had such a good talk."

"Me, too," I said. "You're most welcome to visit anytime. And Homer as well, of course." Homer had risen when Cal did. They both moved slowly down the porch steps into the yard.

Cal looked up. "Would you like to come over to our place in the morning? There's some things I believe you'd enjoy seeing. Things you'd appreciate."

I was stunned and overjoyed. "I'd love to," I said before he could change his mind.

"Good." His head hung down and his voice trailed off to a whisper tinged with sadness. "Good." We set a time to meet and said our good-byes before Cal and Homer crossed the road to go home.

Cal was no longer in view but I heard the faint crunch of gravel as he walked toward home. His humming grew louder then he once again broke into song. A little farther on, I could hear the muffled cry of Homer, howling along as he joined in on the chorus.

I took my time washing up the dishes. With a contented sigh, I walked up the staircase, pausing to look over my living room. I had left an old-fashioned desk lamp on in the far corner of the room. Its light shone softly over familiar chairs, tables, and the few decorative pieces I'd become attached to over the years. I sighed again and continued up to the bedroom thinking, *So nice to be home.*

I tossed about in bed, turning my back to the alarm clock, when I heard a noise downstairs. It was a soft sound, like a single drip of a faucet. I lay still and quiet, but heard nothing for a long minute, during which time I convinced myself that I'd heard nothing at all in the first place.

Weary deep in my bones after the long day, I could feel my body relaxing and my mind crossing over to dreams, then to sleep. I barely heard the second droplike tap downstairs. Just before I drifted off, I thought whatever it was could drop to its heart's content until morning. I was much too tired to fix a leaky faucet in the middle of the night.

six

Jane Tours Cal's Land

The loud chirping of birds outside woke me very early. Still tired from all the excitement of the previous day and late night, I got up nonetheless, anxious to have my breakfast and set out to visit Cal's land.

I looked out my upstairs window to see the sun rising over the treetops and coming gently to rest in my backyard. I hurried into my running gear and downstairs with only a quick stop for my morning ritual of water with lemon, then out into the fresh morning.

Once again, a hint of fall hung in the air. I breathed in as much of it as I could, held it, and let it out slowly. Never have I enjoyed stretching into a sun salute so much as on this morning, the first in my new home. After a short series of more stretches, I set out on my morning walk.

The Colonel saw to it that I kept in shape. He was something of a fanatic about it, actually, and also when it came to teaching me self-defense. His favorite method of instruction was through sneak attacks to test my instincts and reflexes. If you're familiar with the Pink Panther movies in which Cato does the same to Inspector Clouseau, you have the idea.

Mornings are when I miss the Colonel most, for that was when we always ran together through the streets of whatever city we happened to be in. When his health began to decline and he was unable to accompany me, I found I ran less, opting for a run-walk combination. It was difficult watching age catch up with him. I thought of him as invincible. More and more, I slowed my pace until my treks became strolls. Age seemed to be catching up with me as well. Now at sixty-seven, I rationalized it was time to stop pushing myself, that I should be content to walk at leisure.

This first morning in Tullulah, while watching the passing scenery of woods and fields, I felt young again. The sounds of early morning birds chirping with no competition from vehicles, machinery, or other aural assaults of city life absolutely invigorated me. I found myself wanting to step up my pace, to sprint out to a point up ahead as I had done so many times racing the Colonel. I quickened to a slow run. My body informed me straight away that this must be a gradual process, now that the old heart was a bit out of practice. I returned to the house, out of breath but happier than I had been in a long time.

After pouring another glass of water and lemon, I set the coffeepot to brew and stepped outside onto the stone patio just beyond the back porch. It had been my intention to go through my Tai Chi routine there. However, once on it, I realized the surface was too uneven. I decided instead to try a small clearing between three oak trees near the edge of my lawn. It was perfect, just the right amount of space to do my moves comfortably. Once in the movements, my mind and body seemed to leave the world and drift among the high branches of the oaks.

Time reversed. The cool breeze carried me back, the years flying past, as if it were the same breeze I'd felt many years before, learning the slow movements in a San Francisco park not long after the Colonel and I married, the beginning of my life. And here, in the fresh air moving over mountain woods and springs, my arms moved in circles, like everything in life, and came around to start again.

On my return to the kitchen, I thought I might bake a pan of biscuits. I'd have a few with coffee then take the rest in a tin to Cal. After his night of drinking, they might be just the thing for a light breakfast. I turned from the stove and stepped toward the pantry where I'd put a new sack of flour.

I'd reached the center of the floor when something crunched underfoot. With a quick step back, I looked down to find I'd crushed a tiny acorn. I couldn't believe my eyes. In addition to it, another sat beside it, whole, having escaped its brother's fate. I blinked and pushed my glasses up hard against the bridge of my nose for a clearer look.

Surely these had not been here the night before. I'd swept the floor clean before Cal's visit and afterward had gone straight to bed. Then I remembered the sounds I'd heard in the night. Could these tiny things have been the cause? A check of the faucets in the kitchen and the downstairs bathroom sink and tub yielded no leaks. As I returned to the kitchen, I surmised that a chipmunk or squirrel must have come inside while the doors were left open for the furniture to be moved in. Apparently, my visitor was thoughtful enough to bring a gift. I would have to leave the door open again so the little fellow could get out, if he was indeed still inside.

With rich coffee and a couple of biscuits in me, I grabbed the tin of extras. I'd located my binoculars the night before and put them out so I wouldn't forget them. I scooped them up along with a small wire-bound notebook and set out for my day's adventure. To my surprise, Cal was there at his gate, waiting on me.

We began to laugh and talk all at once. Homer joined our conversation in barks and woofs that, on occasion, had an astounding resemblance to speech.

"Hush, Homer," Cal said. "You'll have to excuse him. He gets to talking sometimes and don't know when to quit."

Cal was remarkably sober and quite chipper. Both he and Homer gratefully accepted the biscuits. They didn't last long after we set out, for both man and dog were typical males, always hungry. We followed Homer, who stopped and sniffed occasionally, on a path leading into the woods.

While we talked, I could see quickly that Cal was not only well educated, but quite a gentleman. What a difference since the night before. Without the liquor, his speech lost much of its country flavor and he stood straighter, giving the look of a younger man.

It made me wonder if his unkempt appearance and "hermit" ways were a ruse to fool me, and perhaps all the townsfolk of Tullulah. Perhaps, like myself, he too wanted only to be left in peace. If so, he had certainly gone to the extreme in order to accomplish it.

Before we reached the trees, I saw two boulders in the field to our left. My first thought was of small standing stones, like ones I'd seen in England, those great rocks moved into place in ancient times for religious rites. On top of the boulders, each about three feet high, bottles and cans had been placed in rows.

"That's my practice range," Cal said. "Do you shoot?"

"Yes, but haven't done in some time. I need a bit of practice now that I'm living out in the wild."

"Come out here and shoot anytime you like. Behind the rocks is the bluff. There's nothing else around to hit by mistake."

I immediately thought of Phoebe. "Would tomorrow be too soon? I'd like to bring a friend, if that's all right." I took another look at the boulders. Phoebe had been so generous in giving me the blanket. Considering her new interest in bullets, I thought a shooting lesson might be a small way to repay her.

He hesitated. "No offense, but I don't usually let strangers wander around." He rubbed his chin, thinking intently.

"It's quite all right. I understand perfectly."

Cal stopped and looked at me. "But if it's a friend of yours, and you promise not to wander off the trails, I reckon it's okay."

"Oh, thank you. We'll not stray."

A grin lit Cal's face. "Okay. Come on. Homer's beating us."

We stepped into the woods where to either side of us stood fir and pines. Cal told me his family had owned thousands of acres around here at one time, and that his great-grandfather was one of Tullulah's founders. After more and more immigrants settled in the area, and towns and cities sprang up along the river, the Prewitt family's land holdings had dwindled to this relatively small parcel of one hundred acres.

"Lots of folks have tried to buy this from me. I never budged. My granddaddy told me ever since I was a boy, 'Son, sell down by the river if you need to, but don't ever sell up here. *Tsaluyi Udelida*— it means Secret Forest. The Cherokee and Chickasaw, Yaquis, Shawnee, who knows what other tribes before them, came here for important ceremonies, not far from where we're standing."

Looking to either side, I thought it quite an appropriate name. The white rays of sunlight filtering down to the leaf-strewn forest floor certainly had the look of secret enchantments to me. I half expected to see the wizard Merlin or some native shaman step out from behind a wide tree trunk.

I breathed in the thick evergreen air from the cedars and pines as birds chipped from high above. Hearing their bewitching melodies, I thanked Cal's forebears who gave me this moment by insisting the forest be preserved.

We came out of the trees to a sloping flat area. I gasped, looking out over the bluff where we stood to the scene below.

Far below, a bend of the Tennessee River flowed between rolling hills and the variant textures of crops and fields. The squares and rectangles of soy and cotton ranged in color from emerald to light sea green. Red patches of tilled land stretched out, waiting their turns next spring. The river sparkled in the morning sun, moving swiftly as it narrowed over jutting rock beds and white-capping before rolling out of view. I could see combines in the distance throwing dust up in their wakes, and beyond them, pastures with horses and cows.

"I've never seen anything so beautiful," I said feeling truly overwhelmed. I turned around toward Cal and the forest behind him when I was struck by a different beauty. Surely most people would say I was daft, that the sight of a poorly groomed, derelict-looking old man and his dog of mixed parentage was a beautiful one.

But I tell you, it was. The outward gaze of a man who, according to Vince Murphy was considered "no count" by the locals, held much dignity in this place where he was able to be his true self. His dark eyes glinted as he stood surveying what was his but not his, merely his charge for one short lifetime. Nothing so grand comes without sacrifice. Cal had given up friends, comforts, and to a large extent, community respect that might have been his otherwise. What more, I wondered, to keep this sacred promise of the land's stewardship to family and to nature?

Homer moved to Cal's side and sat, blinking his contentment as he, too, looked out over the bluff. Cal leaned down and rested his gnarled fingers between the Lab's ears. A breeze blew past and rustled in the trees behind us.

"I had a son," Cal said softly. He paused a moment, then said. "He was killed in Vietnam." Homer nuzzled the hand that petted him and inched closer. "My wife died not long after."

"I'm so sorry."

"There's nobody else. Just me and Homer. And my time is coming on soon. I'm getting too old to keep fighting."

His choice of words mystified me but I didn't interrupt. I assumed he meant his health problems were getting to be too much of a burden. His chest rattled. He had a dreadful pallor in his face. Several times during our walk, he had a coughing spell.

We walked for perhaps another thirty minutes with Cal showing me so many beautiful paths. "That way," he said, "is where we're headed." I followed the direction of his crooked finger. "That stream is the same one we crossed in the field near the house. It goes right into the heart of *Tsaluyi Udelida*. The ceremonial hall. *Danitaga*."

In the distance, I could see two very large boulders standing about two hundred yards away toward the center of the wood. A gap of perhaps three feet separated them giving the look of a grand entrance to an ancient temple.

On the way to the huge boulders, we had stopped to watch two squirrels chase each other across the leaf floor when suddenly a noise in the woods jerked Cal's attention away. Homer looked as well, then followed his master's example, holding still and hardly breathing.

"I don't like the sound of that," Cal said in quiet, even tones. "Don't like it at all. I'm sorry, Miz Jane, but I believe it would be better if you weren't here right now." He moved his shotgun up slowly. A few more moments of silence passed. Cal nodded his head ever so slightly. "That path will take you straight back to the main road. It's not far."

"Don't apologize," I whispered. "I'm perfectly content to wait until later to see more." I glanced around us but saw nothing. "Do be careful, dear."

"Don't worry about us," he said solemnly, then changed his worried frown to a big smile. "Me and Homer may just catch us a little supper."

With a nod, I raised my hand in good-bye and left them to their prey.

It had been an act, of course. Had he lied to protect me? Perhaps there were animals here more dangerous than I knew. I quickened my pace down the road. It would be some days before I encountered them, creatures more deadly than I could imagine that first day in the woods.

seven

Jane Gets a Proposition

*A*fter my morning trip to Cal's, I spent the rest of the day cleaning, unpacking, and running errands. I was exhausted by nightfall. I sat the last dish from supper into the drying rack just as someone knocked on my door. I looked out to see Cal, already seated in the same rocker he occupied the previous night. Homer stood and watched my movements behind the blind.

As the screen creaked open, I said, "So, did your hunting expedition this morning go well?"

Cal gave me a puzzled look, then understood. "Fine. Just skunks." The thick aroma of whiskey that already emanated from Cal's vicinity grew stronger when he spoke. "You got to watch people, Jane. You got to watch 'em real good." Ah, well. It was going to be another of those jumping conversations of disparate musings heavily laced with alcohol.

"Right, then. I'll just fetch some tea."

Once settled with our refreshments, including some nice dog biscuits I'd bought for Homer, Cal brought up something we discussed briefly in our walk. "Tell me again what all you did on the digs, you know, back when you'd go around with them archaeology people."

"Well, I was just a digger. Strictly volunteer. I didn't have the college degrees necessary to be anything more. I was never in charge. Never a professor. Strictly amateur."

Cal turned toward me in his chair. "And you liked that, getting all dirty and sweaty and working until your shoulders and arms were wore out? Knowing you'd be doing the same thing again the next day?"

I laughed. "Well, yes. I did it for the love of it. It's true, most of the time you find nothing for your hard work. And yet, on the day when a buzz travels through the workers, when someone has uncovered something, I can tell you there's nothing more exciting. If I am to be totally honest, I loved it just as much on the boring days. Just touching the earth, thinking that someone long ago, someone of a different race in a different country, or perhaps an ancient ancestor of your own, might have touched where you were working, just there where your hands lay. You think of their lives, what they thought, how they worked, whom they loved."

When some time passed without a response, I looked over at Cal. He rocked, lost in thought, then set straight into a new topic. "Miz Jane, I want to apologize if I scared you that first time, me shooting over Vernon's car. He knew better than to do that."

Before I could say a word, Cal's thoughts took another sharp turn, one I'd never have expected. "Anyway, what I'm trying to say is, I've been thinking real hard about you a'wanting my land."

All my tiredness suddenly fell away. I said nothing in hopes his train of thought would continue in the direction I hoped it would go, rather than meander as it had done thus far.

"The truth is, Old Doc Rose says I ain't got much longer." He tapped his chest, indicating his lungs, I assumed. "Hell, I'm eighty-two and I've been smoking since I was eight. It's a wonder I've lasted this long." He coughed and leaned forward in the chair, raising his bloodshot eyes, old and despondent, to mine.

"What I have for you is a proposition," he said. "That is, if you're still interested in buying."

I didn't want to sound too eager, so I merely inclined my head toward him and said, "What sort of proposition?"

"Let me ask you something first. Why do you want it? You've got a mighty nice piece of property now yourself. And it's just you living here, right?"

"Yes. Just me." He nodded and waited for me to continue. "I want it for peace, I imagine." I told him about the military bases, and for the first time, I told someone my true feelings about our moves, how out of place I'd always felt. "Here, I don't feel isolated, rather protected somehow. I suppose you understand what I mean?"

He nodded again. A sly smile stretched across his face as he rocked. "Oh, yes. Yes, I do. That's something I understand well." We sat in companionable silence for a while before Cal took a deep breath and got to the true reason for this porch visit, the previous one, and the short tour that morning on his property.

"I'd like to sell you my land," he said, the words purposeful and with a forced quality, as if he had reached an unsavory but necessary decision and now must follow through no matter how painful. "With a few conditions. First, it's an all or nothing deal. I want you to buy all of it. Every last blade of grass. Second, I want to keep my house and live there, with free rein over my land, until I die. Are you agreeable so far?"

I nodded again. "Yes. Go on."

"Because that's not all," he said, his speech and the direct look in his eyes making him appear suddenly sober. "The third condition is the most important one."

His black eyes bore into mine as he paused. A tremble came into his voice. "You have to make me a solemn promise, so help you God. For as long as you live after I'm gone, you must not sell any part of it for any reason. Every square inch must stay as it is. No developers. No bulldozers. No changes. Period." He paused. "And number four is the toughest one. You've got to pass it on to somebody else, somebody like us, who won't change it or hurt it in any way."

Silence stretched between us as we considered that difficulty. "You're smart, Jane. I trust you can find a way. You have to."

I took a sip of tea and looked away. Still doing my best not to sound too anxious, I said, "Well. I must say I'm surprised. You seemed dead set against selling it at our first encounter."

He nodded slowly. "Things have changed. I thought it was all taken care of. Someone . . ." He shook his head. "I realize I've got to let go of it now or else it will all be lost."

"I'm not sure I can afford it. You didn't mention your asking price."

The figure he gave was so reasonable, it shocked me. In fact, it was so low I couldn't believe it. It was well within my price range, thanks not only to many years of frugal living and my dear husband's wise investments, but also due to money of my own I'd saved from freelance work done during our world travels.

"Here is the thing," Cal said, his voice shaking. "It's special. It has never been sullied by the white man's ways. Better preserved than the refuge. I've spent my life taking care of it the best I can, just like my granddaddy and his granddaddy before him. And a long time before that. It's pure. I can't let that die with me."

He released his intense gaze but sat forward, still and waiting. He sighed. "I can't explain it all tonight. It's too much. You just need to trust me that it must be preserved as it is."

The loud sawing of crickets filled the night, and in that moment I felt a deep contentment, being here, having found the quiet place I'd always wanted. Here was a rare man, one after my own heart.

"Let me be direct, Cal. I want the property and I agree to all your terms. I see no point in playing games, do you?"

A slow smile spread across Cal's face as he put his hand out. "I like you, Jane. It's a deal," he said, shaking my hand. "I appreciate you helping me out this way." His face held such relief, I nearly cried. I could see the truth in his doctor's prognosis. He didn't have much longer.

"I believe it is mutually beneficial. I give you my word to adhere to your conditions just as you wish. I swear it."

The glow of his face told me what I suspected. He didn't care about the money, only that his land be kept intact and in its naturally beautiful state. Having agreed, he nodded and stood, much less burdened than when he arrived.

"It's late," he said. "I think I'll head on to the house. I'm glad, real glad, things are worked out. Now there's lots of important stuff I need to show you and tell you about, but we'll have plenty of time for all that later on."

That sounded intriguing, but I let him enjoy his secrets for the moment and didn't ask for details. "So, you still don't mind if I take my morning walk tomorrow over the property?" I asked. "And bring my friend to shoot? Because if you'd rather I didn't . . ."

"Not a bit. Y'all come on. Me and Homer are going out of town real early. Got some business in Florence."

"And we wouldn't be disturbing anyone else?"

"Nobody out this way to disturb. Just me and you out this far."

"Yes, of course. That's something to get used to."

He rose, thanked me again for the tea, and stepped carefully off the porch. "There's trails all over," he said with a wave toward his land. "Just take the main road and you'll see them. Stay on the trails, don't wander off." He turned from the bottom step with one finger raised in the air. "One more thing. I'll need cash. Please, ma'am. If you don't mind."

Cash? "I'll certainly ask the banker. I'm sure it can be done."

He smiled, waved again, and ambled down the road.

How odd. Perhaps he only wanted the security of cash in hand. Many older people did. Did he have a checking account? Whatever the case, with his doctors' bills, he surely would need money. I could understand but still felt a bit curious, not only about that, but because I knew his land was worth much more. With no family left, he must have calculated only what he would need and saw no point in asking for more.

My knees creaked as I rose and picked up the tray of our cups and plates. With one more glance over what might soon be mine, I closed the screen door. I could still see Cal and Homer in the road, both walking slowly. The security light threw a long shadow in front of him. He passed out of the light's circle and into the darkness as he turned onto his private road.

It certainly was a strange turnabout in Cal's behavior. For the second time, I wondered if he was sincere or, as Phoebe might say, was he up to something sneaky? It was a fleeting thought this time, however, for Cal's motives were clear. He only wanted to preserve his land and pay his remaining bills before he passed away.

Once inside for the night, I called Phoebe. She sounded so happy to hear from me. I asked if she'd like to walk together in the morning and didn't mention the shooting range. It would be a nice little surprise for her. We agreed she would come at eight o'clock. I walked through the house, shutting off lights on my way to bed.

I had only been asleep a short while when a loud noise jarred me fully awake. It sounded like a shot. Sitting up in bed, I turned to look at the clock. I'd been asleep longer than I thought. The clock read 1:49. Just as it changed to 1:50, another shot rang out in the still night.

I couldn't say which direction the sounds had come from, only that they sounded far away. I imagined Cal in trouble at first, but dismissed the thought, imagining it more likely he and Homer were running an animal intruder away from their house. I realized my knowledge of the area was too limited to assume the shots, or whatever the sounds were, had come from Cal's property rather than some other nearby tract. However, the refuge edged all but a slim parcel of land behind my own, a section I had yet to explore.

Next morning, I rose again with the dawn. The morning walk was made even more beautiful with the thought of soon having an even better, larger barrier against the world.

After the walk and my Tai Chi exercises, I put some biscuits in the oven. While they baked, I sat on a pillow for a few minutes of meditation. I began to think of all the things I might do and find here. So many pictures continued to swirl in my mind, such as all the new plants and birds to discover, the memory of the boulder entrance to the ceremonial hall yet to explore, Cal's moving story of Charlie and Little Wren, all stirred my emotions.

What began as a dream, one I carried for so many years, had come true. I laughed out loud at my good fortune and let tears of joy roll down my cheeks, lost in feelings of peace, quiet, and wonderful solitude. No, I would never feel lonely, not here with so much life surrounding me.

A loud banging on my door brought me abruptly out of my reverie. I was so startled, I jumped straight away to the door and flung it open.

eight

Phoebe Drops In

I just barely tapped real light on Jane's front door. For a minute, I worried I'd got there too early, but when I saw she'd been crying and how happy she was to see me, I knew I'd done the right thing. I was just glad to be there when she needed somebody, all lonesome and depressed and by herself in that big old scary house out in the sticks.

I was so glad she called me the night before to see if I wanted to go walking with her the next morning. That day, I'd baked and run around visiting the hospital and nursing home all day until I was wore out. I was sitting there, stretched out on the couch with a bowl of popcorn watching *Missing in Action 2: The Beginning* for about the hundredth time, and didn't have a thing planned for the following day, which was unusual for me. I could hardly wait for morning.

I followed Jane inside to her kitchen where I could smell something good cooking in the oven. She popped off the lid of my plastic cake holder I'd brought. It wouldn't do to visit and not show up with a present. I brought a coffee cake, one of a half dozen I'd baked for the freezer and for times such as this. Jane took a knife out of a drawer.

"This looks delicious," she said. "I've made biscuits, but I think I'll wrap them up for Cal Prewitt, my neighbor, when we go over. He said we could take our walk across his property this morning."

If my jaw hadn't been hinged tight onto my face, it would've hit the floor and broke in a million pieces.

"What is it, dear?" she said. "Did I say something wrong?"

"Cal Prewitt? Crazy Cal Prewitt said that? You actually saw him? I can't believe that ornery old coot would let us or anybody else go over there."

"I assure you he said we could." Jane hesitated, like she was about to say more. Instead, she kind of hem-hawed then started drinking her coffee.

"Well, it's a wonder," I said. "Cal has been known on more than one occasion to shoot at trespassers. He's the 'Shoot first, call the funeral home later' type. People around here take his no trespassing signs seriously. I'm not sure it's a good idea to walk on his property."

"He was very kind to me," she said. "He told me to make myself at home."

"Are we talking about the same person here? Tall, scrawny, not too much going on upstairs? Cal is also known for being drunk near one hundred percent of the time, you do know that, don't you? You don't reckon he'd been drinking when you saw him?"

She hesitated again. "He seemed fine."

When I looked at her like I thought it highly unlikely, she added, "But I believe I did smell a hint of liquor."

"Hmmm. He might not have known what he was saying."

"He said he had business to attend to very early and would be gone, that we should be most welcome."

That sure didn't sound like the Cal I'd heard about but I believed her. I decided I shouldn't alarm Jane anymore. Besides, how could I pass up the chance to look around the Prewitt place? Hardly a soul in town has ever seen anything except from the road.

I threw my hands up. "If that's what he said, then I'm all for it. I'm ready whenever you are."

"First," Jane said as she rinsed her plate in the sink, "you must pick out a gun."

I slapped my coffee cup down on the table. My eyes must've been bugged out a mile. Jane was smiling at me. "What, are you teasing me?"

She laughed a little tinkling laugh. "No, dear. I'm quite serious. Cal has a practicing range. I thought you'd enjoy trying your hand at a little target practice since you expressed an interest in guns."

"That is so thoughtful of you! Hey, we may very well need guns if we go on Cal's place. They say there are bobcats and coyotes in there, you know. No telling what else."

"Bobcats?" Jane said. Her voice rose and cracked a little. "Oh, dear. I had no idea. That is, I'd read a small number were in the area west of here, but hadn't thought of them being so . . . close."

"Well, sure. There's some of everything in there, I imagine, since nobody human is ever allowed to go in. I can't believe I'm getting to walk on Cal Prewitt's own personal property. I'm like the only one in fifty years, I bet you. Maybe one or two exceptions, but that's it. It's a miracle. Plus I get to shoot a gun! What did you mean I need to pick one out? You have more than one?"

"A few," she said. "Come with me."

A few, she said. Ha. I couldn't hardly believe my eyes. They nearly popped out of their sockets when she opened up what I thought was a nice, normal antique chifferobe she'd set in her den.

Instead of clothes hanging up inside, she had a row of rifles lined up and stuffed in there like she was expecting Armageddon. I'm talking about big guns and lots of them. She took the little ring of keys she'd used to open the cabinet out of its door, flipped around and found another key, and unlocked the two drawers inside. I remember my grandmother on my mother's side had used her old chifferobe's drawers to store gloves and handkerchiefs. Jane used hers for spare gun parts and cleaning kits. Grandma's always had a faint scent of rose petals. Jane's smelled like gun oil.

"Now, mind you," Jane said, "I didn't actually buy these myself. They were the Colonel's. It was his hobby, really, scouting out bargains and trying all the different models. He was a bit of a packrat when it came to firearms, I must say."

She studied the guns for a second, then took one of the little keys on her ring and unlocked a padlock. With the lock in one hand, she pulled a chain through the trigger holes of the rifles. She grabbed the rifle she wanted and leaned it against the wall. After rechaining and relocking everything, she said, "Right. Now, let's see about a handgun for you."

"There's more?"

She walked around the hearth of her fireplace to the back wall of the house. One half of the wall had moving boxes she hadn't unpacked yet stacked against it. Jane had already cleared out the other half, closer to the fireplace, and placed furniture along that part of the wall. An old-timey cedar chest sat next to an antique trunk covered with leather straps that you could tell was old by the funny-looking lock.

Jane unlocked the trunk and let the humpback top rest against the wall. I moved around to Jane's right side so I could see better. Down in the trunk were stacks of square black boxes, or cases, I guess they were, some wooden, some made out of molded plastic. Also down in there, I could see pieces of velvet and felt, all different colors, that looked like they were wrapped around bundles. Of what, I couldn't tell.

I let out a whistle as she carefully unwrapped dark blue velvet from around a pistol. "Jane, honey, don't tell me them's all guns down in there."

"I'm afraid they are, dear. More of the Colonel's fancies. Now, Phoebe, I must ask you not to tell anyone these are here. I suppose, all together, they are quite valuable. I wouldn't want anyone to be tempted to break in, you understand?"

"Consider me sworn to secrecy," I said. I crossed my heart and held up my hand. "I promise."

"Good. I do intend to sell them. I've been meaning to ever since the Colonel passed away." She sighed and fell quiet for a moment.

I thought it was a good time to change the subject so she wouldn't start crying again. "Now what's this right here?" I said like I hadn't noticed she was fixing to get sniffly. "Look at that, a trophy." I pulled a gold cup from the side of the trunk. It had a purple ribbon curled up in it on top of a photograph. It was Jane with a bunch of old wrinkled, gray-haired white women holding onto steel walkers.

"I taught a few classes in Florida. Those were my students in a self-defense class for the elderly."

"Good Granny Alive, Jane. As feeble as they look? What did you do to help them? Issue Smith and Wessons?"

That made her laugh. "No, nothing so drastic." Jane took one handgun out of a plastic case and unrolled another one from a black velvet rectangle. "I think we'll try a couple of these and be on our way. Look all right to you?" she asked, holding them both out to me.

"Sure enough," I said and rubbed my palms together. "Yee-hah, let's go."

Before we left the house, Jane reached in a plastic bag and brought out several boxes of bullets. She dropped them in the pockets of her red over-sized shirt jacket. "I stopped by Mister Wriggle's store again yesterday afternoon when I realized we would need a good many practice bullets, much more than I bought before. I'm sure I already have some somewhere in those unpacked boxes, but where I haven't a clue."

We gathered our hardware and Jane's biscuit tin and set out through the grassy section of wildflowers at the very edge of Cal Prewitt's property. I put on a brave face as we walked by two warning signs that said "Keep Out" and "Trespassers Will Be Shot on Sight." Both were hand-painted red in Cal's writing, which was scary enough, him being so uncultured and all. My heart fluttered a little bit. I turned my nose up and kept walking, thinking about what perfect targets we made with Jane's red shirt and my orange Auburn T-shirt and floral stretch leggings. We wouldn't be mistaken for deer, that was for sure.

We came around a bend in the road and could see a dilapidated house. Instead of a car under the carport, Cal had little mounds of old rusty metal junk on the stained concrete. Against the back wall, a long workbench held smaller piles of what looked like tools and tinier pieces of glass and metal.

"Here we are," Jane said. She was too polite to say, "Here we are at this awful-looking, rundown excuse of a house," but that's what it was. "I'll leave this tin by the side door, then we can be on our way."

I shook my head in wonder. "Doesn't look like he's spent a dime on this place in ages."

Jane moved her head to one side. "He does seem quite thrifty," she said, looking up at the rusted gutter as she came out from under the carport. It didn't have a drop of paint on it and looked like it could cave in any minute.

"You're funny. Thrifty's not the word for it. Crazy in the head is what he is. All that dough and it not doing him a bit of good. They say he has gold and money hidden all over the woods. Pots of it."

"That sounds like a story children might invent beside a campfire," Jane said, as we walked past the house toward the road again.

She brushed her hands off like they had dirt on them even though she hadn't touched anything on that nasty porch.

Jane still didn't look convinced. She seemed preoccupied with studying the trees. She kept taking deep breaths and smiling real big.

That's when it hit me. How had I not seen it before? She was one of those nature freaks. I knew it because she had that look, like Gene Miller's boy Hoil always had, but now Hoil was a hippie. Still is. It's the kind of look that makes you think they are a little on the goofy side.

"And," I said, "his granddaddy was the same way with money. Everybody says that's why he told Cal never to sell, because he couldn't remember where all he'd buried stuff and he wanted Cal to keep on looking for it. And not only that, but his grandaddy's great-great on-and-on grandaddy was supposed to have found a secret cave full of Spanish gold somewhere out here."

"Stories like that hardly ever have any truth to them at all. No, Phoebe, the treasure here is the beauty around us. Isn't it wonderful?"

I nodded. She was a tree hugger, all right.

I said, "All I know is what I've heard. I'm just telling you so you won't be surprised if we trip over a fruit jar full of hundred-dollar bills."

With that ugly shack behind us, I enjoyed our walk, especially while we were in the woods. No, I wasn't catching Jane's nature-freakitis. I liked it because it was at least ten degrees cooler under the trees. The morning had started off cool, but it had heated up already and my clothes already stuck to me, even that early in the morning. When we could see the road up ahead going out into the open again, I sure wasn't looking forward to it.

I changed my mind when we came upon something very interesting. Way off to our left we could see the thick pines that marked the beginning of Anisidi Wildlife Refuge. Way to the right, the land was flat and dusty looking. Big rocks lay even with the ground, almost like a rough pavement. Not much grass grew between the road where we stood and some big boulders lined up about forty feet away. Lots of beer bottles and cans, probably fifty or more, had been set in a row on top of them.

"This must be the place," I said.

"It is indeed. Cal has set up more targets for us, I see. Are you ready?" Jane said, while she loaded up the pistols. "Why don't you take a shot?"

I took the gun Jane handed me and walked to a well-worn spot on the ground where it looked like Cal must have stood a lot when he was fooling around and practicing. Jane showed me how to stand, how to hold my arms out, and how to use the sight at the end of the barrel to aim.

"Hey!" I yelled out. "If it's anybody out here, we're fixing to shoot." A little breeze moved in the bushes but nothing else. "Not that anybody is fool enough around here to trespass on Prewitt land."

I tell you what, we had a ball shooting those guns. When my gun was empty, Jane took out a pistol and fired three times at the cans. She hit two of them. I didn't hit a lick.

"Boy, you're good!" I said. "How'd you do that?"

"Luck, most likely. I'm quite a bit out of practice," she said. She smacked the top slide-y thing back like an expert and popped a metal cartridge of new bullets into the bottom of the gun handle like they do in movies. "The Colonel was a good teacher. He made sure I knew how to use every weapon he brought in the house, and as you could see, he brought in quite a few. I think he secretly hoped the Russians would invade so he could make use of them all."

"Kind of like reliving the good old days of the war, huh?"

"Yes. Exactly."

That didn't surprise me a bit. Didn't I say he was a hard-nosed old so-and-so?

We moved back quite a bit and Jane helped me again with holding and standing right when we switched to the rifle. It knocked me backward and hurt my shoulder to boot. I did like the sight better on it, though. My first two tries pinged off the boulders, but the third one hit a can and knocked it over. I whooped and hollered and jumped up and down like a kid.

We finished off the bullets she'd brought. I didn't hit anything else. Jane knocked off what was left.

"Now that is what I call a good time!" I said. "I could definitely get into this. I'm going to take my can home with me as a souvenir. You know, for my table."

We walked together toward the boulders. Jane pointed out that those flat rocks went on out gradually to the bluffs over the river.

"Look," she said pointing way up to the sky. "Look at the wingspan. An eagle or a large hawk, do you think?" She fiddled around with a pair of binoculars she'd brought. "I've been looking forward to studying the local bird populations."

Good grief, I thought, she's a koo-koo birdwatcher, too. I reckon that goes hand in hand with tree hugging.

I squinted up at the sky. "That's no eagle," I said. "That's just one of those ugly turkey buzzards. Nothing special."

While the bird circled and headed out over the big bluffs, Jane shielded her eyes with her hand to watch him. Meanwhile, I stepped behind the boulders.

Grass grew in scrubby bunches right behind the rocks and then got higher, three or four inches, and thicker toward the edge of the bluffs.

I saw my beer can. I knew it was mine because it was on the end and had a picture of a red dog on it. When I reached down to pick it up, I saw something else in the grass.

"Somebody has lost a coat," I said, looking down on the dark green and brown fabric in a camouflage pattern. I stood up straight as Jane walked up behind me.

We had both stepped closer to the coat when Jane screamed like a wild hyena right in my ear. When I saw what Jane saw, I stayed cool and tried to calm her down. Thank goodness I was there with her, or I don't know what she'd have done, as upset as she was. I couldn't really blame her because it sure was a horrible sight.

The coat still had a man in it. A dead one.

nine

Jane Calls the Cops

Phoebe screamed bloody murder, waving her arms in the air and pulling at her hair as she hopped frantically from one tiptoe to the other, wailing and crying uncontrollably for several minutes. I made her sit on a boulder a good distance away from the body and out of sight of it. I encouraged her to breathe deeply. I spoke soothingly, but I doubt she heard a word due to her loud sobbing.

"Did we do that?" Phoebe said, once she gained control of herself. Her voice quivered when she spoke. She clapped her hands tightly over her mouth so her words were muted, as were her hiccoughs. I felt terrible for her. I wouldn't have thought it possible for her skin to be any whiter than it was normally, but all color had absolutely drained from her face.

I'd seen quite a few dead bodies in my day, an unpleasant aspect of the part-time work I did a number of years earlier, never thinking that doing so could be seen as an advantage. I was clearly better prepared than Phoebe for the sight. When I went back for another look, she insisted on coming as well.

Blood stained the man's back. We could see a hole of darker red, almost black, in the center. I bent down to feel his neck, then his wrist.

"No, dear. We didn't do it. He's quite cold."

"For heaven sakes, Jane, how can you touch him?" Phoebe said, as she jumped again, her hands fluttering like birds' wings in front of her face. "I wonder who he is."

I lay my hand on his shoulder to raise him up enough for Phoebe to possibly identify the poor man.

"Don't do it again!"

"I thought you wanted to know who he is. Was."

"Not that bad. I don't recognize him anyway."

"Right. I'll call the police then."

"*We* will. I'm not staying here with the—the—him."

We went to Cal's house first, in case he had returned, to let him know what happened. It was then that the significance of his parked green truck occurred to me. Either he didn't go out of town as planned, or he'd caught a ride. Or he was still home. When he didn't answer the door, Phoebe and I hurried to my house to use the phone.

Both of Tullulah's police cars came within five minutes. The officers asked that we wait by the road for Detective Waters. Phoebe reacquainted herself with each officer. She appeared to have known them since they were children, and verified each man's personal histories, tracing their lineages through mothers, aunts, grandfathers, and distant cousins with whom she was, of course, familiar. Not many minutes later, a white unmarked police car arrived. A tall gentleman in a navy jacket, red patterned tie, and khaki trousers got out of the car and came toward us. The officers followed, all noticeably nervous in his presence. The detective took no notice of any of them.

The stonelike set of his large, rough features and his shiny, solid black eyes invited no pleasantries. It was a face intent on one purpose. From the moment he left his vehicle, he did only two things. He made one sweep across his field of vision, taking everything and everyone in, then he locked his sights on Phoebe as he strode directly to her side. His impassive expression transformed instantly into a friendly smile, in the space of a snap of a finger, when Phoebe saw him.

They spoke at once. "Miz Twigg. You all right?" He placed his big hands on her shoulders. Phoebe brought her own hands down from her face and said, "Daniel, son, I'm so glad you're here. It was the awfulest thing but I'm okay now." His head bobbed as he spoke reassuring words. Then he turned his attention to me.

"Miz Thistle?"

"Yes. Jane Thistle. How do you do?" I said. "I'm the one who called."

"Detective Dan Waters, ma'am," he said as he shook my hand. "You told the dispatcher you found a body?"

"Yes. Not far from here." I pointed toward the road leading into Cal's land.

He nodded, still holding onto my hand, still looking directly into my eyes. When he said nothing more, I felt compelled to continue. I gave him a brief account of our ordeal in a few sentences. He nodded again when I finished. "Thank you. If you don't mind, I'd like you ladies to walk with me a little ways."

I had no objections and Phoebe, though still a bit rattled, had calmed considerably since Detective Waters' arrival. When we all passed Cal's gate and his "Keep Out" signs on the way to the body, the detective said, "You were on Prewitt land?"

"Yes," I said. "With permission. He said we could use the firing range this morning. Phoebe and I had done so when we saw him."

"Saw Cal?"

"No, sorry. The deceased person."

"Cal wasn't with you?"

"No. Just the two of us."

"And have you seen Cal this morning, ladies?"

"No," Phoebe and I said together.

At the boulders, Detective Waters stood looking in all directions, turning slowly as he surveyed the area. He squatted next to the still form and reached into his own jacket pocket. He took out a pair of rubber gloves, pulled them on, and lifted the deceased's shoulder a few inches, just where I had put my hand earlier. To my surprise, Phoebe edged forward as close as she could to the body to see. Her squeamishness had turned into fascination.

The poor man looked very young, in his early twenties, I'd say. I realized the green and brown coat was one a hunter might wear. I shocked myself when the idea that Cal might have shot him for poaching popped into my mind. I didn't believe it for a moment and dismissed the thought. Cal had shown himself to be a careful shot thus far.

Detective Waters stood and spoke to his men. "Everyone, stay alert. Keep in mind where we are. Cal is usually armed, usually drinking, maybe pointing a shotgun at us right now. Let's be careful. See if you can find him and bring him to me, would you please."

The flat tone of his words sent a chill down me. I felt sure Cal wouldn't have killed someone, accidentally or otherwise. Of course, since he was one of the very few people I'd met in Tullulah, I wondered if perhaps I'd assumed too much in thinking he would be innocent. It was, after all, unlikely for anyone other than himself to be on the property. But then, why was this young man here?

"The house is that way," Detective Waters continued. Two officers headed in the direction indicated. "The rest of you spread out. To the edge of the woods and back here first, please." Detective Waters turned us. "So you haven't seen him today?"

"Nope," Phoebe said. "Not hide nor hair."

I hesitated. "No." I didn't like to talk about him. I don't know why. I understood that from the authorities' point of view, Cal would certainly be the first to question since the body was on his land. I felt terrible for him. Hearing Cal talk on the porch may have brought out a motherly instinct, perhaps too much of one.

The policemen's instinct however would surely be to track, question, and possibly arrest him. To their minds, it might seem a quick and easy case. He had a history of shooting at trespassers, he was alone and seemingly poor. At least from the looks of things, he had no money. Phoebe's story of hidden gold and money could be partially true. Certainly it would fit in with his quirky personality.

The radio on Detective Waters' belt squawked. "Go ahead," he said into the tiny black box.

"Sir, the house is empty."

"Ten-four," Detective Waters said and held the radio a moment. "Begin your perimeter search from the house."

"Ten-four," the radio squawked.

An uncomfortable silence followed between us. Detective Waters again scanned the area from where we stood. I had the distinct feeling he was purposely avoiding eye contact with me. He stepped away from the body and walked in a circle around the practicing range.

He came to a stop behind the boulders and looked out over the bluff where Cal and I had stood the day before. The wind ruffled his dark hair as he surveyed the valley below. He didn't move for some minutes. When he did, he turned slowly, his eyes seeking mine. I saw many questions in them until his blank, intent stare changed abruptly to a fake smile, all in an instant, like the slam of a closing door.

The look chilled me, for in it I saw that he suspected Cal of this murder. I had no more evidence than the detective did to go on, yet I was certain that Cal did not do it.

ten

Phoebe Disagrees

here was absolutely no doubt in my mind—Cal did it. Why Jane was so soft on him without hardly knowing him, I couldn't understand. Even if he was liquored up, as usual, and shot the poor man without knowing who he was, that still wouldn't excuse him for not calling the cops. If he didn't have a phone, he could've used Jane's. And where was he at anyway?

I didn't recognize the dead guy. I don't think he was from around here. Of course, a lot of young people have moved to town in the last several years, what with the new plant opening up in Russellville, so I don't know everybody like I used to.

Tullulah's not that big—one high school, probably between seventy or eighty churches, and no shopping malls. Anything we can't get on the square, we go into either Russellville or the Shoals to get what we need. Time was when I knew all the kids from either seeing them at church or at work at the public library, which I retired from five years ago. But now, a whole new crop of people are here, not connected to anybody, so it wasn't much of a surprise I didn't know that young man we found dead on the ground.

Anyway, it was highly likely Cal did it. You add two plus two and you get Cal in a heap of trouble. The fact he was nowhere to be found was mighty telling.

The cops made us leave the scene of the crime. They took all of Jane's guns for testing and promised to return them if they were cleared. Like they wouldn't be. That handsome Daniel Waters was no fool, so we didn't have anything to worry about.

"Ladies, we appreciate your help," he said. "What I'd like for you to do is wait for me in Miz Thistle's house. You'll be more comfortable there. I'll be by as soon as I can. I hate to inconvenience you, but I'm sure I'll have important questions, and I really do need your help."

He has always been so polite, even as a little boy when I had him in my Sunday school class. The Waters were poor as poor could be and didn't have nothing to wear but rags, but they were always clean, and those children were brought up to be respectful and polite. I was proud of Daniel for making something of himself.

I knew what he was doing by making us leave right then. He said all that just as the coroner's station wagon rolled up the road. I thought it was mighty considerate of him to let us go before they started fooling with the body.

By the time we got inside Jane's house, the day was already sweltering hot. Jane got a pitcher out of the refrigerator and poured us each a glass of iced tea.

"Now about Cal," I said. "I know what you're thinking. You act like he's some poor lost soul. You watch him, Jane. You don't know him like I do."

"I got the impression you didn't know him personally."

"Well, I know *of* him. Everybody in town does. He's been causing trouble and raising Hades ever since he was a boy. Been in jail so many times they nearly named the new jailhouse after him when it was built. He killed a man, you know."

Jane looked shocked. She set her glass down. "No, I didn't," she said. "How long was he in prison?"

"Oh, only one night. And not prison, just the local lockup. Several witnesses in the bar where it happened said it was self-defense. Some guy had been drinking all night, went nuts, and Cal happened to be closest to him. One of the witnesses was a judge. Cal's daddy was still alive at the time, too, so he had money to spring Cal. I believe that was in 1969."

"But it *was* self-defense, you say? He was completely cleared?"

"Yes. From then on, he has stayed out here in the wilderness by himself."

"That's sad."

"No, it's not," I said. "He chose to live like he does. His family had all the money and influence in the world. He could have had any one of a hundred different lives if he wanted. But no, he wants to live like a wild animal. A recluse is what he is. He'd rather die than sit down and have a human conversation with somebody."

"Actually," Jane said, "I found him quite an amusing conversationalist. Interesting. Honest."

That was when she told me he showed up drunk on her doorstep in the middle of the night. I could not believe it. The man showed her exactly what a sorry sot he was and she calls him "amusing." Jane really is a little out there sometimes. I knew right then I'd have to watch her back for her since she didn't understand what kind of dog Cal was. It's a good thing she's got me to help her whenever she's not thinking right.

She did pretty well when Daniel questioned us again. We had a little test runthrough in a way, since Daniel had patrolmen take a statement from each of us at the same time, in separate rooms, before he came in and did the same thing again himself. When he was leaving and we were all standing on her front porch together, he asked her again about times, when were she and Cal at the range together the day before, what time did she last see Cal, when did she hear the shots in the night, and when did the two of us get to the range that morning. He didn't ask her sneaky like Columbo either, just straight out so he was sure he had everything right in his head before he left. It was nigh on twelve o'clock before I was finally free to go.

*T*HE LAST THING SOME FOLKS MIGHT WANT TO DO AFter seeing a dead body is buy a gun. Well, I did. When the police finished questioning me, I went home, took a shower, and then puttered around the house awhile. Every time I walked through my living room, my eyes went straight to the table where my new Israeli bullets lay. I thought, *What am I waiting for, a killer to come into my house? When I'd wish I'd bought a gun while I still had the chance?*

No, sir, I was going to be prepared. It was high time I showed a little gumption and started taking charge of my own defense. I smiled thinking how Jane's knowing how to shoot so good had already been a positive influence on me.

I wasn't about to buy a gun from Harvel Wriggle after the way he talked smart to me that day I bought my bullets. He wasn't the only game in town, not by a long shot. I put on some fresh makeup and headed downtown.

I love the town square. Usually I take my time going around it, talking to folks, but it was already almost three o'clock in the afternoon and too hot to dillydally. I pulled my car into an angled space in front of the courthouse and walked a few doors down to Alton's Gun Emporium. I've been friends with Alton for years because he was my husband's cousin. I was glad to throw a little business his way.

A bell jingled when I opened the shop door.

"Hey, Phoebe," Alton said. "I'll be right with you."

Alton looked like he always did, smiling no matter what and his bony arms hanging out of some ridiculous polyester bowling shirt.

I said hey and right then I realized who the customer at the counter was. I patted my hair up and bit my lips to make them redder as I walked closer to the handsomest man in four counties, Jack Blaylock. He hosts the local hunting and fishing show on the public TV station every Saturday night and has even been a guest expert on several cable programs on tracking game through the woods.

I winked at him. "Why, my stars, Alton, I had no idea you catered to celebrities. Mister Blaylock, I'm Phoebe Twigg. I see you on TV all the time, although I'm not a fish and wildlife enthusiast such as yourself."

He nodded at me and said, "Ma'am."

His black hair had hardly any gray in it, even though I knew he must be in his sixties like me. He was handsome enough to be one of those smoking cowboys in the cigarette ads.

We got to talking and it came out that Alton and I were related by marriage. I said to Jack, "That's right. Alton here is my late husband's double first cousin."

Jack Blaylock nodded like he understood. "What exactly is a double first cousin?" he said with a sexy laugh. His deep voice and his long eyelashes made my knees go a little quivery.

"Alton here and my late husband, Ronald, were first cousins on both sides of the family. Their mamas were sisters, who married brothers. In other words, Alton's mama was Noreen Shelton and her sister, Nelda, was my late husband Ronald's mama. Noreen married Bill Twigg and Nelda married his brother, Lonnie, which makes Alton and Ronald cousins, twice. Ronald, my *late* husband. Who passed away years ago."

"I see," Jack said, while he gave me the once over.

"Now, y'all don't pay any attention to me. Go right ahead with what you're doing because I want to listen and see if I can learn something while I browse."

I thought how glad I was I had on my dangling amethyst earrings. They look good with the lavender pant set I had on. Always look your best, that's what I say. You never know who you'll run into.

"Why would a pretty thing like you need to know about guns?" Jack took a pistol from Alton and clicked it open where the empty bullet holder fell out the handle.

I gave Jack's arm a little slap. "After what I've been through today with police interrogation and dead bodies? What, y'all haven't heard about it yet?"

They both shook their heads and said, "What happened?" at the same time.

"Well," I said. I thought a second, took a deep breath, and began. "It all started yesterday about noon. I went in to Wriggle's to buy my brother a tackle box..."

I gave them the whole story, all the way to me coming into Alton's store. "And that's why I need me a gun."

Alton leaned down and hung his arms over the counter, steadily shaking his head at me. "I'm not sure that's such a good idea."

"And why not?" I asked. "Why shouldn't I get one?"

"Well, Phoebe, I don't really know how to say this, but you've been known to be a mite clumsy at times."

I put my hands on my hips and counted to five. "Will you never forget that doggone wedding cake?" I said. I'd had a small accident at Alton's oldest boy's wedding over ten years ago. Ronald was still alive then. We got up to dance and were close to the refreshments table at the reception. Somebody had dropped an ice cube on the floor and hadn't picked it up. I stepped on it with my heel and my feet went flying out from under me. Naturally, I tried to grab hold of something to break the fall. The nearest thing was the cake table. It wasn't my fault the caterers had set the wedding cake so close to the edge. Plus, if it hadn't been one of those fancy five-tiered ones, which are very unsteady, with the fountain spurting out sparkling grape juice at the top, it wouldn't have collapsed and got stomped on, and the band wouldn't have got soaked when the grape juice tube came loose, spraying in all directions so nobody could catch it.

"Then there was that other time," Alton said. "Remember when our cousin Glendell caught that possum . . ."

"Don't even finish that lie, Alton Twigg. I was not aiming at him with that popgun. He ran straight across that clothesline and right in front of me and you know it."

"And then there was that time with the truckload of watermelons at the fireworks shack . . ."

"Will you hush?"

"Okay, okay. Seriously, now, no offense, Phoebe," Alton said. "And it's nothing personal, but it's not ladylike for women to have guns." He stood there, shaking his head back and forth. "It just don't look right."

"That dead body didn't look right either," I said. "I daresay he'd be walking right now if he'd had a gun on him. Besides, I don't have a big strong man at home to protect me." I flashed a quick sideways look at Jack.

Alton started in, trying to talk me out of it. Jack was on my side. "Maybe the little lady is right," he said. "It doesn't hurt to be ready just in case. It's a different world nowadays."

"Thank you for that vote of confidence."

Alton still shook his head. "The world may be different but Tullulah ain't. It's safe as can be here. Just because somebody got shot on the Prewitt place doesn't mean a thing. We all know how Cal is.

Hey, you know, I heard he sold some of his land to some contractors in Birmingham who build big shopping malls. They could build a mighty big one out there. Wouldn't that be something?"

"I heard that, too," Jack said. "Only I heard it was going to be an industrial complex with a small airstrip for Ag pilots."

"There's room for all of them out there," Alton said.

A shopping mall? I'd love that. Then I wouldn't have to drive out of town to get pretty clothes and things for my house. Dreaming about spending money on home interiors wasn't helping me at the moment though. I rapped my knuckles on the glass counter to get the men's attention.

"Look here, I'm buying me a gun today, whether you like it or not, Alton. Don't make me go down the road and get one from Wriggle's."

I took my box of Israeli bullets out of my purse and slapped it down on the counter. "Now. It has to be something that these will fit in," I said.

Alton and Jack looked at each other funny but I acted like I didn't notice. They could make fun of me all they wanted to, I didn't care.

Would you believe, in that whole store, Alton didn't have a single gun those would work in? At least, that's what he told me. I wasn't so sure I believed him.

"These are for a real big gun, like a hunting gun. That's not what you want. You need one of these here smaller ones."

My lips pursed into a tight line. I do like that when I'm trying hard to keep the wrong words from spilling out. What I do is, I let myself think whatever ugly words I want to and then push them out my ears. I play like they float out and evaporate in the air. Then I feel better without cussing somebody out.

"I know what I want, Alton. One of those little peashooters would only make a bad guy laugh at me before he robs and murders me. It's something my own bullets will fit in, or nothing."

Alton snapped his fingers. "Hey, I just thought of something. You know what you ought to do? Sign up for Jack's safety classes."

"Classes?"

Jack cleared his throat and ran a finger over each side of his moustache. "What I do, Phoebe, is teach folks, just like yourself, how to handle firearms safely in a one-day workshop. There's a little on self-defense, but mostly I concentrate on how to load, shoot, and clean your gun. If you're interested, I believe I could get you in this next class. But . . ."

"Oh, I'd love to! Count me in!" I said. "But what?"

"It's strictly for handguns. So you'd need to get you a small one. And the class is tomorrow."

I thought about it a second and realized there was no law against me having more than one gun. I could get me a big one some other time. But I wasn't going to miss out on special attention from Mr. Jack Blaylock, local celebrity and handsome stud.

"In that case, y'all fix me up. I'll do it."

Jack helped me pick out one that fit my hand just right called a CZ-75. It was fairly hefty and the first thing I've ever owned that was made in Czechoslovakia. He told me a few more specifics about the all-day class and gave me directions to the shooting range.

When Jack left, the little bell on the door jingled again. He touched the front of his hat and smiled at me.

As soon as the door closed, I said, "Is he married?"

"I believe he is," Alton said.

"He wasn't wearing a ring."

"And I hear she's real mean. Watch yourself."

"Oh, don't be silly. I'm just curious," I said, although the truth was I was already flipping through my closet in my mind to pick out the prettiest outfit to wear the next day.

eleven

Jane Has Company

fter we found the body, Phoebe and I waited at my house until the police returned to ask us a few more questions. Most were the same ones they'd asked before but we both obliged. Once done, Phoebe had errands to run, so I was alone with my thoughts.

What a morning it had been. I gathered clean clothes and headed to the bath for a nice shower. I bent to pick up my house slippers from the closet floor, and when I stood again, I noticed my grandmother's table was not where I put it.

It was all I had of hers, a spindly, lightweight thing with one pedestal leg and a top that could be folded flat against the wall. I'd positioned the table carefully to hide a small area of torn wallpaper that at the moment I could see clearly. Curious, I thought, that the table now stood several inches farther along the wall.

The floors here are old, I said to myself, and uneven. Of course such a light object might not stay put in certain spots, particularly one with an old, worn handmade base. The path between the table and my bed was narrow, and most likely I brushed the table when I passed causing it to jiggle out of place.

There was one problem with that theory. I didn't remember walking past it, not since I first set it there. And if I had done, going from bed to closet, the table would have moved in the opposite direction and closer to the wall, not farther from it. I carried on to the bathroom with only a brief hesitance and the smallest backward glance.

The rest of the day was uneventful, other than the continuation of my unpacking into the night. I went to bed worried as there had been no word from Cal.

Next morning, I went through my rituals of stretches, ventured a bit farther on my walk, and came home again for a calming set of Tai Chi. I was quite pleased with myself for I'd incorporated a bit of running into my walk that came much easier than the day before.

Once clean and refreshed, I sat on the porch looking out over the meadow. I suppose I was looking for Cal. I couldn't believe he had murdered that young man then left him to lie in the dirt. But guilty or not, he must return and talk to the police soon. I tried to keep another worry at bay, that Cal had also been shot and lay somewhere undiscovered.

I had no choice but to tell the police about Cal agreeing to sell me his land. I wasn't keen on it, as I considered it no one's business but ours. Also, I feared it might implicate Cal further, perhaps making the police think he had fled since he would soon have no land ties here.

This was preposterous, of course. Cal would never leave his land. That was the whole point of our arrangement. He wanted to die there. Running away did not fit into his plan.

Until more evidence surfaced to clear him, I found myself

wishing he might stay hidden for a few days. If not, I prayed he would come to me. I couldn't do much for him except be a friend. That was something he seemed in short supply of here. A poor man with a criminal record and a bad reputation makes an easy target for false accusations, particularly in a small town. This accusation could prove too much for poor Cal in light of his bad health.

I returned inside but left the door open and the screen locked to keep an eye and an ear out for police activity should Cal return.

I began to mull over the possibilities of our proposed land deal as I fussed with rearranging the living room furniture. I was of two minds about it all. For a while, I told myself nothing had changed. The police might find evidence very soon that exonerated Cal. Then I convinced myself he was guilty, would be convicted, and the land would be tied up until his death in prison. What would happen then? With no heirs, the land might be sold by the state and developed, and I would have new neighbors. Many, many new neighbors. Worse, it would mean the death of a beautiful tract of nature, an irretrievable loss.

I stepped over to the front windows. A single police cruiser remained, parked in the shade of the pines that line the entrance to the refuge. Of course, they would be watching for Cal. Perhaps they were also watching me. Dismissing the thought as melodramatic, I continued straightening and unpacking with the uneasy feeling of being in a cage.

Many more questions surfaced concerning wills and land. I considered calling the lawyer who had helped in settling the sale of my house. His office was located on the square downtown. He was such a nice fellow, I was sure he'd be happy to answer any questions about state laws and the like. However, inquiries to a native Tullulian might not be wise at this stage, I thought.

A sudden loud noise at the back porch startled me. It sounded like a box fell over and hit the back wall. My first thought was of the squirrel visitor that had left me acorns in the night. My second thought was of the huge snake. I found that my eyes went immediately to the floor where it had slithered its way across the threshold.

I stepped quickly to the curtain covering the back-door window.

I saw nothing. No further movement was seen or heard. When I opened the door, all was still. The cardboard box I'd packed with tools lay spread about the porch as if someone had overturned it to find the proper one to use.

I smiled as I went onto the porch, imagining a raccoon or rabbit selecting a trowel and planning his flower garden. But how could one have gotten in? The mesh screening all around the porch looked intact. I bent down to scoop everything up and noticed something reddish on the steps going down to the yard. I shoved the utensil box against the wall where it had been and stepped to the screen for a closer look.

They were half footsteps. The imprints looked to have been made with fresh, red mud. I might have thought the movers had left them had I not hosed off the porches, front and back, after they left.

I tried to remember if the police had walked behind my house. Perhaps they had done so while I was otherwise occupied. Or someone else was nearby now. The image of my grandmother's table upstairs flashed through my mind.

I latched the screen door as a precaution. Immediately I thought of Phoebe's assertion that no one locks doors here in Tullulah and felt a slight twinge of guilt.

No sooner had I turned to go back inside when something thumped under the floor very near my feet. All became clear. This time, I unlatched the door, marched down the steps, and opened the hinged piece of lattice that opened to the storage space under the porch.

All was quiet and very dark under there. As my vision adjusted to the darkness, I saw first one set of eyes blink, then another set, lower and to the right of the first.

I looked around me to be certain no one was watching. "All right, you two. You'd better come out quickly before anyone sees you."

One dog and one man carrying a sack crawled out from under the porch. Both looked apologetic and grateful for rescue. Before Cal could speak or Homer could bark, I said, "Not a word. Hurry now. Up with you. Quick as you can."

They did as they were asked with not a sound out of them. Both stayed on the porch close to the screen door after I shut it behind us. Cal's face drooped as much as Homer's jowls. Both looked embarrassed, standing there covered in mud.

"I'm sorry, Jane. We've been pondering what to do, me and Homer. Seems like whichever way we go, it's going to be a bad turn."

I hated to agree. "You must go and talk to the police, you know. It's the only way."

"I didn't do anything! They'll lock me up without even caring. You wait and see if they don't."

"If you are innocent, you have nothing to worry about if you call them before they find you."

He shook his head. His voice was light, weak. "I know that's right. But I can't die in jail, Jane. I just can't."

I sighed as I took in the sight of them. "No more talking nonsense. Right now, you're in need of a shower and something to eat. Both of you."

Homer licked his jaws. I instructed Cal to stay put while I led Homer off the porch. Minding we stayed well out of view of the road, I turned on the water spigot and gave him a good wash down, which he seemed to enjoy. I sent him up the steps and inside again. While the water was on, I sprayed the mud tracks off the steps. Feeling a bit criminal, I also sprayed away all foot and paw prints from the dirt around the lattice that covered the storage area under the house.

Cal sat on a ladder-back chair on the porch and removed his shoes and socks. "That night, several hours after I left here, I heard a shot across the field. I walked toward the road. I stayed near the street lamp at the refuge entrance. Didn't want to get accidentally shot myself. Didn't see nothing. Figured it must've been a car backfiring, going around the refuge next to your place." He pointed to the narrow road that turned right at the refuge entrance and divided my property and the refuge itself. "I waited awhile, still didn't see nothing, so I went back home. I decided not to go to Florence, so me and Homer just made our regular rounds."

I rummaged through a box and found a few old towels I'd saved for rags. "Come here, Homer," I said. He trotted over so I could dry him off. To Cal, I said, "And you didn't go near the practicing range anytime yesterday morning?"

"No."

"You know we found a body? I presume that's why you're here, correct?"

Cal looked up and nodded slowly. "We seen the police. I started to walk up and see what the problem was until I seen that body bag. We decided to take the long way around the refuge and come here. You know, to give me some thinking time."

Cal wasn't telling me the truth, at least not all of it. His story had one large hole obvious to me already. The bag he carried suggested he had been home and also planned to stay away at least for a little while.

"Do you have a clean change of clothes in there?" I asked and pointed to his bag. He nodded. I brought him inside and directed him to the downstairs bath where he could shower. Meanwhile, I cooked a quick meal of ham, eggs, and fried potatoes for the three of us.

I wondered if Cal wasn't planning to steal away from here as he had done from his own house. He may have intended to stay hidden until he could get the keys to my car and drive off, sometime late in the evening. I chided myself for having such a thought. It was an unlikely theory. With Cal's outdoor skills and intimate knowledge of his land, he could easily evade detection under cover of the woods and stay hidden as long as he liked. Yet he had come here. Why?

twelve

Phoebe Gets Her
Hair Fixed

My phone nearly rang off the hook after we found that body, so many people were calling me. I figured they would. Jane and I were the lead story on the five o'clock news. The news reporters from the paper and WTTV, the local station, came to the scene not long after the police did.

The newspaper story showed us talking to Detective Waters. The headlines read, "Unidentified Man Found Dead. New Resident Questioned." They had both our names in the caption. My hair looked awful but that was to be expected, considering.

The next morning, Jack Blaylock's gun-safety class was supposed to start at ten o'clock. Luckily, this would not interfere with my regular Saturday hair appointment at 8:45, so I had plenty of time to get beautiful before shooting the fire out of those paper targets.

The Beauty Barn sits on an odd-shaped piece of land several blocks behind the main drag on the square. It's more like a cabin than a barn. The logs aren't like new fancy ones you see these days. They're real old and black with age.

The cabin sat empty a long time while the history nuts argued whether or not it was historical. Personally, I saw nothing special about it just because it's old. The town council thought the same. They saw no reason to preserve a former home for young ladies, especially when there's a question as to whether they were actually ladies, if you know what I mean.

After that, the cabin was a florist and gift shop for a while. It was pretty nice but the husband of the lady who ran it got transferred. That's when Ray and Bonita Young bought it because her beauty business she did out of her house grew so much that she was out of space.

Now she has plenty of room. She has expanded from two hairdryers to five, all lined up on the right wall. On the left is where they put the big mirrors and twirling chairs where Bonita and two other beauticians style hair. The big stone fireplace straight ahead hadn't been lit yet for the cool weather, but it wouldn't be long. I couldn't wait.

Every Saturday, the barn is pretty full when I get there. That day it was jam-packed. The high-pitched chatter of women yakking ninety miles an hour was so loud a bugler on a horse could've galloped in the door playing reveille and nobody would've heard or even noticed them. But when everybody saw me, the whole place went silent.

Bonita was the first one to move. She finished rolling the last perm rod on top of Shirley Blevins' head and whirled her around in the chair. She stretched a plastic cap on Shirley's head, and then fastened it with a silver butterfly clip. "Now, you sit tight, Shirley. Here's a towel. You're set."

Bonita smiled and tiptoed over to me. "We're ready for you

Phoebe, hon. We've got a sink waiting on you." She led me back to the sinks and whipped a towel around my neck herself. This was the royal treatment. Bonita hardly ever shampooed anybody herself anymore. One of her nieces or some of their high school friends usually did that and swept the floors now that the Barn was so popular. She flicked one of the new capes out and around my shoulders. With a quick snap at the neck, she wasted no time on small talk and got straight down to business.

"Don't keep us in suspense. We want to hear it all, Phoebe, don't leave the least little bit out." Every ear in the place was stuck way out to hear me. I had to holler over the noise of the spray when she rinsed and project my voice a little more since I was bent over backward with my head hanging in the sink.

"Where do I begin?" I said, looking up at the ceiling. "Let's see. It all started Wednesday morning when I went to Wriggle's Sporting Goods."

I got up to the part about giving Jane a blanket when Bonita told me to sit up. She wrapped a towel around my hair and patted my back so I'd go on to her styling chair. She jacked it up high after I sat down and rubbed the towel all over my head. While she trimmed my hair a little bit and put it up in rollers, I told the rest of the story up to the part where the newsmen left.

Treenie Dodd, a stout girl with kinky blonde hair who is my cousin Annette's great niece (not blood niece, by second marriage), sat directly behind me in the waiting area straight across the room. I could see her in the mirror. She quit flipping through a magazine and said, "So you don't think this Jane woman was mixed up with that young guy that got killed, do you?"

"Of course not. For heaven's sake, she just got here. And before you ask, no, she didn't shoot that poor boy either. He was already dead when we found him. He was done cold as a Popsicle."

"You touched him?" Bonita said. Her hands stopped in mid-roll.

I swiped my hair out of my eyes. "New-hoo, new, new. No,

ma'am, not me. I just took Jane's word for it. I wasn't about to touch that thing."

Treenie edged forward on her seat. Her voice was low and husky, like a man's. I think she does it on purpose. "Well, she could've been lying. For all you know, she could've done it herself earlier that morning or even the night before. Was she up and dressed when you got there?"

"Yes," I said, as I thought back.

"Could she possibly have led you over to those rocks, making it look like y'all just happened on them?"

"No, of course not. She told me she already knew they were there. She'd been the day before." That didn't sound good. "She only wanted to go because of me, because I got the idea I wanted to buy my own bullets at Wriggle's."

Treenie's eyes narrowed. "Maybe you thought it was your idea but she really suggested it. You know, subliminal. Put it in your mind."

"Oh, hush that ignert geechie, Treenie Renee Dodd. You're talking plain crazy."

"I'm just making conversation." For as long as I've known Treenie, she's been a hard head. Contrary from day one. Whatever I told her and the other kids at the library not to do, she'd do it. If little girls were supposed to be quiet and play with dolls and wear dresses, she'd play with guns and trucks.

It was no surprise to me when she joined the army. She tried to get on with the police when she got out but she tested positive for marijuana during the interviews. At least that's what I heard. Now, she works for a construction company. No, not answering the phones or doing the payroll like a respectable lady. She runs heavy equipment like bulldozers and bush hogs. They say she's good at it. I say there's something mighty peculiar about that girl. I think she just likes to hang around old men who cuss and spit. They say she laughs and jokes with them that she's got a girlfriend just like them.

If you ask me, that's taking the whole "bonding with the guys" thing a little too far.

I decided it was best just to ignore her. I finished telling my story. I wasn't about to let her think I didn't know exactly what happened, so I said, "We saw all kinds of strange things on that property." I looked all around at everybody and then directly at Treenie and said, "Stuff you ain't got no idea about. Stuff you wouldn't even believe."

"Like what?" she asked, leaning toward me.

I shrugged and looked away, real nonchalant. "Well, I wouldn't want to scare you too bad. I'll say this—there's more in those woods than just a bunch of trees and squirrel poop. Jane and I pretty much figured everything out about that poor boy's murder. But I've probably already said too much. The police wouldn't appreciate me blabbing out things that might be pertinent to their investigation, now would they?"

She looked impressed. That'll teach her to be nosy. I smiled and changed the subject. Everybody was real interested in Jane's house so I told them all about her furniture and how she was decorating. When it was time to get under the hair dryer, I could finally relax. I closed my eyes and tried to think if I was sure my turquoise outfit was good enough for my gun class or if I needed to stop around the corner at Franny's Boutique to buy something new.

thirteen

Jane Hears Cal's Side
of the Story

When he reappeared from his shower, dressed in his clean clothes, Cal reached in the bag he brought with him and took out an old notebook. "After we talked the other night," he said, "I went ahead and wrote out a few things about our deal." I took the notebook proffered and skimmed it. In rough language, he had made a bill of sale, according to our agreement.

"Cal, considering the circumstances, perhaps we should let this go for a while. After all, much more important things occupy our minds at the moment."

"No." He shook his head adamantly. "There ain't nothing more important than this. This here," he said tapping the notebook heavily with a tobacco-stained finger, "is the only important thing there is. I want it to be a done deal."

"Of course I want the same but there's no need to hurry. Right now, we need to call a lawyer for you." Since I knew only my own, I was about to ring him to see if he could refer us to a criminal lawyer.

"Wait." He sat very still. Indecision and pain lined his face. "I got my own." He took his wallet out of his back pants pocket, fingered through a number of cards, and pulled one out. It was yellowed and quite wrinkled, as if he'd been carrying it a long time.

"Come sit down at the table and eat a bite. You look famished. I'll call him for you."

He handed the card to me. I called and asked for the lawyer but was told he was out of town. The secretary said his junior associate agreed to come straightaway.

"Cal," I said when I hung up, "you must be completely honest with the police. If you are innocent but lie to them about something trivial, you will discredit yourself needlessly. You understand that already, I'm sure. Just remember to choose your words carefully."

He nodded. "I know you're right. I've been there before."

I hoped he would also keep jail in mind. He'd been there before as well.

"You didn't have to fix this," he said of the plate of food I sat before him. "You shouldn't have gone to so much trouble."

"You need your strength. It's no trouble at all." I'd scrambled a few more eggs and a bit of ham for Homer, still on the back porch. I set the bowl down next to him and by the time I brought him another bowl of water he'd cleaned his plate.

"Here is what I've been thinking," I said. I sat down next to him with a glass of tea. "When the lawyer comes, we'll talk about the bill of sale, if it will ease your mind. Then, in a day or two, we'll see where we need to go from there."

"I'll be in jail by then, I reckon."

"You mustn't think that. They will ask you questions. A murder was committed on your property. It's inevitable. They'll have no evidence against you."

A derisive smile curled his lips. "Evidence or no, they'll lock me up. He was on my property. And yes, I've been known to shoot at people. But I never hit anybody. Could have if I wanted to. Ain't nothing wrong with my aim."

"It makes no difference. They must prove you shot this time. The past doesn't matter."

For the first time, Cal lifted his eyes to mine. They were full of disbelief but he said nothing.

Not long after, the front doorbell rang. I looked through the window beside the door. I expected to see Cal's lawyer, certainly, but was not prepared to see the lawyer was a she, a young and beautiful lady. Her straight red hair hung to her shoulders with short bangs on top. Her summer-weight suit was pale yellow, the skirt of which just touched her knees.

"Mrs. Thistle? I'm Shelley Barnette from Hannigan and Wade."

"I'm pleased to meet you," I said, as her small hand shook mine. I noted her control as she saw Cal. Only a flicker sped across her eyes before we stepped through to the kitchen. Curiosity? Compassion? I couldn't tell.

"Hello, Mr. Prewitt. Shelley Barnette. Pleased to meet you," she said, as she put her hand out. Cal took it and gave a tentative shake. "Ma'am," he said.

Shelley smiled. "Mr. Wade is out of town. I hope you don't mind that I'm his replacement."

"No, ma'am," he said. His face looked transformed and obviously pleased with his new counsel. He pulled a chair out for her to sit, then returned to his own. She set her briefcase on the table, and we got right down to business.

While we explained Cal's situation, she jotted a few notes in a leather organizer. She didn't interrupt either of us. When we'd finished, she sat without speaking for a few moments, then said, "Mr. Prewitt, first, we need to call the police right away. I'll be happy to do that, but I believe it would look better if you did so yourself."

I took the card Detective Waters had given me and handed it to Cal. He said nothing but took it, walked to the phone on the kitchen wall, and dialed.

"Detective Waters? Yes, sir, this here is Cal Prewitt. I just stopped by Jane Thistle's house and she said y'all were a'looking for me. Say there's been some trouble out at my place?" After a few moments of listening, Cal said, "Yes, sir. I'll be right here then waiting on you."

I must have sighed too loudly as he replaced the cradle, for he laughed at me as his own worried look relaxed. "You ain't got to worry about me. I've been playing with them boys for a long time. You might say it's my avocation."

He drew out the last word with a slow delight. Even at what might be his weakest point, healthwise, with certainly a dark outlook for his immediate future, the force of his personality sparkled out of his eyes into mine.

I would like to have seen Detective Waters' reaction on receiving Cal's call. Naturally, it would be good news for him, but I pitied the officer stationed outside who would surely be reprimanded for letting Cal slip by unseen.

Before Cal returned to his seat, he retrieved the hand-written rough draft of his bill of sale for his land. He tried to smooth wrinkles out of the paper in front of Miss Barnette. "Young lady, there's something else I'd like you to do for me."

She smiled and read over the document. Her eyebrows rose high on her forehead. Her finger slid down the page with a pause at each of Cal's stipulations. "I see. Well, this looks straightforward enough. It brings up a few questions that I'll need to doublecheck first." Her brow furrowed. "I'll look into everything and get it written up in legalese," she said, giving me a wink and a smile. "I can have it back to you in a few days to sign."

"No, ma'am," Cal said. "No, ma'am, that won't do."

"Did you need it sooner?"

"Yes, ma'am. I'd like it to be official now, just like it is. It's got to be right. No confusion. No loopholes. No wiggle room for lawyers. No offense. Just saying it like it is."

She laughed, looking at the rumpled sheet, front and back. "No offense taken. Still, there are some specific points I need to research to be sure what you want will hold up. I want it worded right just like you."

A knock at the door prompted Cal to interrupt. "That's why I need it now," he said, as he pointed toward the door. "I want everything set before they cart me off."

Shelley's eyebrows wrinkled. She looked as if she might want to further her argument.

I stood and offered a compromise. "Let's say this is the temporary agreement," I said. "We can do as you wish now, Cal, then she can draw up a more detailed one from that to override it later, if necessary. After you've approved it, of course. Is that agreeable?"

Cal nodded. He didn't say it, but I believe he thought he might be gone before the second document was drafted.

Shelley looked from the paper to her watch to the door. "Wait. Let me make a quick call. Mr. Prewitt, if you could come with me or wait in another room, that would give me a little more time. I don't want you saying anything to the police unless I'm there. Mrs. Thistle, do you think you could entertain the officer for a few minutes?"

"Certainly," I said, heading for the door. "Use the phone in the kitchen, if you like."

"Thanks. I've got mine." She held up a tiny cell phone. She grabbed the bill of sale and stepped quickly to the kitchen.

"Tell him I'm in the restroom," Cal said, as he turned in the opposite direction toward the hallway.

I let in the police officer, who was extremely young and quick as well, judging from the short amount of time between Cal's call and the doorbell's ring. Detective Waters must have radioed him from the station, and this man would surely be the one I'd seen parked in the shade of the refuge trees.

I asked him in and told him Cal would be just a moment. "Make yourself comfortable, officer. May I get you something to drink?" Shelley was still on her phone when I entered the kitchen.

"Okay. Will do. Talk to you when you get back." She disconnected and turned her phone off before putting it in her briefcase. "Now, let's get the two of you to sign this."

Shelley gathered her things, the bill of sale last, and went to the hall where Cal walked slowly toward us. We stopped at the small hall table and put our signatures at the bottom of the document. "And you have the money?" she asked.

"Oh. No. That is, I don't have it in cash."

"I'll take one dollar in earnest money," Cal said. "The rest to be made payable by, say, one week from today. Does that suit you?"

"Very well."

Cal waved his hand over the paper. "Write that down, Miz Shelley."

She did so while I got a dollar bill from my purse. We checked her amendment, I gave Cal the dollar, and we shook hands. Shelley then locked the document away in her briefcase. Cal offered his hand to Shelley as well. "I thank you. I guess I don't have to tell you that this is strictly confidential. Don't tell a soul."

"You're my client. You have my word."

Cal took a deep breath. "Good. I appreciate that."

"Mr. Prewitt?" Our officer had stepped into view. "Detective Waters asked if I'd give you a ride to the station."

Cal turned to him. "Thank you. That's mighty kind."

"May I go, too?" I asked. "I can drive him home when you're through and save you the trouble."

"Not sure what time we'll get done, ma'am," the young officer said.

Shelley stepped forward. "It's all right, Mrs. Thistle. I'll be glad to bring him home. Shortly." She gave the young policeman a quick glance. "Mr. Prewitt has volunteered to answer a few questions and has graciously agreed to do so at the station so as not to inconvenience the very busy Detective Waters. Considering Mr. Prewitt's health and age, I think he's being more than cooperative, don't you agree, officer?" The policeman blushed a little and looked away, as if something in my china cabinet suddenly caught his interest.

Shelley tucked her briefcase under her arm and patted its side. "Now then. All official and no wiggle room." She winked at Cal. "Shall we?"

Cal smiled and crooked his arm for her like an escort at a fancy ball. He was smitten.

I followed the three of them outside. Shelley steered Cal to her own car without a word and deposited him in the passenger seat. The poor young policeman looked like a helpless pup. Shelley's charms had an effect on him as well. "I'll follow," he said. I suppressed a smile.

Cal rolled his window down. "Cal, dear, don't worry about Homer," I said. "I'll enjoy his company this afternoon." The humor present only a few seconds earlier in his dark eyes was replaced by a bleak stare. He nodded and whispered, "Thank you," as Shelley started the engine.

fourteen

Phoebe Goes to Class

The R. D. Basham Recreational Sporting Range was built right on the line between Winston and Bankhead counties. The land looked a lot like Cal's place, only taken care of and prettier. Off behind us in the distance was Bankhead National Forest about a half-mile away from where we set up to shoot.

We registered for the one-day workshop at the welcome desk inside the lobby of the office building. It looked more like a lodge. It's a real popular place for the men in town, especially on Saturdays when the wives run their husbands out of the house. Men of all ages milled around the place while I signed up. The old guys held coffee cups and the young ones drank Cokes from the vending machine.

I was the only woman there. That didn't bother me a bit, not with that handsome instructor. Ever since I first heard of Jack Blaylock, he has been winning one championship or another for shooting or hunting. He travels all over for tournaments and the like so we hardly ever see him in Tullulah. He'd make a good movie star with his dark hair and moustache, kind of like Tom Selleck but in camouflage or waders. His hair color looked natural even though he had to be near my age. I figured he was part Indian like a lot of people around here. I've tried and tried to find Cherokees or Chickasaws or Choctaws in my genealogy. I haven't yet officially, but I know way down deep that I am part Indian. I don't care if I never find it out for certain on paper, I still know it. Just because it's not written in some white boy book doesn't mean a flip. They don't know everything. They want you to think they do, but they don't.

We had a class in one of the rooms first. Jack handed out a stack of papers about gun safety, cleaning your guns, storing your guns, and first-aid tips in case you shoot yourself. Everybody in the class but me was a young boy, about a dozen of them. Their dads stood back out of the way because Jack didn't want them to "distract" the boys. I think he really meant "interfere."

I wasn't surprised I was the only woman. Around Tullulah, probably in all Alabama, females fall into one of three categories when it comes to guns. A few have been shooting since they were kids; they were tomboys with older brothers and wanted to do whatever they did, so they don't need lessons. Or they're the kind who don't believe a lady should shoot when there's a perfectly good man right there in the house to do it for her.

The biggest category though is women who just don't have time. They're so busy doing for their families and friends and church that they wouldn't dream of taking time out to learn to shoot, especially on a Saturday, when their husbands aren't able to be much help since they're out in the woods with their buddies getting sloshed and looking for something to kill.

The classroom stuff was boring and not worth paying attention to. Outside was a different story. We lined up thirteen across with thirteen targets in front of us. The shooting center rents ear and eye protection, but we got to use them free. We spent about thirty minutes getting used to firing with Jack walking down the row to check everybody. He helped people to stand and hold their guns right.

He took special care of me. The first few times I shot my CZ, which was a lot more powerful than I would've thought, it jerked around in my hands so bad I dropped it. Jack looked after me real good after that. The most thrilling moment was not when I hit the target, although that was pretty fun. The best part was how Jack put his arms around me while showing me how to aim. One time he put his cheek against mine, you know, to see the target better, and he gave me a little squeeze after I shot. Talk about motivation.

I tried not to get too flustered, him being so close and all. Instead, I concentrated on the lessons, so I'd know how to load and unload when I was by myself. I wished I had Jane there with me to help me remember things, but since she already knows how to shoot, she would've been bored. Besides, it felt good to not have a tag-along with me. Especially one as cute as Jane. Competition is mighty tough when you're our age.

We went inside for a box lunch, also included in the registration price. The eating area had tables and flimsy chairs with plastic seats and metal legs. On the other end of the room they had a sink, microwave, and a refrigerator. Jack sat with us students, but the daddies sat away from us.

You'd think I wouldn't have enough in common with this particular group of boys, all young enough to be my grandchildren. True, some of them snickered at me because they thought I was a decrepit little old lady. They changed their tune when one boy said, "I know you! You were on TV about finding that dead man."

This drew a good bit of respect from a crowd usually only impressed with video games. They wanted all the details, being curious just like all little boys. "Tell us! Tell us!" they said, so I did.

"Well, all right. Let me see now. It all started the other day at Wriggle's Sporting Goods..."

We shot for another hour or two after lunch. Jack paid more attention to me than anybody else. Later, Jack and a couple of other men demonstrated how to walk or run with your gun ready, which was harder than you'd think. They did a few rough and tumble moves to show how to handle an armed attacker without getting shot. After they finished, we learned how to clean our guns. Jack came over to the folding table where I worked. "You did a fine job, Phoebe. I hope you got something out of the class."

"Oh, I did. You're an excellent teacher."

"It does my heart good to see a lady learning to defend herself." He smiled at me. "A weaker woman would've stayed in her house the rest of her life, after a horrible experience like you had." He smiled as he took my hand and rubbed the back of it.

Ooh-wee, who turned the heat on. "Not me. No, sir, I intend to do just like I always have. I give everybody the benefit of the doubt. Then if they turn out to be scum, I'm ready for them." I patted the gun and took a deep breath. "I appreciate your help so much. Why don't you come over for supper tonight?"

He looked away so in a hurry, I said, "My friend Jane, that was with me when I found the body, is coming over, too. There'll be plenty."

"I wish I hadn't already made other plans."

"Maybe another time," I said. He winked and went over to shake hands with a few of the boys.

I fanned myself with the safety handout he'd given us as soon as he turned his back. My whole body felt like it was on fire.

*T*HREE HOURS LATER, I WAS FINISHING UP THE DIRTY POTS and pans I'd used to fix supper when Jane rang my doorbell. She carried a bouquet of flowers and handed them to me as she stepped into the living room.

I went in the kitchen and poured us a glass of tea. "Everything's ready whenever you're hungry."

"I'm famished. It has been a very long day. I hope your class went well. Did you enjoy yourself?"

"I sure did. I didn't hit anything much. I believe my target was cockeyed." We talked about all the shooting and what all we did. And of course I talked about Jack.

She told me about finding Cal under her house. What a lowlife. Didn't I say he was no account? I took a bite of squash casserole and pointed my fork at Jane. "Watch out for him. He may be old and sick but he's still sharp upstairs." I pointed at my head. "Sly. Conniving, is what he is. He's liable to tell you anything to get what he wants."

"Really, Phoebe, he has done nothing."

"I wouldn't be too sure. He must have something up his sleeve. We just don't know what it is yet." The lime and pineapple Jell-O salad had turned out good, if I do say so myself, so I spooned a little more on my plate while Jane talked.

"I called the police station before I left home," Jane said. "He and Shelley are still there. I thought I'd stop by on the way home."

"You're too soft-hearted, Jane. I understand how you might feel sorry for him, him being sick and alone. It's sad, I give you that, but he's still low class. You shouldn't be worrying about him." I got up to take our plates away and poured us both a cup of coffee while I was up.

"Look here," I said. "Let that cute little Shelly Barnette take care of him. She has always been one smart young lady. Her mama and daddy are so proud of her they could bust. Not just anybody could have got all the scholarships she did and then get a plum of a job at Hannigan and Wade. There's no more respectable business in the whole area. Mighty good folks. So don't worry about any of that. She knows what she's doing."

Jane sat staring into space. "I like him. I want to help him." She took a sip of coffee. "And I am convinced he is innocent."

I sighed but didn't say anything else. When somebody's hardheaded, you might as well just hush. She'd just have to find out for herself.

I'd fixed a peach cobbler the night before. I took it out of the refrigerator and put it in the oven. Meanwhile, we took our coffee with us and walked through the house to my front porch and sat while the cobbler cooked.

My porch isn't like Jane's. Hers is big and rich looking and goes across the whole front of her house and wraps around to the side. Mine is the poor folks' version, a little screened-in box. But you know what? Jane said it was so comfortable she'd stay out here day and night if it was hers. She meant it, too. She liked the pots of geraniums and ferns I had around us. We got to talking about Gladys Philpott, my next-door neighbor, and her mums, and then walked over to her yard so Jane could see the ones just now blooming.

It was about six thirty, still light outside and still fairly hot. A little breeze helped cool us off but the gnats were swarming. We got tired of fighting them off and walked back toward the house. "The oven buzzer should be going off any minute anyway," I said as a bug fell in my coffee cup. We reached the grouping of dogwood trees set about midway between the house and the street.

"What sort of ground cover is this?" Jane asked. She bent down to touch the leaves.

"That's a variegated periwinkle my sister from Augusta brought me. If you want some, you're welcome to them. They'd look pretty out there around that big maple tree in your front yard. Here, let's go ahead and get you some clumps."

I bent down to pull up a handful for her when all of a sudden we heard glass breaking around the back of my house and the sound of tires digging in and slinging gravel in the alley out back. We both looked up and right then *Boom!*—an explosion rocked the ground and fire shot straight out all my kitchen windows.

Jane and I screamed and hugged each other while Lowell Tuten, my next-door neighbor on the other side, came running out of his house with a red-checked napkin tucked under his chin. He took one look at us and the house, and then ran back in to call the fire department.

You never heard such a roaring. That fire sounded like a locomotive coming at us. The explosion took out the whole outside kitchen wall and the whole back porch blew clean off. Flames just kept getting bigger and they shot out all over the place, higher and higher. I worried they'd burn up my shade trees before the fire trucks got there.

"We could've been killed," I said. "If we'd been in that kitchen, we would've flown out of there like two slices of burnt bread popping out of a toaster."

"Was it the stove do you think?" Jane asked. "The gas line, perhaps?"

"It's electric." By now, the shock was wearing off. All I could think of was my brand-new rug and matching kitchen towels I got at Dillard's and paid full price for.

"How then? I've never heard of an electric oven exploding."

"I have no idea," I said. "But I know one thing for sure. That peach cobbler is good and done."

Several neighbors came over to talk to us and watch the firemen work. Once they finally cut off the hoses, and the smoke and steam cleared, I could see there was nothing left whatsoever of my kitchen, other than the oven and the refrigerator, but they were ready for the junkyard now. It looked like a black hole in there—melted appliances, woodwork, linoleum, all black as a pit.

"Molotov cocktail," the fire chief, a big guy with soot all over him, said as he came toward us. "Folks that live behind you said they saw a pickup truck, no tag, driving down your alley, and saw it earlier going real slow past in the street. We'll be running some tests, but right now I'd say it looks like this fire was set deliberate."

"Arson!" Jane gasped. She put her arm around my shoulder and said, "There, there, dear. Don't cry. We have much to be thankful for. No one was hurt," she said, as a policeman with a notepad walked over.

I watched the smoke billowing out of the ragged opening where my kitchen had been. "No one has been hurt yet, you mean," I said. "Mr. Fireman, I sure hope y'all catch whoever did this before I do. Jail bars are about the only thing to keep the dirty dogs safe from me."

"Now, Miz Twigg, these people are obviously dangerous. You let the experts handle this. We'll get them."

"This is my fight, too," I said, shaking my head. Those "experts" couldn't possibly understand how this hurt me. It had taken me two weeks to pick out just the right artificial flower arrangement to match the colors in my wallpaper. They matched good now, all right, seeing as how walls and flowers alike were all one new color, Charcoal Briquette.

Jane gave my shoulders a squeeze. "You'll come stay with me. No question."

"Oh, I couldn't impose," I said.

"Nonsense. I have plenty of room. I insist. At least until you can see about getting some sort of temporary wall in place and a new door and lock."

I didn't have much choice. We couldn't stand there looking at the firemen all night. Luckily, the upstairs closets kept my clothes fairly smoke free. I picked out a few outfits and other things I'd need for a few days and threw them all in a suitcase. Smoke and dust covered everything downstairs. It would take me a week of steady cleaning to get everything back to normal. We gave the chief Jane's phone number. He said he'd let me know as soon as they found anything and promised to stay in touch.

fifteen

Jane Brings Phoebe Home

I bundled Phoebe and the few belongings she'd need while staying at my house into my car. On the way home, we stopped by the police station to see about Cal. Shelley Barnette was just coming down the steps to the sidewalk. She was alone.

"They've taken him into custody," she said, confirming my fear.

"But why? Surely he didn't confess?"

She shook her head. "I don't know what got into him. He went wild and tried to hit a couple of police officers. He tried to cooperate at first, but after awhile, he became belligerent. Nothing I could do. They'll keep him overnight. They're just letting him cool off. He'll be free in the morning."

"What about bail? Can't we get him out?"

"The night judge is on the same hunting trip as my boss."

"But he's so ill. Surely they could see that."

"Yes. The police assured me a nurse would be there if he needed medical attention. Don't worry. Cal said he'd be fine in jail for one night."

This gave me pause. I couldn't believe he said that, not when he'd been terrified at the very thought of jail when we talked.

When Shelley walked on, I turned to go back to my own car. Phoebe's head and arm hung out the window, the better to hear our conversation. "So they're hanging onto him for a while, huh?" she said. "Doesn't surprise me."

"Phoebe, I should go in and make certain Cal doesn't need me for anything. I won't be a moment."

"I'm fine," she said. I walked quickly toward the building. "And you're too tenderhearted," she said from behind me.

Dusk settled around the police station, a modern square of concrete and glass with three stories. It sat on a block of its own across from the west arm of the town square. Care had been taken in the design of windows and doors for they echoed those of the much older buildings of the downtown shops. The landscaping visible in the lights along its sidewalks was as lovely as could be and also matched the quaint, colorful decorations along the square's storefronts.

Inside, florescent lighting dispelled any connection with the past. I stopped at the high black counter that stretched across the width of the room. "May I help you?" asked the burly officer who manned the desk. He tapped a stack of papers together, stapled them, and set them aside.

"Yes. A friend has been taken into custody. I hoped I might be allowed to see him."

The desk sergeant studied my face. "Cal Prewitt?" he asked.

"Why, yes."

He nodded. "I'll check for you, ma'am." I thanked him and only had a short wait. The desk sergeant instructed me to walk through a metal detector at the door that connected to the inner offices. I left my purse in his care then followed his directions to the end of the hall where I was to turn again.

A familiar figure prevented me from doing so. Detective Waters stood immovable, like a mountain, with a resolute, expressionless face. Once again, his look switched to an instant smile. "Come this way, please."

I did as he asked, although we went in the opposite direction from that given by the desk sergeant. Detective Waters waved me into his office and politely pulled out the chair reserved for guests and interviewees.

"Shelley Barnette told me Cal had been arrested. I thought I should come and see about him. I'd like to talk to him, if I may."

The detective nodded in a friendly, attentive way as I spoke. "No, ma'am. That won't be possible." I was taken aback momentarily, as I'm sure was his intent. "It's a nice thing, you coming down to check on him. Very nice, since you haven't known Cal for long. I can appreciate that." His head nodded again as he tapped his blunt fingertips in a little tattoo on the desktop. "Cal is fine. He's not too happy, but we're going to make sure he's comfortable for the night."

"Yes. I'm quite sure, it's just that he's in such poor health . . ."

"A nurse will be by to check on him around eight o'clock."

"Ah," I said. "Good. That's a relief then. That was my main concern." I looked him straight in the eyes and said, "I imagine you rarely hold men of his advanced age overnight," with the most innocence I could muster.

The on/off smile lit up and relaxed his facial muscles in what was the closest to a real smile I'd seen so far. "It's a first," the detective said. "Even for us backwoods hicks."

"Oh, dear," I said, "I meant no offense."

A loud, hearty laugh filled the small room. "I'm just playing with you," he said, his Southern accent now more prevalent. "And if it'll make you feel any better, I'll tell you a little secret. Cal isn't as weak as he looks. I know, because I'm the one he tried to knock to the floor." He nodded at my shocked look. "That's right. Ordinarily, I'd have set him down and let him cool off before sending him home. Couldn't do that this time. He went flat out of his head. And he hadn't even been drinking. That would've changed once he got home. He's better off being here, where we can make sure he doesn't hurt himself or somebody else."

"I see." His concern for Cal's welfare made it impossible to think of further argument. "Yes, I suppose you're right. Thank you, detective."

He rose, so I did likewise. When I stepped into the hallway, I saw a flash of red and orange clothing disappear around the corner ahead, Phoebe hurriedly and stealthily making a getaway with long, tiptoe strides.

"What time will Cal be released?" I asked Detective Waters when he caught up with me in the hall.

"We'll feed him a good breakfast and let him go about seven."

"Good. I'll pick him up then."

"No need. I'll have a patrolman drop him off. At your house, if it will ease your mind."

"That's very thoughtful." I shook his hand in the lobby and said good night. He smiled then, but when I turned for a quick look a second time, his face had fallen again into a blank but serious stare.

Phoebe sat in the car exactly as she had when I'd left her, only now she was well into a nail manicure. "Everything okay?" she asked without looking up.

"Yes. All is well." It was a relief that Cal was all right. I would sleep more easily, except for a small new thing that now hung in my mind, a scribbled note I'd seen on Detective Waters' desk. The word "ex-military" caught my eye. Below that followed a man's description, age thirty-two and one distinguishing mark, a scar down his neck. It was stacked with a paper about Cal.

HOMER GREETED US WHEN WE ARRIVED HOME. HE LAY on the top porch step and perked up his head when the car rolled into the driveway. He was particularly friendly toward Phoebe but she would have none of it.

"I can't stand old nasty dogs," she said. "And they all know it and come right to me first thing and want to lick and paw all over me. Git outta here!" She flung a foot in his direction.

Poor Homer. He looked positively dejected. Needless to say, I didn't bring him inside with us. I'm sure he preferred the outdoors in any case. I fed him outside and let him wander for the night.

Phoebe ranted a bit as she bustled about, putting some of her things away in the upstairs bedroom across from mine. Cal, naturally, was the reason and the topic of conversation. "He has done every mean thing known to man."

"What specifically?" I asked.

She described a few incidents, all involving a drunk Cal, all done when he was quite a bit younger and fighting other drunken young men, none so terrible for the reputation she, and according to her, the town, ascribed to him.

"But nothing in many years, correct? He seems very different then from the man he is now."

Phoebe huffed. "A raccoon does not change his stripes, Jane. Get real. Dead bodies don't just show up any old where."

Phoebe's remarks often required a moment of thought.

"Well, he's just no good, that's all," she said in summary as we went downstairs to wash the clothes she'd brought. The smell of smoke on them was faint, barely noticeable at all, but I knew she would feel better if we ran them through the wash. I brought out an old bottle of brandy. I felt a little indulgence was called for due to the disturbing events of the day.

"Oh, my," she said, as we went out the front screen door. "I'm not sure I can drink this. It's awful thick."

"Try to take a few sips and relax, dear. It will do you good."

"All right. I'll try." She took one tiny one, barely enough to wet her lips.

She grimaced but quickly took another sip. "What a day," she said. "I'll get things squared away at home as soon as I can. I don't want to be an imposition at all. In fact, I could get a good rate at the hotel tomorrow."

"I won't hear of it. Please, I'd like you to stay as long as you wish. It will give us a chance to get our strategies together."

Phoebe stared at me wide eyed. "Strategies?"

"We have much to consider. The fire chief made it quite clear. Your kitchen fire was no accident."

"Strategies," Phoebe whispered as she looked into the distance and gulped a mouthful of brandy. "You're right. If those sorry criminals think they can get the better of me, they're dead wrong. Why, the very idea of bombing my house and making us find a dead body."

"Let's not get overly excited. I agree the two are possibly connected. I don't mean we will interfere with the authorities' murder investigation."

"I wouldn't dream of it," Phoebe said.

"Nor would I."

Phoebe moved her lips as she thought. "It's just that while they're looking under microscopes and testing dumb things, like your guns for instance, somebody needs to be doing important stuff."

"I'm sure the police are busy pursuing all leads and covering all aspects of both cases. However, it occurs to me that we certainly have something of an inside track as far as the two locations. When Cal is released, I think we should ask his opinion. I think he has been holding something back from me. Perhaps we should concentrate on getting him to open up."

"That won't be tough. I'll pick up a bottle of whiskey in town."

"Isn't Tullulah dry? I thought there were no liquor stores here."

"Oh. I'm not going to a store. Don't worry. I know just how to go about it. Me knowing the ins and outs of everybody and everything in town will be a big help. See, I make a good partner. I like taking care of business. I can be the muscle, and you can be the brains."

I laughed. "I don't know about all that. I do know this, I'm certainly lucky to have found such a wonderful friend."

Phoebe grinned and raised her glass. "Here's to Friendship."

I clinked her glass. "To Friendship."

She sipped, puckered her lips and squinted her eyes shut momentarily. She held out her glass again and said, "To Justice."

We clinked again. "To Justice." We sipped once more.

"And to Revenge," she said.

I stopped my glass midway.

"Aw, come on, Jane, don't be a wuss."

I thought of the macho videos in Phoebe's living room. I didn't comment on the possibility that she might be too influenced by them. Perhaps I'd been hasty in giving her a shooting lesson. Surely she wouldn't go overboard with her tough-guy fantasies. No, I thought, she's just having a bit of fun. Nothing serious. Nothing but a couple of harmless little ladies, the both of us. I touched my glass to hers. "To Revenge."

After a good laugh, she downed the last of her brandy and smacked her lips. "Now," she said, "how's about another look at your gun collection?"

sixteen

Phoebe Can't Sleep

I think I took the house-bomb thing rather well, considering. Thanks to my Midgette genes (that's my maiden
name, Midgette), I was able to withstand the stress and horror of
watching my beautiful little kitchen burn without me falling apart.

Jane made sure I was comfortable in her guest room and then
went on to bed herself. I sure was glad to finally lie down and rest
in that big fluffy bed. I felt like I was a kid at Grandma's house.
Even as worn out as I felt, I still didn't drop off to sleep right away.
Too many things churned in my mind. I kept seeing those firemen,
working at putting my kitchen out.

Was it possible it was just a mean bunch of kids? But whose
kids? Nobody in Tullulah had any that bad. Any that mean
would've been whipped into line good by their parents long before
they got old enough to drive a truck or make a firebomb. And why

me? What if it wasn't because of that body at all, but was something else entirely? Why would anybody pick my house out of all the others? Have I not been a good person? Did I cut somebody off on the highway? Did I say anything that offended anyone?

It was no use. I couldn't sleep. I figured I might as well get up since my throat was dry and I needed some water. I cut the light on and picked up my watch. It was almost midnight. I tiptoed downstairs to the kitchen and was surprised to hear steps following me soon after.

"What's the matter, dear? Can't sleep?" Jane said, as she shuffled in.

"Not a peep." I filled a glass with water from the tap and took a big long swig. "I'm thinking you're right."

"About what?" Jane went through the back door and looked out the porch screen. Homer woofed at her from the backyard. "Good boy," she said.

When she came back, I said, "Somebody threw that bomb because of us finding the body. They think we saw something or know something. That's how it always is on TV. We're going to have to be on the lookout. They might try something here, too."

Jane nodded. "I hadn't thought of that. It's possible. Think back, Phoebe. Has anyone, other than the police, shown particular interest in our discovery of the body? Have you talked to anyone about it?"

"I believe I might have mentioned it to one or two folks."

"Good. We can start there. Not that we'd interfere with the police."

"Nooo. Not in a million years." We sat there straight-faced for all of five seconds before busting out laughing.

Jane got her breath and said, "Of course, anyone could have seen the news coverage on television." She got up, went to a drawer, and took out a legal pad. "Still, we should make a list of what personal connections we can think of. It will help us remember everyone later on. We can mark off anyone with an alibi or anyone we find otherwise unsuitable for our purposes." At the top of the paper, she wrote "Suspects" in big letters. "Right, then. After talking to the police, whom did you see?"

I thought a second. "Well, I went to buy my gun so I saw Alton Twigg."

"He's the owner?"

"Yes. And Jack Blaylock was in there, too," I said and let out a big sigh. He was such a hunk.

"Good. Only two. That's a short list."

"Then I needed some groceries so I stopped at the Pig. Let's see, I saw June Freeman. Deb Wiley and her husband. Then Rennie May Adams was in the checkout lane when I got there, talking to my cousin Lois and her sister Dean, who isn't able to drive anymore, so Lois carries her to get her groceries, to the doctor, or wherever she needs to go."

"I say. That's quite a few more than . . ."

"And then John Purnell was one aisle over, so he probably heard me. We went to high school together. He asked me out once back then but I said no. We haven't said two words to each other since."

"That would've been almost fifty years ago. Surely he wouldn't still remember."

"Oh, he remembers, all right. But that's probably not enough to make him bomb me."

Jane finished writing and said, "Do you consider any of them serious suspects?"

"Oh, heaven's sake, no. If anybody, it'd be Rennie May. She's mean as the devil, but she's eighty-six. Even so, I guarantee she could throw a bottle from the alley to my kitchen, and farther probably. But she doesn't have a truck. Wouldn't have used one anyway. That's not her style. She'd have just come storming up the street, took a couple of long side skips, and flung that thing like one of them Olympic hurlers."

Jane inclined her head as she marked a line through Rennie May's name. "So many charming people to meet," she said. "But did anyone act differently toward you than they normally do?"

"I don't think so. Oh, I forgot. I had my regular beauty appointment at the Barn this morning. There must've been fifty people in there. Come to think of it, Treenie Dodd sure did ask a lot of questions. Oh! All those young boys at the gun class! I didn't recognize but a few of them. No telling where those others came from."

"Did any behave badly toward you? Or did you have an argument with them?"

I shook my head. "No. Nothing like that. Jack was the only one I talked to, other than when I told them about finding the body."

Jane held her pen in the air. "Well then. I think the curious lady at the beauty shop sounds most promising at the moment. Don't you agree?"

I did. "I'll check her out first. It was strange her being down at the Barn at all, now that I think about it. I've never seen her there before on my regular day."

"Then we might assume she came specifically to question you?"

"Could be." I sat there thinking real hard for a minute. "What I'll do is, I'll ask Marlene if Treenie was a walk-in that day. Then, I could go down to where she works. I know Melissa, the secretary there, real well. She can tell me if Treenie was on the job at the time in question."

"Where does she work?"

"All over the place, really. She works for a construction company."

Then I remembered some of her trashy-looking coworkers. I mean, what kind of a man wears a scarf on his head? The no-good kind, that's who, and Treenie fit right in with that bunch.

seventeen

Jane Has
Midnight Visitors

*M*y pen hesitated over the notepad. A construction company? A chill went up my spine, for I remembered driving by a construction site on the outskirts of town. As I went by, I heard a loud blast. My face must have reflected my thoughts, for Phoebe said, "What's wrong?"

"You must promise me to be extra careful, my dear. Construction sites often have explosives."

"Oh, I won't go near anyplace where they're blasting . . . Oh." She covered her mouth with her hand as the implication sank in.

"The explosives they use aren't in the same category as a Molotov cocktail. Still, a little caution is in order."

"I know where she lives. I'll find out if she did it or not. I have my ways."

We sat and talked about other things. I saw no point in keeping Phoebe in the dark any longer in regard to buying Cal's land. She promised not to tell anyone. I didn't tell her all his conditions, only that we agreed he would remain there until he died. "After I go by the bank tomorrow, I suppose I could go by Shelley's office to see if the land-sale document has been drawn up. I doubt she will have had time but I can check. She may do it quickly since Cal was so anxious about it."

While I spoke, I looked beyond Phoebe into the center of the kitchen and became aware of a small reflection of light about the size of a dime a few feet beyond her shoulder. The light disappeared almost as soon as I noticed it. It left me with the impression of candlelight shining on copper. This was only a fleeting impression, for not only had it disappeared by the time I fully registered it, but my attention was drawn away by noises outside.

Phoebe said, "What was that? Did you hear something?"

Homer woofed once, quietly, from the backyard.

We both rose and peered out the window over my sink. The moon was full. Even at midnight, we could see a good distance, across the wide side yard all the way to the locked gate at the refuge entrance, thanks to the high security light above it. We saw nothing else there in the light or farther along the refuge boundary and the narrow road that ran between it and my land. But as we looked to the back corner of my yard into the darkness, moving lights bounced near the access road that edged my property and ran through the woods.

"What in the world," Phoebe said. "There's somebody fooling around in the graveyard out there."

At first, I wondered how she knew about the cemetery since this was her first visit. I wasn't thinking. Of course Phoebe would know every inch of the county very well.

Before I could comment, Phoebe was through the kitchen, the back porch and its screen, and fast walking across the yard, tightening her robe belt around her waist as she strode. I grabbed a flash-light out of a kitchen drawer and stepped into my gardening shoes beside the outer screen door.

"Come along, Homer," I whispered. "Not a sound." I put my finger over my lips then dropped it, realizing how foolish it was to think a dog would understand my words or sign language. Foolish or not, he obeyed. He was a hunter, after all, and would be accus-tomed to stealth and perhaps similar signals from Cal.

Phoebe was well ahead of me so I hurried to try and catch up. The graveyard she referred to was that of the Hardwick family, where the remains of five generations lay. I hadn't as yet found time to study the tombstones or the family history, but it was high on my list of priorities once I'd settled in. The moon illuminated the open yard. I turned off my flashlight. I didn't need it to see the fig-ures moving ahead.

Three lights bobbed in the darkness. We could hear hushed voices coming from near the lights. I could make out five or six forms moving about in the moonlight. I had a moment of regret for charging ahead rather than phoning the police.

Phoebe called out to them as she neared the cemetery bound-aries. "Hey! What are y'all a'doing out here?" The three flashlight beams jerked in our direction and shone on us as we approached. Those holding the flashlights stood still; two others fled and hid behind trees beyond the farthest tombstone.

"Stay with me, Homer," I said. I ran a hand over his head. "Stay right here." He sat first then slowly lowered himself onto his belly. I clicked on my flashlight again to better see my visitors' faces, one male and two female, who immediately put their hands in the air.

"We're sorry," a young woman, about twenty years old with braided pigtails, said. Various tools and other objects I couldn't readily identify stuck out the many pockets of her denim overalls. "We didn't mean to disturb anyone."

The blond girl next to her, heavier and taller than her friend, nodded agreement. Her white T-shirt stretched across a wide middle and rode up due to the weight of a leather carpenter's belt slung low on her hips. The belt was also full of various accoutrements that made her jeans sag at the waist, revealing a few inches of skin.

Phoebe put her hands on her hips and addressed the young man. "Riley Gardner, is that you behind that wild getup?"

The getup was something I recognized—an out-of-date set of infrared night visors once used by the military, looking like a rectangular box strapped tightly around his head and eyes. He wore an olive drab T-shirt with the word "Army" across the chest and a pair of camouflage pants, a type the Colonel had been fond of. The pants legs were tucked into shin-high military-issue boots. I immediately thought of the memo on Detective Waters' desk regarding the man with the scar, the one I'd seen, presumably, in the grocery store's parking lot a few days earlier.

He lowered his chin down and into his neck while raising the visor to rest on top of his head. Large dark eyes cast a pleading look to us each in turn. No, this was not the same man I'd seen. Riley had long hair. He was taller, thinner, and had a slight stoop in his shoulders. I remembered now that the other man was clean shaven. Riley had a long, drooping moustache.

"Ah apologize," he said in a deep voice. I didn't understand him at first. He dragged out each syllable to double, perhaps triple its normal length, the flow of them thick and glottal like a Slavic dialect. This gave me pause at first as I considered, then rejected, the languages of several Balkan countries before realizing, of course, that this was a variation of the native tongue.

Phoebe huffed and inclined her head. "You better do more than apologize, and be quick about it. Explain yourselves. And, for goodness sake, put your hands down. We aren't carrying and you're not under arrest. Yet."

"We were on the refuge trails," the stocky blond girl said, "We come out here sometimes to...well, when it's a full moon." She and her companions looked up, as if the fact that the moon was full and visible somehow lent credence to her story.

"Aren't you Shelby Taylor's granddaughter?" Phoebe asked her.

"Yes, ma'am. I'm Sarah," the girl said.

"Wouldn't she have a fit if she knew you were traipsing around in the middle of the night on private property and scaring poor sweet little Jane. Those refuge trails close every night at sundown and you all aren't supposed to be over there either."

The two girls looked to each other for support, shuffled about a bit, then the blonde said, "Please don't tell Granny."

She looked too old to worry what her grandmother might think but, as I was quickly learning in my short time in Tullulah, things were different here.

The girl in pigtails said, "It's kind of a secret."

A hissing sound beside me of Phoebe slowly inhaling through clamped teeth facilitated a more prompt and complete confession.

"We've started us a group," Sarah explained in a hurry. "A little club. Completely harmless. There's lots of other groups like it around the country, so it's perfectly respectable. It's just that it's a little...unusual. We've never told anybody around here about it."

I couldn't wait to hear what someone in this delightfully strange community would consider "unusual." We waited as Mrs. Taylor's granddaughter gathered her courage.

Could it be they were Druids or New Age Witches? Many worship nature on nights of the full moon. Their clothes looked wrong, however, and I couldn't imagine what use night visors and their other various tools might be to those who practice the old religions. "Are you Wiccans, dear?" I asked.

Sarah fervently shook her head. "Oh, no, ma'am!" The three of them looked to one another in horror. "We're not a bit wicked. We are good, completely good, I promise."

Like many other things in the outside world, the word "Wicca" apparently had yet to reach the fair boundaries of Tulluluh.

Phoebe folded her arms across her chest and cocked her head to the other side. "And what kind of a club are we talking about here?"

The three of them began babbling together until Phoebe said, "Sarah! What in tarnation is it?"

Sarah hung her head. "We're ghost hunters. We got some readings, and then got excited and followed them and ended up over here. When we didn't meant to."

Phoebe and I looked at each other, both perplexed. Riley raised his hand, as if Phoebe were a teacher who must call on him before he could speak.

"What, Riley?" she said in an exasperated tone.

"Ah can explain," he drawled, coming almost to a stop between each stretched syllable. Fascinating. I determined to begin a notebook on local accents as a reference tool, much as I had done when working on digs in India, Southeast Asia, and remote areas of Eastern Europe.

"See," Riley continued, "Went in yonder." He pointed to the refuge land on the other side of the road. "Callie," whom he indicated by sweeping his arm and pointing to the girl in pigtails, "got strong, strawwwwwng vaahhhhbes. Then me and Sarah," here he indicated the blond girl, "did the same."

As the girls' heads bobbed in unison, I caught a glimpse of the other figures I'd seen run away. They peered out from behind tree trunks in the near distance. In the dark beginnings of the wood, I could barely make them out, but as they moved slowly forward into the moonlit cemetery, their shapes became clear.

One was a tall young man who looked about the same age and height as Riley. The other couldn't have been more than a teenager, perhaps only a boy of ten or twelve years old.

These two were different. The most obvious thing was that they carried no hardware, presumably ghost-hunting equipment, as

Riley and the two girls did. Secondly, they did not have fear in their faces, nor discomfort at being found out. They both looked at me, with not even a glance at Phoebe or the others, smiling as if they might laugh at any moment. An inexplicable feeling of calm came over me, or more precisely a wave of loveliness, of something innocent and untouched, embodied and standing there beside Riley and the two girls. Strange, I know, but there it is.

"So," Phoebe said, "there's just the three of you? Nobody else running out here like a wild Indian?"

I was about to tell them that I had no objection to them "hunting" to their hearts' delight, tonight or at any other time, when Phoebe's comment made me realize another thing different about the very young boy's attire. He was in a skin of fur wrapped about his lower torso and a necklace made of what looked like shells or bones.

As I processed this, the other part of Phoebe's comment suddenly dawned on me. "Three, did you say?" I asked.

Riley nodded. "That's rahhhght. Us three. Hope to get more. Y'all like to join us?"

The boy in the fur skin and his older companion, also in a costume of sorts, I then realized, grinned widely. The tall, older one had Anglo features. His clothes looked ordinary at first, but on closer inspection, the collar on his plain white shirt was something not worn since the late 1800s. His feet were bare. Suspenders held up plain trousers. Both shirt and pants looked handmade.

He raised a finger as if to say, "Watch this," then he turned his head so that it was even with Riley's. He blew in Riley's hair, continuing down his ear and bare neck.

Riley shivered. His eyes bulged as he ran his hand over his head and neck. "Did y'all feel that?" he said.

"Feel what?" Phoebe said.

Riley jerked the infrared glasses down over his eyes and began scanning the area in a one hundred eighty degree sweep, high and low, and straight through the young man who stood beside him.

It was only then that I understood. How stupid of me not to see it earlier. The newcomers were not dressed in costume at all. The tall boy bowed to me first, then the young one followed suit. I must say I felt positively impolite to not respond at once but what could I do? Phoebe and the three ghost hunters obviously couldn't see them. Only me.

While Riley continued sweeping the area with his infrared visors, his two friends took tools from their pockets. Sarah held what looked like a voltmeter that might be used to test electrical outlets. Callie, the girl with braids, took two short metal rods out of her pockets, one in each hand like a gunslinger drawing revolvers, and dropped to a half crouch. She held the rods before her with the long ends sticking forward and the short bent ends serving as handles.

Once I had a few moments to become accustomed to the idea of the two boys as otherworldly, I noticed a vague halo shimmering about them, as if the moonlight reflected differently off their bodies. I suppose you'd say "bodies." They looked solid enough to me, enough to fool me at first sight. Watching them run away through the tombstones, a difference in movement became apparent. They seemed to float. Their feet appeared to touch ground but at the same time they bounced a bit as if gravity didn't hold them down.

Riley took long, slow strides forward, around and around, edging toward the middle of the cemetery. He pulled a camera out of a pocket, turned, and held it toward me. "You don't mind if we take pictures, do you, ma'am?"

"Not at all," I said, wondering what he thought he would take pictures of when he obviously could see nothing. "Is your camera special, then? In capturing ghost images?"

"Not special. We get some mighty strange things sometimes though." He patted the top of the camera. "Get something good, be sure to show you."

"Thank you. I'd like that. Feel free to roam about here as you wish. Look all you like. Next time, I'd appreciate a word beforehand though, if you please."

"Ah sure do appreciate it, ma'am," he said, bowing slightly and touching his visors as if they were the bill of a cap. "Thank you, ma'am," the two girls chorused. Sarah turned to Phoebe and said in a pleading voice, "And don't forget about not telling Granny." Phoebe didn't answer. She still had her arms folded tightly across her. She was shaking her head at the sight of Riley and the girls making their way to the center of the small cemetery.

"Have you ever in your life heard such nonsense? They're all old enough to know there's no such thing as ghosts. The very idea. Come on, Jane. It's too chilly to be standing out here watching a bunch of crazy fool younguns."

She was right, it was a bit nippy with us only in our nightclothes. Still, I hated to turn away at that moment. The ghost boys were playing some sort of game with Riley. I couldn't see well enough to be certain, but it looked like they were playing catch or juggling with small balls of light. Phoebe turned toward the house and, as I was about to do likewise, the boys smiled at me and waved good-bye. I waved back, which caught Phoebe's eye and brought a curious look from her since the ghost hunters took no notice of our leaving.

Homer had been so quiet and still, I'd forgotten he was there. His eyes tracked the movements of the visitors until I turned toward the house. Another long glance satisfied him the intruders wouldn't follow and he turned with me, staying well clear of Phoebe.

I kicked off my gardening shoes once inside the back porch. Phoebe, who had run outdoors without her shoes, stood on the mat at the kitchen door to peel off her soggy socks. "Could you hand me a paper towel? I don't want to track dirt in on the floor."

I stepped inside, tore off two sheets, and handed them to her. Just as I turned to go sit down, I stopped myself. Halfway between the door and the kitchen table, a small object lay on the floor. I walked forward slowly.

It was a leaf, bright red and quite large, about the size of my hand. I was certain it had not been there before Phoebe and I left the house. I picked it up and turned it over in my palm. Neither of us had been so far into the room, so I knew we hadn't brought it in with us from outdoors.

"Isn't that pretty," Phoebe said. "Is your maple tree out front turning already? I hadn't noticed, but then we've had so much excitement, I've been distracted. That's the first red one I've seen this year." She gave it a look, front and back, then said, "I'm bushed. I believe I'll just head on up to bed, okay?"

"Certainly, dear. I'll see you in the morning. Sleep as long as you like." I ran my fingers over the red leaf, wondering how it could have gotten inside. The maple in my front yard had not turned yet, nor had any in the back. This one came from somewhere else. I carried it with me upstairs and placed it next to my bedside lamp before getting in bed. It was several hours later, while I lay awake between foggy dreams, when I realized the leaf had lain in the same spot as the two tiny acorns.

eighteen

Jane's Phone Acts Up

*E*arly next morning, a police cruiser drew up in front of the house. Phoebe and I were up, dressed and having breakfast. Homer, who had eaten already, was prowling the grounds out back near the cemetery, nose to the ground, tracing the movements of our previous night's visitors. When he heard the car, he dashed to the road and reached it before I did.

Cal seemed ill at ease as he stepped from the police car. He met us with a sudden cheery smile, though he looked even thinner and weaker than the day before.

Cal bent down to rub Homer's black coat, sending his tail wagging into double time. Phoebe watched from the porch. Cal waved to the departing patrol car, and man and dog walked slowly to the house.

"Cal, this is my friend, Phoebe Twigg. Phoebe, my neighbor, Cal Prewitt."

Phoebe frowned but nodded her head in acknowledgement. "Nice to meet you," she said unconvincingly.

Cal squinted his eyes and looked her over for some time. "You're Ben Midgette's daughter." He said it as a fact, not a question, and with great fondness that made his lips curl up in a big smile.

Phoebe was astounded. "You knew Daddy?"

"Sure, everybody did. He was a mighty fine fellow. Seems like yesterday he was walking you around down on the square to show you off. You was a pretty little thing with that long red hair. You haven't hardly changed a bit. Couldn't have been more than six or seven at the time but you could talk up a storm, just like a grown-up."

"I don't remember that." The change in Phoebe amazed me. The mistrust in her face had melted away at the mention of her father. She took Cal by the arm and led him inside and into the kitchen, listening to another story, chiming in herself with several comments.

Homer stopped at the door when I stepped inside. He looked up with sorrowful eyes.

"One moment. Stay here," I told him. I crossed quickly to the kitchen and got paper towels. He allowed me to wipe each paw thoroughly with no complaint. "Now. We couldn't very well have a welcome home party without you." He hopped over the threshold and trotted jauntily past me to follow his master and friend.

"Yes, I liked Ben. He was always kind to me," Cal said. "Back in them days, not everybody here was. It was a bad time. I was young and wild. Not the most upstanding citizen."

We sat at the table while Cal told us about his interrogation. The longer he talked, the more Phoebe warmed to him. She asked question after question about his treatment at the station. He insisted he was treated well and had been given breakfast just as the detective told me. He felt terrible for losing his temper with Detective Waters. I cooked up a bit more for him as we talked, though most he reserved for Homer who thought a second breakfast was an excellent idea.

"I don't think they believe me, Jane."

"But they have no proof."

"That don't necessarily mean they think I'm innocent. They just had no choice but to let me go. For now."

"Shelley must have done a good job for you then."

Phoebe waved her hands to get our attention. She pointed to the small TV on my kitchen counter. "Y'all come look. They're showing us again on TV."

We missed most of the news footage showing us talking to police at the scene. Cal hung his head, seeing for the first time his own land in the video and the news reporter mentioning his name. "They'll be back for me."

We watched quietly. Suddenly Phoebe got up and strode to the television. With a hard smack, she turned off the set and faced us. "That's enough of that." We drank coffee and talked a while longer. Phoebe told Cal about her house burning.

"Oh, no," Cal said softly. He sat and rocked in his seat. His eyes took on a far away look. He was obviously deeply disturbed at the news.

"What is it, Cal?" I said. "Do you know of someone likely to do such a thing?"

He shook his head but I wasn't sure if he meant no, or if he thought of something else. From his expression, it appeared he was thinking hard in order to solve a difficult problem.

"I'm sorry about your house," he finally said. "We'll have to see what we can do about that." He coughed a little, which made me realize he'd been coughing less since arriving than usual. Perhaps they had not allowed him to smoke in the jail.

"I need to get me and Homer on home," Cal said. "I do appreciate the hospitality." His knees creaked when he rose. "Come on, Homer," he said, then to us, "I'm old but not completely useless. I'll see what I can find out for you, Miz Phoebe, about your house."

"The main thing, Cal," I said, "is that you get plenty of rest now. I'll come over to check on you later with a little lunch, all right?"

He agreed as he and Homer left us. Phoebe and I looked to each other. "I wonder how he thinks he can help with the shape he's in?" she said.

Cal was hiding something, something important. "I don't know. I just hope he's very careful." The police car that brought Cal home sat down the road in plain view. Cal waved to the figure seated inside as he and Homer crossed over to his property.

My telephone rang inside. "Heavens," I said to Phoebe. "You're the only person I know who might call." Before I reached the phone, Phoebe's muffled voice came from the porch. "The po-lice, maybe." Yes, she was probably right. I had given Detective Waters my number.

"Hello?" Static buzzed in my ear. "Hello? Anyone there?" I thought I could make out faint noises in the background that might have been speech, but I couldn't be sure they were even words. The static sputtered a bit more. Phoebe stood behind me.

"No one there," I said, replacing the receiver. "Just static. Sounded like something wrong in the wiring."

"You might have varmints in your walls or attic," she said. "When Ronald and I first got married, our doorbell would ring but nobody would be at the door. It turned out that squirrels had got in the attic where the doorbell wire was. They'd chewed it up until it was frayed, and then every time their little legs ran across the wire, it made the bell ring."

"Amazing. I would never have thought of that. Yes, the house is so old and was empty so long, there very well may be something of the sort happening here. If not 'varmints,' perhaps just old phone wire." Perhaps the squirrel that brought me acorns was a resident rather than a visitor.

Phoebe and I each had business to attend to in town. We'd agreed that I'd drive her to her house where she would meet with her insurance adjuster. I needed to make a stop at the bank.

nineteen

Phoebe Goes to the Gun Show

e left Jane's house not long after Cal did. We both had business in town, and I needed to get my car so I could come and go as I please and run my errands.

Jane told me the night before that Cal was selling her his land, which nearly knocked me on the floor. That's why her first stop was going to be the bank. She wanted me to swear I wouldn't tell a soul about Cal selling, but I told her that was against my religion so I'd just have to promise, cross my heart, and spit on the ground.

That insurance adjuster, Eddie Free, was the cutest thing. He couldn't have been more than twenty-five, and had a blond crew cut and a turned-up nose just like his daddy. I've known him all his life since all his family goes to my church.

Eddie was on the job. He told me he'd take care of everything, not to worry. He already had a crew lined up to come redo the walls that day, and then they'd get everything painted and fixed just like new within the week. I was so impressed. You always hear horror stories about lazy insurance people and construction workers not showing up when they're supposed to. Well, Eddie wasn't having any of that. We walked around the outside and inside of my house, looked at every little thing, and Eddie wrote it all down, money estimates and all.

"Have you ever seen anything like this? I mean, in your line of work, you must see damage you know was done on purpose. I don't suppose there's been a rash of firebombings in Tullulah or I'd have done heard about it."

"No, ma'am," he said and laughed. "Most everything I've covered has been accidents or natural causes. You know, acts of God. Tornado, lightning, flood damage. The only thing other than those was when Jody Taylor's boy jumped on a bulldozer when the River Glen condominiums were being built. It got away from him and he ran across the road into a neighbor's garage. But that was unintentional. This? No, ma'am, I haven't ever handled a case like yours."

"I can't understand anybody doing this to me. Or to anybody around here."

Eddie clicked his pen and stuck it in his shirt pocket. "I did see something interesting several weeks ago. May not have any connection. We get a monthly report at the office of claims filed from all over the state. Usually I just scan it for what's happening locally. Two weeks ago, there was an incident in Lawrence County that caught my eye. A business had a fire claim. The inspector said it looked like arson."

Lawrence County. That was the next one over from us, on the other side of the river. "So, was it like regular arson? With a gas can and a match?"

Eddie shook his head. "No, ma'am. Bottle firebomb. No witnesses. Done in the middle of the night."

"Where was this?"

"A honky-tonk by the railroad tracks, right at the Highway eighty-seven and fifty-one junction. The Pool Cue. They mostly attract the afterwork crowd from the plants at shift changes, plus, being at a major intersection, they get a lot of travelers and folks from the outer-lying areas. I talked to the adjuster that handled the claim at a regional meeting last week. He said the bar's owner thinks he knows who did it, some guys who've been coming regularly for several weeks. They play pool a lot, sometimes get a little loud. Some other drunks hassled them one night and a few got punched. The owner threw everybody out, even the ones who hadn't started the fight. When he did, they threatened him. The next night, the place was burned."

"I don't see how the police haven't arrested them, if they know."

"They don't have any evidence. The police did question them like everybody else in the bar. Fortunately, the bar only had a small area damaged. The clean-up crew was still there when the fire started. They were able to get the fire department out in a hurry. So, the bar was reopened for business after only a couple of days."

"And the suspects were never seen again, right?"

Eddie shook his head. "No. The owner said they still come in, like they're innocent. Maybe they are."

Once Eddie and I had done all the figuring we needed to, I picked out some more clothes to take to Jane's. After that, I stopped at Tullulah Appliances on the square and looked at the stoves and refrigerators. They said they'd take my old melted burnt-up ones as a trade and haul them off for me, so I was thankful for that.

That left just one more thing on my to-do list. Revenge.

That's right. I'd been thinking about it and stewing over it and getting hotter and hotter over the bombing. I'd come to the conclusion that I needed a real gun. Sure, the little pistol I bought from Alton would've been fine before, especially since I hadn't really planned on using it much. I mean, it's one thing to discover a body completely unknown to you and not your fault for being dead. But it's quite another to have your house destroyed, not to mention the lives of you and your friend endangered. That is personal. What if those boys from down the street had been in my house? That right there officially used up all my sweet reserves. I mean every lick of them. Having spent sixty-five years under the regime, I had precious little left to begin with. Next stop, the Gun Show.

I called Jerry Nell Gillispie, who runs the ceramics class I go to, to find out if this was the right weekend for the Gun Show and if her husband, Donnie, was setting up this month like he usually does. She said he was and that she would be there, too, since this month the fairgrounds were having two shows, a combination Gun plus Arts and Crafts.

Jerry Nell makes the prettiest baskets and floral arrangements. She can make anything. She painted and framed all my living room pictures and made all the wall doodads, too. I expected to see lots of her hunting-dog pictures at her booth since the men who are Donnie's customers like that kind of thing.

Of all the ladies with talent I've seen in ceramics and other artwork, Jerry Nell is definitely the best. She and Donnie also personalize T-shirts with an airbrush. Car tags and coffee cups, too. Donnie isn't a bad artist himself, and he can make anything out of wood—cabinets, lamps, duck decoys, you name it. They are one talented family.

I walked inside one of the air-conditioned buildings at the fairgrounds. The smell of hot dogs and cotton candy hit me as I pushed the heavy door open. I stopped for a cold drink and looked over the booths on the way to the very back. Some things interested me but when it comes to true art I'd never buy from anyone but Jerry Nell.

She and Donnie had one of the biggest booths there. It took up the whole left back corner of the building. Donnie stood in it, front and center, behind five or six huge tables set out in a rectangle. Gun stuff covered them. It would take all day just to look at every single holster, ammo box, knife, and Lord knows what all that he had laid out.

Donnie's a fairly good-sized old boy. He was wearing his usual white T-shirt with the sleeves cut off, a ball cap, and worn-out jeans slung under his belly. Today's cap said, "Para Hawg." I didn't know what it meant but I liked it. He was busy showing a pocketknife to a fellow from out of one of several glass cases with small items in them so I didn't interrupt.

Jerry Nell was sitting in a folding lawn chair a few tables down to the right, painting the finishing touches on a vase. Her area for her crafts was just about as big as Donnie's. All her tables were full, too, with decorations crafts mainly. Their airbrush machine was up against the wall.

"Oh, Phoebe! How are you, darling?" she said. Jerry Nell always looks nice. She keeps her hair colored and knows how to fix it as good as a beautician. That day she had a little pink dogwood blossom, artificial but it looked real, stuck behind her ear where her glasses hook over. She's pretty hefty. I would be, too, if I cooked like she can. All the girls in her family were taught right by their Grandmother Genie. Not a county fair goes by but one of them wins a blue ribbon.

"I'm sure sorry about your house," she said. "I heard you weren't hurt or I'd a done been over to see about you. Lord, what kind of times are we living in. I heard the whole kitchen was blown apart. Mama said Gladys said her dogs licked the screen on her porch all night after it happened." Gladys, my next door neighbor, is Jerry Nell's first cousin.

"They licked the porch screen because they liked the taste of smoke and ashes?"

"No. I believe Gladys said it looked like peach cobbler. But now listen, if there's something me and Donnie can do for you, you know all you have to do is let us know."

"As a matter of fact, that's why I'm here. Y'all can help me a lot.

I was hoping Donnie would have a good rifle he could sell me this weekend."

"Sure he can. He can fix you right up. But now, come on over here and look at some of my new stuff while he finishes helping that other customer. You know how these men are—they could talk forever about a stupid knife."

We walked down to a section of new crafts she'd made. Ladies were swarming down at that end, all looking at a nice Christmas display Jerry Nell had set up with snowmen, Santas, and some little angels made out of raffia, cotton balls, and pipe cleaners.

When Donnie's customer left, Jerry Nell went and told him what I was looking for. He motioned me over. I said, "Now, Donnie, I want me a big gun. Some kind of rifle. Something nice." He led me past several upright glass cases and pegboards full of hand-guns to where a locked cabinet held the bigger rifles. Some were old and ugly looking. Antiques, I guessed. Others shined like they had been spit polished.

He showed me some newer ugly ones first. They were the least expensive, which I thought was considerate of him. He also tried to tell me that, if he was me, he'd get a good shotgun. They were easy to use and even a lady like me could stop somebody with it, if I had to. I appreciated the advice and he made a good point. Maybe I'd get one some other day. But right then, I knew a shotgun wasn't what I'd buy.

"What I want," I said as I reached into my purse, "is one that these here bullets fit in." I showed him the box.

He jumped back a couple of steps. "Hoo-wee, Phoebe," he said and tilted his ball cap back.

"Yeah," I said, patting my hair and trying not to sound smug. "Israel."

He scratched under the cap's brim. "I'm not trying to tell you what to do or anything, but have you thought about maybe just buying some different bullets?"

I closed my eyes and shook my head. "No. I don't want that. I want these. They're lucky."

He stared at the box a little longer and shrugged. "Okay. I've got two a lady might could use that this ammo will work in. And I have to say, they're both real high now but you can't find no better."

One of them he brought out was the scariest gun I'd ever seen in my life. It was love at first sight. I didn't even have to hold it or anything to decide.

"That one right there," I said.

"But, this other one . . ."

"No, sir. You might as well put that one back in the cabinet."

Donnie's front two teeth have a sliver of space between them. So, when he drew in a breath, it whistled a little bit as his eyebrows rose. He didn't say a word though. He leaned the big, long ugly one carefully back into the case.

Meanwhile, I took my rifle from his other hand. It was black and shiny with a couple of pieces of wood on the top and back. Not too heavy either. My palm fit around the grip just like it had been made for me.

"Was this what Rambo had in the jungle?" I held it up and looked through the sight up at the ceiling. Oh, yeah. I wouldn't have any trouble aiming at a criminal. A gun like that? A bad guy with a lick of sense would run at the sight of it without me firing one shot.

"Real similar to Rambo's. That was an AK-47. This here is an AK-46 and a half. Ladies' model. Made small for a woman's hands, lighter body. The magazine only holds twenty rounds, though."

"Twenty is plenty. I'll take it."

While Donnie took my check and wrote up my receipt, another one of Jerry Nell's displays on the other side of the booth caught my eye. Of all the kinds of art she does, my favorite by far is her Native American stuff. She's got paintings of all sizes, cross-stitch patterns, ceramic statues, whatever you can think of, of Indians. She did the two pictures in my living room of warriors on horseback, did them made to order because I wanted the orange and turquoise to match a blanket wall hanging I already had over my couch.

Right when I saw some new T-shirts Jerry Nell had personalized by airbrushing people's names on them, Donnie looked up and said, "I tell you what, you'll be good and prepared now. This here will fix somebody's wagon before they can give you any more fire or smoke damage."

"Hah. I'll fire this baby up and smoke them good, is what I'll do." I looked over at those T-shirts again and had what they call an epiphany.

"What I have to do," Donnie said, "is run a background check on you, even though I know you're an upstanding citizen. Federal law."

"What? You have got to be kidding me. If you can't buy a gun in Alabama when you want to, something is wrong."

He shrugged his big shoulders. "Alabama will let you, just not the Feds. It won't take long. Like checking a credit card, is all. You'll be ready to go here in a minute."

"You know what, it doesn't matter anyway. I've got a little work I want Jerry Nell to do on it before I take it home."

He looked at me funny. "She don't know nothing about guns."

"No, but she knows about other stuff."

twenty

Jane Goes to Cal's House

*A*fter I dropped Phoebe off at her house, I stopped at the bank. I had a very pleasant chat with Mr. Roman, the local manager there. We'd met on two previous occasions when I opened new accounts and settled my house purchase before my move to town.

My first thought in regard to buying Cal's land had been to simply transfer the money from a credit union savings account I'd used for years when depositing my part-time freelance money. I'd never touched it, and many times the amount Cal asked for had been growing in interest there for some time.

The night before my trip to the bank, I had a better thought. I decided instead to take out a loan, as a way to support the local bank. I could easily transfer payments electronically from my credit union account when they were due. Mr. Roman seemed quite pleased and assured me the necessary paperwork and the cash Cal requested would be ready for me within a few days.

I worked in the house the rest of the morning, unpacking boxes and putting things away. I wanted to give Cal plenty of time to rest before going over to see about him. Around noon, I had a nice lunch made for him and a few extras for later.

The inside of Cal's house was a bit messy but not so bad as I expected. The kitchen was outdated and in need of paint. We passed an old wood stove in the middle of the house and stepped into a small sitting room. No paintings or photographs hung here. There simply was no room. Floor to ceiling bookcases filled the walls and their shelves were stuffed with books.

I made Cal sit and eat while I looked over the spines of his collection. Homer received a treat as well then lay on the floor beside Cal.

"Miz Jane, I sure do appreciate you being so nice," Cal said, as he tucked into his meal.

"My pleasure. Now, let's talk about something serious. I want to call a nurse for you. You need someone reliable who will come see after you regularly."

His mouth was full but his eyes had the look of "No." He shook his head.

"Please, Cal. How long has it been since you've seen a doctor?"

"A few weeks ago. Doctors can't do me no good anymore."

I didn't want to pry. If he'd seen a doctor as recently as that, I had to assume that doctor would have advised him to get a nurse if he needed one. Whether or not he had, and Cal was being uncooperative, was another question. "And are you following his instructions?" I stared at the cigarette butts in the ashtray next to his chair.

He smiled, following my gaze. "Not too good. He only gives me six months, so I figure why quit smoking now?"

"I'm sorry," I said.

"Don't be. The main thing is, we've got to get our sale settled."

He was very happy when I told him that it should be done within a few days. Mr. Roman saw no problem in getting the correct amount in cash for Cal but doing so would delay things a bit. "So, I should have it by the weekend? That's good." His back relaxed into his chair as he breathed out a heavy sigh of relief. "It'll be over by the weekend. That's good."

I didn't pester him about his doctor's orders. Two bottles of prescription medicine sat on the end table next to the ashtray. One of them contained painkillers in a strong dosage. The fact that Cal had filled the prescription encouraged me. The other side of the coin was not so good: that the pain must be nearly unbearable for him to have done so.

"Something has been on my mind since this morning," I said. "I must ask you, when you heard about Phoebe's house being set fire, you looked as if there was something you might know about it. Have you heard something?"

He sat very still. His eyes lost their focus. "I don't know if you've heard much about me, Jane," Cal said. "Rumors always seem to include me around here, no matter what."

"I don't listen to gossip," I said.

"Me neither. But sometimes you hear things that sound convincing, even when there's no truth in a bit of it."

"Such as?"

"Such as, people say I've hoarded money and gold out here," he said with a laugh. "That I filled up mason jars and plugged them in the ground like planting corn."

"My, how imaginative. Is there any basis for it, or is it one of many silly stories about you?"

Cal smiled. "Maybe it is."

"Which?" I said. My knowledge of Southern speech was limited, but there was no mistaking the playfulness in misdirection here, particularly with Cal.

"What I'm getting at," he said, "is that people will assume if something bad happens, that I did it. Been that way for years."

"Yes, well, we can't escape that in regard to the murder on your land. Yet in the case of Phoebe's fire, you couldn't have a better alibi. You were a guest of the local constabulary."

I resumed looking over his books. I moved a stepping stool aside as I gazed over the book spines. History, many on the two world wars, and fiction, nature books. Native American customs and histories filled one entire bookcase, perhaps more.

"I have some of the special books over here that belonged to my father and grandfather." He led me to a barrister's bookcase with old glass doors over each shelf. Here I could see the pride Cal felt for his family and his land. Inside, books and mementos were carefully spread in displays.

He smiled as he opened one of the cabinets. He took out a black wooden shadow box with a glass top. Inside lay a small fragile-looking string of beads, once white but now yellowing with age. Next to it lay a small dagger with a bone hilt and a sewn leather sheath. Cal placed the box in my hands with reverence.

"Did these belong to someone in your family?" I asked.

He nodded. "My great-great-great-grandparents, Charlie and Jenny. Not the oldest things I have, but the most precious." He took out other treasures in turn. It pleased him to have someone to share his joy in the objects. From beside a pair of gold rings, he brought out a wedding photo.

"My Livvie. She had a laugh that could cure your soul." He gazed lovingly at the image of her and of himself, neither of whom looked yet twenty. He took out another, older photograph, a tintype, showing an elderly couple. "That's my grandparents."

She was small and dark. Her long black hair was braided and hung in two plaits past her shoulders. Her dark eyes shone with character and pride above high cheekbones. Cal's grandfather stood tall beside her, his strong, rugged body protective, his mischievous face very much like Cal's. "She was Cherokee?"

"Yep. He was one-fourth."

I leafed through book after book, looking mainly at pictures taken of the area some time ago. Many were of the construction of Wheeler Dam in the 1930s. Much earlier ones showed downtown Tullulah when its stores were brand-new.

One picture shocked and, frankly, sickened me. Three men with rifles stood beside the carcasses of two magnificent bears. One man held the heads up for the photographer. The shocking part was the caption, which said the animals were "killed on Old Anisidi Road near the bluffs." Not far from where I sat. I looked more closely. One of the men named was Cal's father.

Cal wanted to take a walk. I didn't object, though I could tell he was more tired than usual. He led me off the gravel road in a direction away from his house. Soon his house and the surrounding meadow were behind us. The trees and underbrush of his woods all but erased the slim path we'd been following. Just like that, we crossed to another world.

"Now up here," Cal said, "is the spring. This is good water. You can drink right out of it." He stooped, cupped his hand and drank. "Good cold water." A tiny springhouse made of metal sheets straddled the stream. Inside, shelves held cans of beer. Cal took one down and offered one to me as well.

"No, thank you," I said, "but you go ahead and have one yourself."

From the way the trees fell away from us, I sensed we were on another path of sorts. It continued to rise to a tree with a trunk as big around as the width of two cars. Its bark and limbs looked like no other around them.

Cal saw my astonished look. "Pretty, huh? I've seen it so many years, I forget sometimes how unusual it is."

"What is it?"

"A Canadian hemlock. Over three hundred years old. It and four others you see there across the way are the only ones in this part of the country."

"How is that possible?" I felt the bark with both hands as I walked around the large tree.

"Don't know. The experts say seeds may have come down so far on a glacier. I'm thinking it could've been a traveler that brought them."

A thrilling thought. Over three hundred years, which would be in the late sixteen or early seventeen hundreds. I nodded. "A native down to hunt? Or possibly a European explorer."

"A fellow from a university looked at them. He said it was unlikely explorers were here then and that I just didn't understand. I understand one thing—the trees are here and that's for sure."

We walked along as the path widened. Cal pointed out a fork that led to a well-known native trading route, one that stretched from the Smoky Mountains in North Carolina, across northern Alabama, and connected to the Natchez Trace.

"I spend a lot of time here. The path is so worn, it doesn't need much up-keep. But I feel like I need to keep it open. I like to go along with my scythe and cut back where I need to. Here, try it."

I took a few swipes at a clump of weeds. We walked on and as I got the hang of it I cut back here and there along the path.

"That's right," Cal said. "There's maps I've drawn of all the trails, so you'll have them. I've been writing things down for thirty years or more. My daddy and granddaddy did the same, so you've got plenty to read up on whenever you get the notion."

"Wonderful. I look forward to it. Cal, there's something I want to say. I want you to know that I will never intrude. As long as you live here, and I hope it will be for a very long time, I will consider this your place. I want to be sure you feel the same way, no matter if I'm the official owner."

"I appreciate that. We aren't going to have any problems, you and me." He stopped and looked around us. "Now then. We're here. The ceremonial hall."

We had arrived at the two gate-like boulders, but from another direction than before. They had been completely hidden from view on our approach by large firs.

Cal took a folded piece of paper from his shirt pocket. "This is just a rough sketch. I wrote down the main points. There's better ones at the house that show everything." I unfolded the lined paper torn from a wire-bound book. Held horizontally, a stream ran from left to right. Trails ran along the length with offshoots to paths Cal and I had already traveled.

Cal's crude handwriting scrawled out words that made me stop in my tracks. All along the trail, place names in Cherokee tickled my imagination and rang in my head like fire bells.

"We're here, at the main entrance." He tapped the map. His finger touched a crude drawing of the entrance stones. Across from it, the map showed a wall opposite us with the words *Nvya Noquisi* on it. To the right, he'd drawn several waterfalls, one with the intriguing name Maiden's Tears. To the left, he'd written one large word, *Danitaga,* above two trees, and in smaller print, *Tseni Usti, Tsali Skatsi,* beneath them.

We sidled through the entrance rocks. Cal waved to the old trail, a precipitous drop that a goat would have difficulty navigating. To the right, Cal walked on a short stretch of flat earth and onto a wooden plank bridge. It had no rail, no rope on the sides, but on its right, more huge boulders served as a wall as the path led steadily down. We were headed into a deep valley, like a canyon, with steep sheer cliff walls towering on the other side of the stream, as on Cal's map.

I puzzled over the scene. "The stream, had it once been a river? The canyons out west were carved by water, but here the rock looks much different."

"That's right. It's not a real canyon. All these boulders are from an earthquake. Many, many thousands of years ago. They formed a big circle and isolated the forest here."

Cal stood on the planks, turned toward me, watched my expression of delight. A wordless communication passed between us, and he smiled while a pair of cardinals swooped between us. We walked round a bend of the stream, taking care to avoid the more slippery-looking rocks covered with wet green coats of moss. I could hear the sound of water rushing somewhere nearby, though here the stream meandered slowly along a thin curve.

"First stop, Invisible Falls," Cal said. I expected to see a waterfall for the sound grew louder as we progressed. True to its name, there was sound but no falls, only an indentation in the rock about ten feet square, dry as could be.

Cal answered my confused look. "It's an echo of another fall, that way. It bounces off the boulder across from it and again into this hollow." Farther ahead past dappled shadows through the rock maze, I saw the bottom of a waterfall where a rainbow hovered in a patch of bright sunlight over the stream's bed. In many more places, water fell from the rocks above us, some trickled flat against the walls, others in little streams as if spraying from a water hose. None were so breathtaking as the next spot I remembered from Cal's map.

"The Maiden's Tears," I said when I saw it. It couldn't be anything else. A large sandstone outcropping above us had been worn into the shape of a human face. Drops of water fell from the downturned eyes to a small pool about fifty feet below.

"The U.S. Government rounded up all the Indian tribes in the southeast at different times over a period of years. They held some here in the canyon, then forced them to walk to Muscle Shoals. From there, they started on the Trail of Tears on the way out West. She cries for them."

I could no longer hold back my own tears. I'd suppressed my

emotions when I first saw the canyon from just inside the boulder portals. I hadn't wanted Cal to think me daft. Even as wonderful as the outer forest was, on first seeing the canyon below us, I could hardly take in the beauty. I had to steady myself with a hand to the entrance and remind myself to keep breathing.

And now, gazing upon the Maiden, so lovely not only in form but also in meaning, I could hardly bear it. How small and insignificant now were the sculptures I'd admired in museums, the paintings that provoked thought and emotion. So small now, our best human efforts, and so very pale beside this magnificent work of nature.

The reality of it all, the responsibility of this place that would be mine, fell heavily on me. I needed to sit down. Cal led me to the center of the canyon to a huge open area with a solid stone floor. This was the ceremonial hall, as awe-inspiring and holy as any church and every bit as regal, more so by virtue of its natural architecture of stone wall and floor, and the ceiling, part thick green canopy and part wide openings of blue sky.

Cal showed me the wear in a section of the rock floor made by human feet at dancing ceremonies over millennia. He'd said Chickasaw, Cherokee, and other tribes lived here in recent history. How many thousands of generations of unnamed, ancient peoples before them?

I had to step back for a moment to collect myself. There was too much to take in at once. "You okay?" Cal asked. "Come over to these steps and sit. I want you to see at least one more thing today."

The steps were not wooden ones made by Cal or his father or grandfather, as some we had passed on our trek. These were rock. Three individual "seats" faced a section of particularly damp and mossy stone walls where water dripped into larger pools than we'd seen before now. At this spot, no trees grew behind the wet boulders for, on the other side of them, were the high river bluffs. Above this section of boulders we could see only a large patch of blue sky.

It had the look of a panorama, like a high screen showing a director's cut movie, with our seats facing it as if we were an audience. My seat was one slab of rock with a natural indentation for a footrest. Cal sat on a stack of three flat rocks that were fashioned like the third seat to his right.

"Star Rock," he said, motioning to the wall before us. He rose, walked to the nearest pond, and dipped his hand in it. He held out his palm to me. In the little well of water lay a small cylindrical thing that looked like a cocoon.

"You can't see it now in the daylight, but at night these little critters glow. See them?" he said, as he pointed to the wall.

I did. The damp rock face was covered with small brown spots like the one Cal carried. He put it back in the pond, also teeming with brother "critters."

"Glow worms? Oh, my. I've never seen one. What do they look like when they glow, like fireflies?"

"No, not like that. They don't go on and off, and their light isn't yellow. It's more of a blue or blue-green. Spooky the first time you see it."

"I can hardly wait." I started to cry again. I never expected such wonders and wasn't handling myself very well. "So sorry. I'm not like this normally. Not at all. It's all so overwhelming. You should have warned me about this place, that it would be so astonishing. I don't know what to say."

"Don't have to say anything. It's enough to see you understand now. Why I've had to protect it the way I have."

So many questions buzzed through my mind. I wasn't sure I did understand why he'd kept it all to himself. It was much too grand and important a place, historically, to not be shared with all. If not open to the public, then why not to scholars and scientists who could learn so much here? Then there were also the interests of native groups who would surely feel entitled to its use, even if it were on a limited basis only. Cal's respect for the tribes that were here, as well as his own Indian heritage, were evident. Why had he not made the canyon, at the very least, a temporary retreat for those like him, who sought to revere nature and the ways of the area's original peoples?

I was too tired to tackle such questions. Cal was worn out too, though he tried not to show it. His breathing was more labored and I knew he needed to rest. As we made our way out of the forest, Cal stopped occasionally and named different plants we saw that he used for medicines.

Once back in his house and with Cal comfortable in his chair, I made him promise to come over for breakfast in the morning. He didn't put up much of an objection, I was pleased to see. If I could keep him fed reasonably well, we'd both feel better.

I walked toward home. I'd passed through the hedges at the entrance to Cal's land and stepped onto Anisidi Road when a truck came barreling from around the corner. It squealed its tires and flew past me. Two men were inside. I didn't think quickly enough to get a license plate. Only when I reached the house did I remember that the truck seen at Phoebe's was also red.

twenty-one

Phoebe Deciphers a Phone Call

ane thinks she's sneaky. She was quiet, I grant you that, when she left the house the next morning before six o'clock. Personally, I don't go in for getting up with the chickens. What's the point? It's not like I've got farm animals to feed, not since I was a child. Let me tell you, you do that when you're a kid and you're cured for life of this rise and shine at the crack of dawn business. Not Jane. She asked me the night before if I wanted to go for a run with her early next day. Ha. Me, run. Not likely.

Anyway, that wasn't the sneaky part. That was when she got back. She didn't come directly in the house. She went out, way on out yonder to the far side of her yard where her oak trees are.

She took a few long drinks from her water bottle and set it against a tree. Thinking nobody was looking, she stood up real straight, took some deep breaths and then Lord help my time if she didn't start doing the Tai Chi. Yes, Jane. Sweet little-bitty British Jane. Out there hiding in the trees and swinging her arms and legs around like she was Bruce Lee or somebody.

There are folks around here who, if they saw her doing it, would think she was weird and would avoid her from then on. Not me. It impressed the chili peppers out of me. She did it good, too, like she'd been at it a long time. Did I tell you that in addition to being a nature freak, she's also an exercise freak? Well, she is. I didn't know it until I saw in her sunroom on the other side of the kitchen that she had set up weights, weights now, like they have at those fancy gyms. I knew she looked trim, but dang, that's ridiculous and going a little too far if you ask me.

That Jane is full of surprises. You wouldn't know from looking at her she knew anything close to the Tai Chi, but while I was watching her, I started thinking about that husband of hers. I bet he taught her some mean Ju-Jitsu, too, and I bet she taught a little of it when she did those self-defense classes. Maybe I could talk her into teaching me.

I didn't mention I'd seen her when she came in. Cal was coming for a late breakfast, she said, brunch since he's the type who can't eat early. Jane and I had coffee and biscuits to hold us over until then.

Cal looked much better than the day before. His eyes were clearer and he looked happier, too, like a weight was off him. He laughed and joked with us, telling stories while we ate.

Homer barked outside. We had a visitor. Jane went to answer the door and when Cal heard who was there, he got up and went into the living room where Detective Daniel Waters walked in. Cal didn't look too happy to see him.

"Everybody relax," Daniel said. "I'm just here to return Miz Thistle's guns." He held up a big leather bag in one hand. Jane held her rifle she'd taken from him at the door.

"We're clear?" I said.

"All clear. Fortunately for you two ladies, our murder was committed with a .45. So we didn't have a match. If I could get you to sign this to show I returned them all, I'd appreciate it, Miz Thistle."

Jane set the bag on her living room couch. She took out the guns we'd practiced with and put them side by side on the cushions. Once she was satisfied they were all there, she took Daniel's pen and signed the paper.

He thanked her, folded the paper up, and put it in the bag. He looked over at Cal. "How you feeling today?"

"Fairly well, thank you." Cal looked embarrassed. He started to say something but Daniel interrupted him.

"Good, good. Listen, could we step outside for a minute?" Jane's face was a sight. She didn't like that one bit. She didn't tell Cal he should have a lawyer present, but that's what we were both thinking.

"It's okay," Cal said to soothe her. "Everything's okay." They stepped through the front door and out to the yard. Jane and I went back to the kitchen to get our coffee. Not two minutes later, we heard Homer start barking again and a car door shut.

Jane looked worried. "Are they leaving?"

When we walked outside, we saw another car at the curb and Chalmers Wade, the best lawyer in town, out in the yard rubbing Homer's belly.

"Let that poor dog alone, Chalmers," I said. That boy is some kind of good looking. It's not just because both his parents were, either. It's because he has a beautiful smile and he's nice to everybody. Sure, he's rich as the devil but that hasn't made him the least bit stuck up. He's always in the news from giving to charities. I understand he goes to church every Sunday. He's the best thing the Episcopalians have going for them around here. He handled my husband Ronald's will for us. Couldn't have been nicer.

Chalmers laughed and said, "Why, Miz Twigg, what a surprise. I don't think Homer minds."

He stood up when he saw Jane and said, "Miz Thistle? I'm Chalmers Wade, Cal's attorney." He shook her hand while he nodded his head at the unmarked police car at the curb. "Surely Dan Waters isn't here interrogating my client this early in the morning."

I was just about to tell him he was when Dan and Cal walked from the backyard around the side of the house past Jane's nandina bushes. Cal stopped when he saw Chalmers. I think his brain wasn't working quite right. It took him a second to get it together and realize who he was looking at. I guess all the stress of being in jail is what did it. Anyway, he finally came around and smiled at Chalmers and said, "Son! Where you been hiding?"

Chalmers went to him and gave him a big hug. I could tell it hurt him to see Cal looking so poorly, even though he put on a good show. "You all right? This guy been bothering you?" he said.

He gave Daniel a little boxing punch on the arm before they shook hands. You know how guys do, especially former football players like them. "What's this about you assaulting my client?" Chalmers said, as they tussled a little bit.

"Other way around. Lucky I got witnesses," Daniel said, giving Chalmers a good punch back. "What've you been doing this time, murdering deer or murdering fish?"

They all had a big laugh out of that one. That's what you call diffusing the situation. Chalmers and Daniel knew what they were doing. You wouldn't see that kind of thing in a big city. If somebody like them would go teach the *NYPD Blue* and *Law and Order* people how to act, they'd get those cases solved in thirty minutes instead of an hour. The other thirty minutes they use up with just a bunch of hollering, pouting, and talking smart.

All three guys joked around, acting like everything was okay, which it was since they were making it okay. Nobody had to act up with his lip poked out about past offenses, and goodness knows there were plenty of them with these three.

As a kid, Chalmers was several grades ahead of Daniel. Back

then, people weren't so openminded as now, and I have to say poor Daniel took a lot of guff from Chalmers and the other rich kids. Now that they're grown, things are different. They've put the past behind them and now are practically colleagues, although at times like this, and with Cal involved, they worked on opposite sides of the fence. They knew they'd have their chance to officially lock horns later.

They didn't need my help, but I thought I'd jump in anyway and steer the conversation in a completely different direction. "Chalmers, you know all about what's going on in business around here," I said.

"Not hardly, Miz Twigg," he said.

"Yes, you do, don't play like you don't. I've got a question. Is it true we might be getting us a shopping mall in Tullulah? Somewhere out this way?"

He shook his head and looked off. "Not that I've heard," he said.

"Not even a little one?"

"If it is, you're more plugged into the grapevine than I am. Although George Deitz out on Mill Creek has threatened to sell his place."

"He's been saying that for years," Daniel said. "I wouldn't count on it."

"Shoot," I said. "I wish he would. Why don't you use your clout, Chalmers, and see if you can't get us a Dillards out here so I won't have to go to Florence."

Jane asked if everyone would like to go in for coffee. Daniel excused himself since he needed to get to the police station. Chalmers came in and we caught him up on all the excitement from the last few days. He told us about his hunting trip in Montana, and how he flew into Huntsville late the night before, then had to drive home which took another good hour. It was too late to check on Cal by that time, so that's why he came over early that morning.

"I hated I wasn't here for you, pal, when you needed me."

Cal shook his head. "Everything worked out fine. Miss Shelley did a good job. Don't fault her any for me having to stay over. I did it to myself."

We talked a little while longer then Chalmers said he had to get to work. He and Cal had walked through the house when Jane's phone did that weird thing again. It rang, she picked up, but there was just loud static in her ears.

"I think I hear faint words," she said. "It may be my imagination."

"Give me that." I took the receiver from her hand and listened. I had to strain real hard but she was right. Way down in there, I heard "Come over" and "Burn."

"Burn? Is this Junior Burn? From Pale Holler?"

"Pale Holler," the voice said, a little louder than before.

"My stars. Is everything all right? I can't hear you. If you can hear me, I'll come down yonder and see what you need, okay? You hear?" I think whoever it was said "Come over" again but I couldn't be sure.

"You understood?" Jane asked.

I hung up. "Yep. I believe it's your other neighbors way on the back side. The Burn family. They're a little backward. I've only seen them two or three times. They keep to themselves. Have a big garden. They go to an independent church one county over. I know because this was my territory when my church had a gospel meeting one time. I went door to door with flyers, personally. Reckon what they want? We need to go see."

"But, Phoebe, are you sure you heard correctly?"

"Positive. He said, 'Pale Holler' and 'Come over.' Can't get much plainer than that."

"But I haven't met them yet. It just seems . . . peculiar."

I nodded. "That's them, exactly. There's nothing wrong with them, per se, they're just old-time country. Never learned how to act normal in social situations. Always lived out by themselves. No socializing, so everything they do is a little peculiar. I hope they're just being friendly and nothing is the matter. I'd hate not to go if something was wrong."

Jane didn't look like she understood. It was hard to explain and I didn't do a good job of it. She'd get it after she lived here a while and met a few other families like the Burns.

"Perhaps you're right," she said. "I trust your instincts in such matters. I certainly wouldn't want to offend." She stepped over and gave me a little hug. "I'm so glad you're here. You're a godsend."

twenty-two

Jane Meets the Burns

*P*hoebe was certainly right. The Burns's house and their surrounding acreage had a decidedly primitive look about it. The area's name, Pale Holler, was apt, for as we came over the hill, the center of the valley looked like a large spot of gray. The road was gray mud with puddles, large and small, pitting the driveway to the house. Two outbuildings were also gray, a barn and what looked like an unattached garage with simple wood doors open. A large puddle in the road reflected the wood-frame white house and the gray clouds behind it that held the promise of a cold rain.

As Phoebe's car slowed, a man and a woman came out onto the front porch. They eyed us with suspicion, their bodies still, their heads slowly following our progress. We parked just beyond the house where the road ended in a small parking area of gravel with small shallow pools of rain and mud. Four aggressive dogs of various canine parentages surrounded the car and barked loudly. Phoebe turned off the engine.

"What do we do?" I said, unsure of the etiquette procedure. Were we to wait for our hosts to come to us or call their animals? Or were we to step into the midst of the snarling pack?

"It's okay. They aren't going to bother us." Relieved that Phoebe must know some country or Southern way of gently deterring unfamiliar dogs, I waited. She eyed them a few more moments and seemed to reach a conclusion.

With a sudden great force, she swung her door wide open, knocking two of the dogs back. She reached out her hand to what appeared to be the alpha dog, the largest and loudest of the group, and immediately slapped him on the muzzle.

"Heah!" she said, something between a yell, a nasal utterance, and a growl deep in her throat. Although I'd never heard that particular exclamation before, the dogs apparently had and understood its meaning, for it effectively scattered them away from the car.

"Hey, Mister Burn, Miz Burn. How y'all doing?" Phoebe called with a lilt. Her voice was completely calm as she gave a friendly wave. She motioned for me to get out of the car then shut her own door and walked toward the porch. I joined her quickly, keeping an eye on the dogs who, for now, kept at a distance but still barked. Phoebe ignored them. She marched toward the house as if the dogs didn't exist.

"Hush that," Mr. Burn, a tall wiry man with jet black hair, said to the dogs. "Get up here." He wore an open-neck cotton shirt and dark work pants, both neatly pressed. His gruff voice was instantly obeyed as all the dogs ran to his side, lay down meekly, and said no more.

It occurred to me that I'd not given a thought to what I might say. How does one broach the subject of mysterious phone calls with a stranger?

Phoebe came to my rescue. Just as she had taken charge with

the dogs, she used her larger-than-life personality to commandeer the situation with ease and aplomb.

Mrs. Burn, a plain woman with her brown hair pulled back in an old-fashioned bun, neither smiled nor frowned as she said, "Y'all come on in for a spell," with a hint of curiosity in her voice.

"Why, thank you so much," Phoebe effused and began talking in a steady stream of compliments and small talk. Her speech patterns altered slightly, using different words and syntax that combined into an interesting country accent, stronger than her usual one.

"This is Jane Thistle. She's your new neighbor up at the old Hardwick place. The one y'all called?"

Mrs. Burn turned to her husband. She looked confused, then there was a brief flash of horror in her eyes before she quickly turned away. Mr. Burn's back stiffened slightly. I thought I detected embarrassment when he met his wife's eyes. Oh dear, I thought. We've surprised her. She wasn't expecting us at all. Had Mr. Burn phoned? Or had Phoebe misheard the caller entirely?

Phoebe pressed on, oblivious to the currents passing between the couple. "You know, I haven't been out here to your house in, what, almost twenty years?" she said continuing her monologue, effortlessly switching from one topic of conversation to another without a pause. "Remember, my church was having a gospel meeting and I was in charge of handing out leaflets to everybody living from Highway Seventy-six to the county line, and Gaynord Phelps came down to preach, all the way from Detroit, Michigan, and . . ."

Mrs. Burn was nowhere in sight, I noticed, after we stepped inside. Mr. Burn, Phoebe, and I stood in a comfortable living room, decorated with no particular color scheme and filled with antique mahogany furniture. The overstuffed couch and three chairs took up most of the available floor space. A small ornate coffee table was dwarfed and completely surrounded by the couch and chairs, so much so that we had to squeeze through the tiny openings between them and sit with our knees very close to one another's.

A small television sat on a desk to our right. To the left, an end table held a figurine lamp with two courtly porcelain dancers as its base. Next to the lamp on a starched white doily sat an old black telephone with a dial that looked like an original from the forties.

Mr. Burn, expressionless, stood beside the couch until Phoebe and I took our seats. He hiked his trouser legs up at the knees and sat on the couch, just as Mrs. Burn came into the room carrying a large tray.

"Oh, my," I said, on seeing she had prepared quite a large tea. She set the tray, which must have been very heavy, down in front of us. In only a few minutes time, she'd produced a carafe of hot coffee, four cups and saucers in a beautiful Old World rose pattern, and a plate filled with slices of coconut, chocolate, and angel food cake.

"There's apple pie and ice cream, if you'd rather have that," Mrs. Burn said in a flat voice as she poured coffee into a cup. She handed it to her husband, making no eye contact. She then hesitated, holding the pot in the air. "Y'all like coffee? Because we've got tea and some good homemade cider if you'd rather have that."

Phoebe and I assured her that coffee was fine, and that her array of refreshments was more than suitable and quite generous. I marveled at her ability to produce such a delight on short notice. Mrs. Burn allowed a quick smile to flit across her lips, though she performed her hostess duties without looking directly at either of us.

Phoebe swallowed a bite of coconut cake and dabbed a spot of white frosting off her lips. "Mmmm, boy, that is mighty good. Now, like I said before we, or rather Jane, got your phone call. I was worried something might be wrong." She paused, waiting for one of the Burns to respond. "We could barely tell it was you, the static was so bad."

The Burns froze in place, Mr. Burn with his cup poised in front of his mouth, Mrs. Burn as she set the carafe on the tray. Phoebe continued her narrative.

"... And we couldn't hear very good, but I thought I heard 'Pale Holler' and 'Come Over,' so I looked in the phone book to call y'all back but didn't see you listed there."

Mr. Burn took a sip of coffee. "No, we don't have a phone," he said.

"Well, see, that's what I figured, or that your number was unlisted," Phoebe said cheerily. Her eyes slid to the right, nor could I control the natural inclination to look at the hulking black phone on the end table beside us.

Of course, they noticed our interest in it. Mr. and Mrs. Burn spoke at the same time. "It don't work," they said in unison.

I was suddenly aware of the smell of pipe smoke in the air. I hadn't noticed it when we came in. It was faint, as if a smoker had walked through the room.

Phoebe took a breath. "I see. So y'all don't need anything? I'm sorry, we came and barged in on you because I thought you did need something, or maybe just heard about Jane moving in and wanted to meet her since she's practically your neighbor now. But I reckon it wasn't you then, seeing as how your phone don't work and all."

And at that moment, the phone rang. Phoebe and I jumped in our seats. It was extraordinarily loud, much like the clanging of a ship's bell.

Mr. and Mrs. Burn stared at one another. The phone rang insistently yet neither moved nor spoke. Finally, on the fifth ring, Mrs. Burn picked up the bulky receiver and held it to her ear. She did not say hello or any other greeting. We could hear a faint noise as she listened. She looked at her wristwatch. Without a word, she recradled the receiver.

"Nobody there," she said, and then she did a very odd thing. She rose from the couch, walked across the room, and turned on the television. She adjusted the volume so it could be heard but would not interfere with our conversation. She returned to her seat. Both she and her husband ignored the TV.

"Probably some kinda e-lectric surge," Mr. Burn said, having trouble looking us in the eye. I didn't point out that the lights hadn't flickered. "So you live in the old Hardwick place now?" he said to me. Mrs. Burn continued to ignore the television as she put her napkin on her lap and took a sip of coffee.

"Yes," I said. "Please stop by sometime so I can return your kind hospitality." From the TV, we heard the sounds of a fight scene with kicks and grunts. Only Phoebe turned to watch.

"I'm enjoying it here very much," I said, trying to keep conversation going. "Everyone in Tullulah has been so kind and most welcoming."

The fight scene ended and a commercial began. Immediately, the phone rang once again. This time, Mr. Burn picked up. He closed his eyes while listening, then rubbed his free hand over his face. "Uh . . . ," he said, holding the receiver away from his ear for a moment. "Don't . . . ," Mr. Burn said, but the voice on the other end of the line didn't stop.

Mr. Burn sighed. A glance to his wife was answered with a stern shake of her head and one mouthed word, "No." The next instant, she turned to us and grimaced as she forced a smile. She lifted the cake plate from the coffee table and said, "Another slice?" I declined.

"Yes, sir," Mr. Burn said. "Yes, sir. Yes, sir." With another sigh, Mr. Burn held the receiver out to me. "It's for you." Mrs. Burn's eyes widened. Phoebe slowly turned her head away from the television. I tried not to look shocked.

"Oh. I see," I said. Gingerly, I took the receiver from him. "Hello? Jane Thistle here."

A scratchy male voice came over the line. "Hello, Miz Thistle. Welcome to Alabama. I hope you like it here."

"Thank you." The faces around me looked on with rapt attention, Phoebe with curiosity and the Burns with acute anxiety. "I like it very much."

"Good, good. This here is Nelton Burn. That's my boy and his wife at the house. You can call me Dad. I appreciate you coming over so quick." The voice was that of an elderly man, and though some static crinkled in the background, I could hear him clearly.

"Yes, well," I said. "My friend, Phoebe, and I weren't altogether sure we got the right information. I'm afraid we had quite a bad connection at my house. I must have that checked."

"No, ma'am, it's not your wiring." He drawled out the last word, *"wah-ren."* "It's cause I ain't never called nobody anywheres else. Tell the truth, I didn't reckon it'd work a tall. But my little great-niece said you was real nice and she liked you, so I thought I'd give it a try."

"I've met your niece?"

"Doreen."

I was puzzled. Not only had I not met a Doreen in Tullulah, I was certain I never knew anyone by that name.

"She probably didn't tell you her name," Dad said. "You saw her down on the square them first two times you came here before moving." My breath caught in my throat. The little girl in the white dress. I'd told no one I'd seen her. Not a living soul.

Dad's voice continued over the intermittent background static. "Now, there's people where I'm at who see better than I do. They wanted me to tell you something. They said Cal's mind ain't what it used to be. They say he has done messed up and he's going to be sorry. Tell him to quit thinking he can do it all by himself."

Dad coughed and caught his breath before continuing. "You both need to be real careful about trusting people right now. I told my friends, I said that you were smart and not to worry because you wouldn't be here if you weren't the one. I may not see as good as they do, but I tell you one thing, I can feel a whole bunch of meanness prowling out there in the woods, right up next to you. You be extra careful."

"Sorry, I don't understand. What did you mean, 'the one'? The one for what, exactly?"

"The one who's gonna save the woods and Cal's sorry hide. He has always been a stubborn old cuss. Never would listen to nobody. And the woods, well, that's the main thing, isn't it? That's why it's so important. Now, I'm sorry if I've upset you. I know this is a lot for you to take in all at once. I wish we'd had time to get to know each other first. But time is something we don't have much of. I felt like I had to try to reach you now before it was too late."

On the television, the commercial ended. A young blond girl in a graveyard came onscreen. She held a wooden stake in her hand. Phoebe was entranced.

"Well, Jane," Dad said, "it was sure nice talking to you. My story is back on, so I'll let you go for now. Don't forget what I've told you. Oh, something else. Don't you worry none about Boo. He's a good boy and he knows you've come to help us. And we sure do appreciate it, Miz Thistle, more than I can tell you. You let me know if I can do anything for you, you hear? I'll try you again at your house soon if I can figure out how to do it. And please excuse my boy there next to you. I'm afraid I've embarrassed him and his wife."

I was about to ask precisely how I could get in touch, should I need to, but the phone clicked. I held it to my ear a little longer, waiting for the dial tone. None came. The line was dead. "Hello? Are you still there?" I said. When there was no answer, I handed the receiver back to Mr. Burn. Both he and his wife had red faces and looked quite uncomfortable.

"I'm sorry about that," Mr. Burn said. "I take it he called your house. We didn't realize he could do that. Nobody else ... ah ... that is, you're the first person he's talked to other than us."

Mrs. Burn cut in. "It's a crank caller. He has messed up our phone to where it doesn't work except for when he calls." She looked to Mr. Burns to back up her unlikely statement which, from the fear in her expression, I was sure was a complete lie.

Mr. Burn looked torn. He rubbed a hand over his face and did his best not to contradict his wife. "We've gotten used to his calls. I'm sorry if he has started pestering you, too."

"Not at all," I said, unsure now if the man on the phone was actually Mr. Burn's father or not. "He was quite charming. He only wanted to welcome me to the area."

"I don't suppose he, ah, told you his name?" Mr. Burn obviously hoped he did not. Perhaps his father was right, that his son was terribly embarrassed by him.

"Yes, he did. Dad. Dad Burn."

Phoebe's body shook beside me. She was trying very hard not to smile or giggle. I had no idea what she found so amusing.

Mr. Burn cringed. Mrs. Burn gasped and looked as if she might faint.

Phoebe couldn't suppress a giggle any longer. "I'm sorry," she said. "I'm sorry. I just thought of something funny."

I stood and pulled Phoebe up with me. "We really should be going," I said. "I'm so sorry if we've imposed." Amid assurances to the contrary, we thanked the Burns for their hospitality and made our way to the door. Something on TV caught Phoebe's eye. The blond teenage girl fought off three large men who, on second look, were actually zombies. The girl was winning. Phoebe stared, wide-eyed and impressed.

"Come, Phoebe, dear." I tugged her arm until we reached the door and stepped off the porch toward her car. The dogs watched but made no sound or gave any indication they wished to follow us.

As soon as our car doors shut, Phoebe had a fit of giggles. She drove us onto the main road, shaking and laughing. "What's so funny?" I asked.

"Dad Burn? Ha ha! Somebody is pulling your leg good, Jane. And was that weird about their telephone, or what? See, I told you. They are severely country. What did old 'Dad Burn' have to say, anyway?" She laughed and shook, wiping the corners of her eyes while muttering the name over and over.

"Just pleasantries. Welcoming me to town, that sort of thing. Very nice, really. He said he's Mr. Burn's father. I find it puzzling that his son and daughter-in-law didn't want to openly recognize him. Even if he is eccentric, I don't understand why they don't just come out and say he was family."

"No, hon," Phoebe said. "That's not possible. Junior's daddy, Old Nelton Burn, died years and years ago."

"Good heavens. Are you sure?"

"Sure, I'm sure. I remember when it happened. A telephone pole got hit by lightning and fell on him, sparks a'flying everywhere. Lit him up like a Christmas tree. He glowed in his casket the whole time he was in the funeral parlor. No lie." She held up a hand as if giving an oath. "He had the highest attendance, yet to be topped, of people viewing a body during visitation. Folks that didn't even know him, even from other counties, came every night to see him. Look here, it doesn't matter. Somebody is having a good time fooling with you, that's all. No harm to it and we had some mighty good dessert while we were there."

I sat quietly as we drove, trying to sort out the mysterious phone call. Presently, I asked, "Phoebe, who is Boo?"

"Boo who?" She started laughing again. I couldn't help from doing so myself. What a silly friend I'd found.

"Don't know. Someone Dad mentioned," I said.

The rest of our phone conversation I kept to myself. I wasn't sure what reaction I'd get from Phoebe if I told her I didn't believe the caller was a crank at all. She might not take it very well if she knew that I, sensible Jane, had just talked to a ghost.

twenty-three

Phoebe Hits
The Pool Cue

After we left Pale Holler and the rest of the boonies behind, Jane and I drove past the first building in town,
which was Grace Baptist Church. Grace Baptist has a nice new
building, complete with a lighted sign like at the Pig, where they
can change the letters depending on the specials that week. Grace
Baptist changed their sign like that, too, only with different Bible
verses.

"What did it say?" I said. "It was too long to read and drive at
the same time."

"'For in Him all things were created, in heaven and on earth,
visible and invisible.'" Jane's voice was so low I could barely hear
her, and she sat there, staring out the windshield, like she was pondering something real hard.

"Huh. Not a very deep one this week. Tub Ashwander must be

on the sign committee again. Speaking of invisible, that reminds me. Ricky Blaze, who is working on my house, told me something you might be interested in," I said. "He said there was a murder in your house and that's why it's haunted." Jane turned her head to me. She looked a little scared. "I don't believe it's haunted, Jane. He said that, not me, and when he did, I told him, I said, why it's not haunted a bit, and that's when he told me what happened. But if you don't want to hear it . . ."

"No, I do."

"And it doesn't have anything to do with ghosts; it's just what happened. Cold, hard facts. It was way back in my granddaddy's time. The Hardwicks took in a retarded cousin whose family was poor and ignorant and didn't treat him right or know how to take care of him. They took him in, and then one day, a little girl from town went missing and he got killed."

"How do you mean? Was there a connection?"

"The little girl's daddy thought so. Him and a bunch of other folks in town blamed the retarded boy because he was out walking in the road, right down from your house, and he was carrying a doll that belonged to the girl. Her body was found close to where he was seen, somewhere on your property, I expect. The daddy went berserk and went home, got his shotgun, and tromped straight into the Hardwick's living room. Didn't even knock. Blew that poor boy away."

"How horrible."

"Yeah. Ricky Blaze said they never got the blood off the floor. I haven't seen any, have you?"

"No. It must be one of those lies you mentioned."

"Yeah. I knew it was. You can't believe a word anybody says."

Once we got settled in at Jane's again, we looked over her living room floor for dark spots on the wood. Nothing. Just like I figured.

I followed Jane into the kitchen and almost ran into her. She stopped in the middle of the room, bent over, and picked something up off the floor.

"What's that?"

She didn't say anything and her face was pale when she showed me. It was a bullet.

"How did that get there?" I said.

She shook her head. "I've no idea." That's what she said but I got the feeling she was fibbing.

I hated to leave Jane by herself that night but I had a date. I'd seen an old friend, or should I say, old flame, at the gun show. When I settled up for my AK-46 and a half that day with the Gillispies, I turned around and there stood Bernard French, towering over me, looking like a gray-headed lumberjack.

Now you'd think a guy named Bernard wouldn't have much in the looks or brains department. Bernard French was different. He hadn't let himself go to pot like most fellows my age. Sure, he had a little less hair and a few more wrinkles than when we dated in high school, but still. I'd seen him jogging around the lake at times over the years, so he was in tiptop shape.

He looked down at me and smiled. "Law, Phoebe, what's a good-looking lady like you doing here?"

I explained how I needed a gun on account of my house blowing up.

"I heard about that. With you by yourself, I don't blame you a bit for getting some protection." Bernard has flirted with me for I don't know how long. After his wife died, which was several years after my own husband died, I'd see him over in Iuka on Friday nights at the Regency Hotel for Dance Night. They had a live band and everything. Bernard was a good dancer and always wanted me to do the fancy numbers with him since I took ballroom lessons.

I had a sudden inspiration. "Bernard, I wonder if you'd do me a favor. I need to go to The Pool Cue."

"Whatever for?" Bernard looked liked I'd slapped him across the face. It's not exactly the kind of place where ladies hang out.

"It's kind of a recon mission." I knew he'd like that. Bernard joined the Marines right after school. He gave me a sly look.

"You spying on somebody you ought not to?"

I shrugged. "Somebody that maybe needs spying on. Are you with me?"

He grinned. "I reckon I better be. Just in case you need some backup."

I was pleased as punch. If a big man like Bernard went with me, those rednecks who bombed The Pool Cue wouldn't suspect a thing. If they were there.

And I believed they were. When we drove into the parking lot, the first thing I saw was an old beat-up red truck. I sure was glad Bernard agreed to go with me.

I'm telling you what, that place was rough. A few women sat at the bar but they weren't too dainty, if you know what I mean. The room was mostly full of big, ugly men on their way to drunk at full speed.

Bernard and I got a table over by the wall under a neon sign of a moose drinking a mug of beer. Bernard brought me a Shirley Temple, which was mighty nice of him since he remembered I liked them from the old days at the dance club.

After he settled down and looked around, he turned to me. "Well, you got me here. Now will you tell me what you're up to?"

"I'm not up to nothing."

"Come on now, Pebbles."

"Oh stop that," I said with a little smack on his arm. He always used to call me that because of how I wear my hair up on top of my head.

We giggled and drank a little while. I decided he was one I could trust and so I told him the truth. "It's like I told you. I'm here to spy on some guys," I whispered.

He leaned back and looked at me. "Why? Have you had a hot tip about your house bomb?"

"Possibly."

"And you think the ones who did it are here?"

"They might be."

"What do they look like?"

"I ain't got the slightest idea."

Bernard laughed. "How can you spy on somebody when you don't know what they look like?

I changed the subject. "I overheard some mighty interesting stuff at the gun show. When I was looking at gun accessories at the booth, I heard a man saying he was in Special Forces when he was in the service. Then, he went over to a rack of magazines and books and picked up one that said *Homemade Devices*."

Bernard stared at me. "That's it? That don't mean nothing."

"No, that's not it. Those guys talked about a meeting at a base camp. Said they might be having a survival crisis in this country soon and wanted to be stocked with supplies and ready to fight. They badmouthed the government the whole time I listened."

"A lot of people complain."

"Yeah, but these guys were scary."

"Well, you've got to remember sometimes guys talk, but when it comes down to action, they're just as big a sissy as everybody else."

"I know what I heard."

"Don't get upset, Pebbles. What can I do to make you feel better? I tell you what, let's go over to that booth. We'll be closer to the pool tables and those rough-looking characters. We can play like we're double-aught spies on a case of international intrigue."

"You're making fun of me."

"No, ma'am, I am not. I would a lot rather be with a woman who wants a little adventure than one that just sits in front of the TV all the time."

"Oh, Bernard!" He knows how to talk to a lady.

The booth had a low wall on one side, a little higher than the table, that divided the sitting area and the pool-table room. The divider was made out of dark paneling with a piece of wide crown molding across the top. Rings were all over it from where rednecks with no upbringing set their beers, right straight on the wood.

Bernard was right. We had a great view of some scary fellows and could hear them good. Of the three pool tables, we were only out of earshot of one way on the end. That didn't matter though because there were only a couple of girls shooting on it. They looked mighty rough in their tight pants and tank tops. Obviously, they were not from Tullulah.

Neither were the guys at the table next to them. They had all the hallmarks of thugs. Like maybe redneck mafia. Or even small fish used by international terrorists to infiltrate northern Alabama. The one racking up the balls was short and scrawny, the little buddy of the bunch that does all the scut work. His dirty blond hair was greased with big comb marks from his scalp down to his neck. He laughed like a hyena when he didn't have a cigarette in his mouth. He needed a dentist in a bad way.

A big guy waiting to shoot stood by the end of the table, chalking his cue. His hair was greasy, too, but at least he had it pulled back into a neat ponytail. He wore a muscle shirt so his blue-green tattoos would show. A chain with dog tags hung down when he bent over for the break.

Another guy stood in the shadow by the wall. I pegged him as the leader. He was a tall man and stood with a straight back, his legs apart and firmly planted. He was all muscle with a burr cut. His movements were slow and purposeful. The whole time, he looked out over the room like he was expecting trouble or maybe hoping for some. I knew the type. He stays quiet and gets a crazy look in his eyes to make the others scared of him. He wasn't drinking. He held his pool cue like he'd rather smack somebody with it than play pool. He looked just like the type who would throw a bomb into some nice lady's house, and then go have a beer and laugh about it.

I squinted at him like Clint Eastwood. Wouldn't Clint and I make a good team against this here bunch? Son, we could clean house, him with his .44 Magnum and me with my new AK-46 and a half. The first thing I'd do is hold my rifle out like a WeedEater and mow them beer cans off that ledge. Then I'd make those boys put coasters down.

"I know what you're thinking," Bernard said. "Just because these guys look rough doesn't mean they did it."

"I realize that. I don't expect to sit here and overhear them say, 'We sure had a good time blowing up Phoebe Twigg's house on October eighteenth.' All while an upstanding citizen and former Marine just happens to be here to hear their confession."

"Good. Now don't pout. If these ain't your bad boys, we'll go find some other ones. We can hit all the low-class hangouts. How does that sound?"

"There's not anymore but this one, you know that." For another thirty minutes or so, we laughed and had a good time while the other ones played pool. I've never heard so many cuss words. Those boys were mighty lucky Bernard was with me or I'd have found me some soap. That's all right. I knew their time would come.

twenty-four

Jane's House Is
Inspected

The next day, Cal asked me to bring my car to his house. He'd been busy gathering books and other materials into boxes that he insisted I take. The number of boxes he had stacked and waiting for me was more than I expected, seventeen of them numbered with red marker. I hurried so I could load them all myself. Cal was so stubborn about taking it easy and I worried he'd overexert himself. Once home, I stacked them next to my own boxes that I had yet to unpack in the den.

I'd promised Phoebe I'd go into town with her that morning. She wanted to keep a watch on the progress of her house repairs and also needed help in choosing new colors for the painters.

We passed the Piggly Wiggly before the turn onto her street. She gave a little yelp, goosed the accelerator, and drove past her street to the square up ahead. She pointed to a man walking into Wriggle's Sporting Goods.

"Look, look, look!" she said. "That's Jack Blaylock, the one who had the gun seminar."

I only had a glimpse of his face, saw that he had a moustache, before he entered the store. His hat and boots looked expensive. Phoebe covered her heart with her hand. "Oh, he is so handsome. Do we need anything from Wriggle's?"

"Was he there the day we met? He looks vaguely familiar."

"You must have seen him on TV. He's got his own show."

"What sort?"

"Fishing and hunting and other outdoors-y things."

"I don't think that's it."

"You'd like it, seeing all the local fishing spots on the river and all. I'm sure they show plenty of trees, too."

Then I remembered. He was the size and build of the man I saw at the grocery giving the ex-military man a fishing rod and duffel bag.

We stayed at Phoebe's only a little while. At home, I baked an apple pie and spent the rest of the day about the house. Only two events in the outside world caught my attention. At about one o'clock, I heard the rumble and chug of Cal's truck as it came out of his road and headed toward town. A few hours later, Shelley Barnette's yellow Volkswagen turned into Cal's driveway and disappeared from view.

Later that night, Phoebe and I had unexpected visitors. Phoebe answered the door. She put her hands on her hips. "Now what are y'all up to?" she said, then turned to me. "It's them crazy ghost-hunting kids again. You want me to tell them to go haunt somebody else?"

"Of course not," I said with a laugh. "Do come in. Are you off on another trek tonight?" Sarah, the tall blond girl, turned herself and walked in sideways so her leather tool belt wouldn't knock against the door frame. Behind her, Callie did likewise.

Riley brought up the rear. With care, he let the screen door close behind him while he took in his immediate surroundings. He did a thorough, steady sweep from left to right. Several times, his hand reached up and touched the night visor atop his head. He wanted badly to yank it down for a good look, I was sure. He had his hand in the air again but caught me watching and instead adjusted the visor's band slightly to a more snug fit. "Yes'm. We might go around a little."

As I looked at the three of them, all rigged in full ghost-hunting complement, I smiled. Each gazed about the inside of the house with wide eyes and a studied nonchalance that told me they "might" be hopeful of an in-house hunt.

"Brought these," Riley said, as he held out a packet of photos. "Said you'd like to see 'em." The photos showed various shots of the graveyard from our previous encounter. Most had little in the way of photogenic scenery, considering they contained only badly lit tombstones and tree trunks in the night. Riley touched the edge of the photo I held.

"This is for real. We didn't doctor it up in developing neither. Dropped them off at Wal-Mart. Unbiased second party. And we sure didn't do nothing funny when we took the pictures. You know that. That right there," he said, as he tapped the images with his finger. "You didn't see them orbs floating around like that, did you?"

I hesitated. "Ah. No, indeed I didn't." I failed to mention I distinctly saw them thrown, not floating around.

I could feel Phoebe breathing over my shoulder. She reached around and snatched the pictures from my hand. "What kind of foolishness are y'all talking about?" She eyed the top photo from several vantage points, up close, at arm's length, held upward toward the chandelier light, and down again at the end of her nose. "Huh," she said.

"You see?" Riley asked.

"No. I need my bifocals." With that, she turned on her heels and strode to the kitchen with the photos clutched in her hand.

My guests hardly noticed. All remained intent on surveying the living room, all stepping in slow circles to take in everything. "You sure have a pretty house," Callie said in soft, slightly awestruck tones.

"Why, thank you, dear. Have you never been here before then?" All shook their heads. "Perhaps you'd like a small tour? Even though I've not finished unpacking?" They answered together with "Yes, ma'am" before I'd finished the sentence.

Riley held up a finger. "Have you had any . . . oh, say . . . strange things happen? Like we did the other night?"

"Well, I've certainly not seen any orbs."

"Because if you have, or if you ever did, we'd all be glad to check the house for you, official like," he said, with indications to the others and his own equipment. "Free of charge. Anytime."

"How kind. But of course I wouldn't want to impose." Another louder round of comments came from the group, all protesting that I was most welcome to both their time and detecting talents. "In that case, feel free to . . . do whatever it is you do."

A collective sigh of relief arose as they each busied themselves in taking out and readying their devices. Phoebe returned with her glasses to see the young people settling into their new search. "What in the world are y'all up to now?"

"Riley and the girls have kindly offered to check my house."

"For what? There ain't none of them light balls in here."

"No. No anomalies here," I said.

Phoebe leaned closer and whispered, "That's a mighty big word, Jane. Around here, we call them 'dee-lusions.'"

I laughed. "What does it hurt to give them a little fun? They've come with the hope of discovering something exciting. I couldn't deprive them, not when they're so obviously enjoying themselves. They're just kids."

Phoebe's suspicious, hard stare softened as her lips turned up in a smile. "You're right. Let them look all they want. They aren't going to find anything. And maybe looking around will get it out of their systems so they won't come messing around bothering you anymore."

I didn't tell Phoebe that they might actually be useful. There was no point. I doubted anything would come of their testing, but I was interested to see if they "read" anything unusual in the two spots where, in fact, there had been instances of "anomalies."

The makeshift, home-modified look of Riley and the girls' equipment didn't instill much confidence. Yet I couldn't deny the photos of the orbs. Riley may not have seen them as I did, but his methods did produce results in the photos. Tagging along behind these three might prove to be fun as well as informative. I certainly intended to watch closely in case they turned something up. As it happened, that didn't take long.

"We got something," Callie said from the front room. She held her modified voltmeter out and over the corner of my maroon Persian rug and the intervening floor space between the rug and my fireplace. The black hand of the meter jumped behind its clear plastic casing when she moved the device over that particular spot, and each time she did so, with no exceptions.

The other two joined her and immediately deployed their own instruments, Sarah with her handheld scanner-like device, red lights pulsing, and Riley with his night visors snapped into position.

Phoebe closed her eyes and shook her head. She waved her hands in our direction in a dismissive gesture. "I'm fixing coffee." She shuffled away in her house slippers toward the kitchen.

"Okay, everybody," Riley said. "That's good. That's something. Now." He took out his camera and gestured for us to step back. He snapped pictures from all angles, some with and some without benefit of flash. The girls moved away from the spot with reluctance when Riley gave the order to move on.

"What would you say that means? In your experience?" I asked.

Riley shrugged. "Everybody be sure and write everything down real good," he said and turned to me. "We'll sit down and do some analyzing once we get some hard data."

"A scientific approach," I said. "Excellent." He sniffed authoritatively and pocketed the device, held together by duct tape, before leading the troops onward.

We turned our attention to the upstairs. All took great interest in the staircase itself, which I admit does have a certain air about it. Its design and workmanship speak from another age, but apparently not from another dimension, as nothing registered on the devices.

We passed down the upstairs hallway, entering each of the three bedrooms. As Sarah passed the bedside table in my own room, we heard a quiet blip from her scanner. She paused at the telephone, ran her device over it, the table, and the wall just behind it several more times with more corresponding blips. "Weak," she said. "But something."

Once all had written down their notes and measurements, we returned downstairs. We had two rooms left to explore, the former dining room that would now serve as my den, and the kitchen. In the den, Callie flipped her pigtails behind her back and took the outer perimeter. It was therefore she who first found what we came to call the Hot Spot.

I'd lingered by the door, watching the three of them and their slow, methodical search. Riley went straight to the fireplace there, hoping, I suppose, for a repeat of the success in the front room earlier. Sarah started by turning left and testing the large built-in china cabinet. She opened each door, scanned each shelf. Meanwhile,

Callie began her search, going along the right wall. It contained only stacks of boxes and the next wall contained the new bookshelves I'd installed, still empty, so she had relatively little to test.

It was when she reached the outer wall and the large bay window that overlooks the backyard that her equipment went, in her words, "doggone bozo." We knew immediately she'd found something, for she yelped and jerked the device in her hand. When we all turned to see what was the matter, she said, "It's . . . it's warm. It's warming up in my hand."

We gathered round and witnessed an astonishing sight, that of the meter knocking repeatedly into the red. Sarah reached into a pouch on her leather belt and withdrew a digital video camera, hardly bigger than her palm, to record the phenomenon.

I was suddenly aware of the aroma of coffee and remembered Phoebe. She hadn't responded to our outburst, so I called out, "Phoebe, come look!" She didn't hurry. I kept looking for her over my shoulder as Riley and the girls used every gadget, including ones I'd not seen, from belts, lanyards, and inner pockets. All did not give a reading, but most did respond in some way.

"What?" Phoebe said when she finally arrived at the doorway.

The blonde said, "Callie's meter is getting hot."

Phoebe came across the room, stood beside her, and put an arm around her shoulder. "Let me see if I can fix that," she said. She eyed the gadget, noting its jumping meter with raised eyebrows, but remained unimpressed as she turned her attention to the bay window. She bent to the floor, swung down her arm, and flicked the heater vent shut with one motion. Once standing straight, she dusted her palms together.

"Y'all holler when you find Elvis," she said as she turned to go, her slippers flapping away on the wood floor.

Riley, watching Phoebe's performance from behind his visors, shook his head. "Skeptics. Can't tell 'em nothing."

Much time was spent in gathering and recording information

until, weary from the excitement, we retired to the kitchen, which was the last room left to scan. When I first walked in, Phoebe was looking closely at the photos scattered about the table. She quickly pushed them all together and neatened them into a stack before the others followed me in.

Sarah's scanner blipped as she walked through the center of the room. After several tests of the area, it appeared only a small spot prompted the blips, and it wasn't on or around an object but in mid-air.

Phoebe ignored them as they made a cursory sweep around her. Riley took pictures, as he had throughout the house, with a camera containing special film. "Good for auras," he said with an arcing gesture of his long, skinny arm. "Spectrum. Everthang."

They stayed for coffee, chatting about the house, all so very excited about their readings. The photos from my graveyard had apparently been their greatest success to date. Now, they had ever so much more to talk about, a thought that worried me a bit.

"I wonder if I might ask you a favor," I said. "It's rather a big favor, I'm afraid." They took my request to keep our evening's adventure to ourselves quite well. There was a little disappointment at first, but all agreed it would be best to evaluate things first.

"Plus," Sarah said, "people might start bothering you. You wouldn't want strange folks coming around." Phoebe said nothing as she gave each of our guests pointed looks. A small silence ensued, during which the unspoken idea of keeping my house and its supernatural possibilities our own little secret hung between us.

twenty-five

Phoebe Walks on
the Refuge

*T*he next morning, I left Jane's and went to my house to see
how the Blaze boys were doing. They only had a little bit
more framing to replace around where the oven was. Bless their
hearts, they moved my old oven and refrigerator to the backyard,
out of the way, so their cousin Judy's husband Darren could lay the
vinyl flooring down that I picked out. They said I could have the
appliance store bring my new oven and refrigerator the next day.

The painters, some young boys that were friends of the Blazes,
were making progress and doing a fine job. They were done with
the upstairs and had all the downstairs finished except the kitchen.
Ricky said they'd have it ready before Darren got there later in the
afternoon. I tell you what, it was a relief to have those boys taking
care of everything. All that was left was to pick up my drapes and
living room rugs from the dry cleaners. I'd do that last.

Until noon, I spent my time wiping down and polishing my tables, picture frames, and everything else in sight. I went to the kitchen and said, "Is that door going to be done today?"

"Sure will," he said.

"And it'll lock good?"

"Yes, ma'am. She's ready to go."

I'd promised Jane I'd come back for lunch and then we would take a walk. I suggested we go out to the shooting range on Cal's place. She didn't like the idea.

"Cal said you could come anytime you wanted, didn't he?" I said.

"Yes. Still, I wouldn't want to without talking to him first."

"He doesn't care. It's practically yours, or will be in a day or two."

"Only in name. Nothing will change. I'm a little surprised you'd want to go there, after the bad experience we had."

"Oh, pooh. I'm over it. Besides, we need to find some clues. We've got to find the perps so the fuzz can throw 'em in the slammer."

Jane laughed like little tinkling bells. "We've not done very well so far, have we?" she said.

"We've been distracted."

"Yes. Don't worry, dear. They'll find who killed that young man and those responsible for burning your house."

"Jane, quit thinking like a girl scout. They would've arrested somebody by now if they had a clue. We're gonna have to crack this case if it's gonna get cracked. And who better to do it?"

"The police who have years of experience in these matters?"

"You know what I mean."

She put her hand on my shoulder. "I understand it's frustrating and it's hard when you want to feel useful. But Detective Waters seems quite capable of handling the job himself."

"But what if he missed something?"

"After combing the area, as they've surely done several times over by now? No, dear, we wouldn't find anything after such thorough searches."

I let it drop. There's no convincing some people. If they're hardheads, you might as well be hollering at a slab of concrete.

We headed out to take our walk on one of the refuge trails. A police car was still stationed between the entrance to the refuge and the road onto Cal's land. We waved at the young boy behind the wheel.

"Is he spying on us?"

"I rather doubt it. More likely, he's here to deter the curious." It's true that Jane and I had noticed lots of cars on the road lately, going slow and gawking at Cal's gate.

"Yeah, but they're watching for Cal, too. To make sure he doesn't run off before we find who really killed that boy." After we got well out of earshot, I said to Jane, *Beverly Hills Cop.*

Jane cocked her head, thought a second, and said, "No, Phoebe."

"No what?" I said all innocent but half giggling.

She gave me one of those looks. "You know perfectly well. I am not going to distract that poor young officer with food while you stick a banana up his tailpipe."

"See there. We're thinking on the same wavelength."

"A fact that disturbs me greatly," she said all serious, but then she grinned and we both laughed. She looped her arm around my elbow. "I remember Cal showing me a place where this trail curved very near his land. Let's see if we can find it."

"We won't get lost, will we?"

"No, no. From where we stood that day, I could see the trail clearly. It was no more than thirty feet away. The clearing had very distinctive rock formations. I'm sure I'll know it. I have my compass, just in case."

The refuge is okay but it's nothing special. Just trees like everywhere else around here. The walking trail is nice new asphalt though, so you don't feel like you're too far from civilization. I wasn't sure I wanted to traipse through the woods without even a dirt path to go on and no road or trail in sight.

Jane found the spot she was talking about. We didn't have to walk far away to be square on Cal's land. We stomped our way through bushes with some sticky bristles and then went over a little hill. I turned around to look back, but the hill hid the refuge trail.

"I saw the roof of a cabin last time, just past these rocks. Let's take a look." We hadn't gone far when Jane bent down to pick up something in a stream running across our path.

"Whatcha got?" I said.

"It's a shell." Jane didn't sound too pleased.

"What, a mussel shell? There's millions of them around here."

"Not that kind." She held out her hand. There was something gold in it. "A bullet casing," she said.

"Huh. Cal must've been hunting something over this way."

Jane shook her head. "No. I don't think so. Not so close to the refuge. I can't be sure what guns Cal might have that I've not seen, but I know one thing—this is not the type of ammunition common to hunting guns." She slipped it into her pocket and kept walking, searching the ground as we went.

I stood there and stared at her. Something was different about Jane all of a sudden. It was almost like her face got flipped around and another one, her real one, came out. The sweet one I'd seen up until then was really her, too, I guess, but this new one had a whole lot of serious in it and it changed her features just enough to make me think Mob Boss or SWAT team commander or some such. I kept a couple of steps behind her.

We went on a little ways until we came to a clearing with a log cabin set back near the trees. Out in the middle of the clearing, a stuffed dummy had its waist and neck tied to a pole. Straw stuck out of bullet holes all over its chest. Farther to the left was another homemade archery target. It looked like a child had drawn the red rings. The bull's eye was torn so bad it was just about gone.

"Look at this stuff!" I said. "Cal must really like to practice to go to all this trouble. What's wrong?"

"I don't like the feel of this place," Jane said. She bent down a moment and inspected the ground around the stuffed targets. "This doesn't look like Cal's work. He wouldn't use bullets of such large caliber."

"It's got to be. Nobody else would have the guts to come here."

Jane shook her head. "He wouldn't litter the ground with trash either. Look. Nor with cigarette butts. He's certainly too thrifty to leave casings about. He reuses them." She picked up a few more of the spent shells nearby. "Look at the size of them."

I whistled. "Goodness. I believe those are bigger than my Israeli bullets."

"Yes. I've seen the type before. I know of several military-issue rifles that use them."

"Oh, really?" I said. Maybe the Colonel had those particular military rifles. Or maybe she learned about them herself somewhere else. "So, this place is a military camp?"

"No, dear. It's much too crude."

I snapped my fingers. "Those guys from the gun show! They talked about their base camp. This is it! I know it!" I ran over and went in the cabin.

It was one room furnished with only a pine table and three chairs. The old fireplace was a small one. It looked like somebody had been using it to burn trash. Cigarette tips were all over the floor. A couple of Styrofoam cups had an icky mixture of black ash and coffee.

"Trashy. Needs a good cleaning."

Jane looked around real nervous. "Come, Phoebe. I don't like this place. Let's not hang about." I didn't argue. It felt creepy to me, too.

"Are you sure this is Cal's land right here?" I asked once we were outside.

"It must be. I saw the top of the cabin, but from the other direction, on the other side of that ridge. We saw nothing like this," she said, as we passed the straw dummy, "and Cal certainly didn't say anything about such things."

We went back the way we came, over the hill again, slid down through the leaves and bushes, and got back on the refuge trail. Jane didn't say much at first. She looked off into the sky, distracted like. Once she started noticing all the birds and trees around her again, she was more like her normal nature-freak self. I figured I better start a real conversation before she started taking deep breaths and got to talking about "Save the Bark" or some such foolishness.

"I don't know, Jane. It's weird. Bullet casings. Calibers. Military-issue rifles . . . ,"

"Yes, it's all quite confusing."

She looked away from me, like she was hiding something.

"No, that's not what I meant. What I meant was, I'm amazed at how much you know about guns and military stuff. Are you sure you never worked for the Feebs or for the CIA or somebody?"

twenty-six

Jane Confesses

*I*t had always been such an easy lie. Over the years, I never had a problem when asked what I did nor in replying I was quite content in being a housewife. Everyone thought it natural for me, a childless military wife with nothing but time on my hands, to find a hobby, and they accepted my desire to be a volunteer digger at whatever archaeology site I could find.

No one queried much further when I explained it was just dirty, tedious work and nothing like the excavations of Egyptian tombs that most people were familiar with. Real riches were found rarely, even bones or plain pots were only found occasionally. No one ever questioned my long absences from home. And on the rare occasion that my shooting skills came into conversation, I shrugged it off and said I shot to please the Colonel. And that was that.

I made friends wherever we moved, of course, but it was best not to have any too close. My freelance work meant staying away from others, which suited me, really. I've always been one more for reading and studying than socializing. My work also meant a fair degree of danger, not always a high risk, but still all of a sensitive nature. For you see, my part-time work was for the government, and the archaeological digs I worked all over the world were my cover. In reality, I was a spy.

One of the Colonel's colleagues approached me after attending a dinner party at which the Colonel and I were goaded into doing a self-defense demonstration. The colleague, a higher-ranking officer than my husband, already knew I was working on a nearby dig. The next day, he came home with the Colonel for dinner.

They'd already talked it over between themselves. Both seemed to think I'd be a good candidate to surreptitiously listen to and watch someone at this particular dig, a professor from China, who was under suspicion of buying state secrets.

I was in a perfect position to see who he talked to, when he left camp, and also to take photos of any meetings with noncamp staff without drawing attention. It wasn't until I accepted the assignment and was watching him do exactly what he was suspected of, that I realized the CIA would also have been watching me. My recruiting officer had not been at the dinner party by chance, nor was our demonstration there a sudden lark on the spur of the moment. They would have checked my credentials long before I was approached, would have watched my own movements for some time. And the Colonel would have known this. It was a good lesson. He never told me the truth. I never pressed, and I never took anything at face value again, even from him.

One assignment led to another, and before long, I found myself taking more undercover jobs while working various digs whenever my husband was transferred. The CIA proved to be a good job finder for digs. I was hired on excellent jobs I'd never have gotten otherwise. They paid very well and the assignments were low-risk at first. Gradually, they grew a bit more dangerous and gave me more than a few good frights.

I did this during tumultuous times, politically, when it was difficult to always rationalize that what I did was right. I only spoke once of my misgivings. The Colonel could be a bit strong in his opinions. He certainly had no doubts as to service to country, as was appropriate for a man in his position. To him, assisting the government in this way strengthened the country. Finding information as I did prepared the authorities against any sort of outside threat and, in turn, meant a safer, more secure America.

Most of the time, I agreed, though there were days in which the gray areas between right and wrong made me think otherwise. For this reason, I never spent a cent of my earnings. They sat safely in a credit union account, provided by my employer, as an emergency fund. That was what my husband called it. I thought of it as a charity fund, for the day when I would be free to give it to a deserving cause.

When the Colonel was near retirement and assigned a more permanent job in the States, I also, in effect, retired. We settled into a slower pace of living. I still volunteered occasionally for digger jobs that weren't too far away from the Colonel's work. We moved several more times around the country, and I did take on a few more freelance assignments, but I generally considered myself out of the game.

My coming to Tullulah had been a purposeful step toward true retirement. Oh, yes, I still subscribe to archaeology magazines and others on anthropology and wildlife, but haven't felt compelled to dig since the Colonel's health took a turn. When he died, I wanted a new, clean start, free to think as I liked, to speak the truth as I saw it without worrying if the Colonel or my former freelance bosses agreed. No more snooping, no more lying or telling half-truths as I had done for so many years.

This time, my evasion of Phoebe's question did not sit well with me. Not at all. As Phoebe might say, it "bugged the fire out of me," a phrase that sprang into my mind immediately after I answered her, for I understood the words' suitability at last.

I didn't want to start wrong here. It didn't fit. I didn't want to lie. Still, I knew no good would come of being frank about my government work with Phoebe at that moment. Perhaps later, but now my worries about Cal's land and these new disturbing finds filled my mind.

One thing became clear as we walked home together. I now had a most worthy charity for my emergency fund, one solely dependent on me, one that would require much more than my money. It needed my protection. Its very survival depended on the actions I would take for its future, and I would see it done. I touched the bullet casings in my pocket as threats I hadn't considered before began to form in my mind.

When we walked up onto my porch, we saw something propped against the front door. It had been set inside the screen. I slowed my steps as I approached, but quickly recognized the familiar yellow and red photo-processing logo.

A sticky note had been attached to the packet. It was from Riley. The note assured me these pictures were mine to keep, and that if I should need any further assistance, he would be most happy to oblige. At the bottom, he'd scribbled his phone number. I smiled, wondering what he and his entourage had captured on film.

Phoebe looked at the first picture. She gave it a dismissive wave and said, "I'm taking a shower. Don't forget, tonight is when I meet Bernard for dinner."

"All right, dear." I took the photos to my desk and turned on the banker's lamp.

I couldn't deny Riley's results. Definite patterns of color, colors not on my walls or floors in the present world, seemed to hang in the air in certain shots. Riley was right in calling them "auras" for they glowed in the photos. Some had a fixed look, oblongs and rectangular shapes that seemed more solid than others. For example, the area near my fireplace in the front room where Riley got his first reading had an orange rust aura shaped in a rough square. It extended across the rug to the fire screen and up as high as the top of the mantel.

A few smaller areas, such as that by my phone, had a greenish cast and ranged in size from say, that of a quarter to that of a shoebox. These were not the most interesting. The Hot Spot by the bay window of the den certainly held the most wonders. Here a virtual rainbow of colors swirled about the glass, the bookcases and other walls, and filled the center of the room, though there the colors were not so vibrant.

One photograph taken in the upstairs hallway showed a small circle of blue on the wall, but what caught my interest was the top of the picture. A narrow swath of blue and green hung down, much fainter but definitely there. It hung like a vapor over the height and width of the attic door.

I replaced the photos in their packet and set them out for Phoebe to see. She would enjoy looking at them when I wasn't watching her, of course. After she left to meet Bernard, I had a light supper and went upstairs, intending to lie down until I heard her come in again.

I settled down under the bed covers at last, with thoughts of the day moving farther into the background in my mind, submerging and getting more quiet as they mixed together with the night sounds outside the window and the creaks and sighs of the house.

A little pop across the room made my eyes flutter open for a moment, long enough to see my grandmother's table inch forward. *I'm tired,* I told myself. *My eyes are playing tricks on me.*

Just then, it wobbled again and rocked to a stop. *It's only a rickety table that would fall over at any rate unless I take more care in setting it up properly.* My eyes closed halfway, noting as they did so the table's slight but decided scoot to the right.

My eyes snapped open, fully awake now. I lay still. The house was completely silent. As the moments passed, the table remained as it was. I remembered the wave of Sarah's hand over the table and wall, and the soft blip of her device as it passed over them. The photo Riley took there, if I remembered correctly, showed a small dash of green. I waited a bit longer, then threw back the covers. I put on my robe and slippers and was downstairs in a flash.

In my previous occupation, I used a pair of Russian night visors on occasion. They should be far superior to the out-of-date pair Riley wore. I unlocked the old trunk in the den and quickly found them among the other specialized supplies I'd used when at work for my former employer.

The table had remained where it was, so far as I could tell. With the lights still off, I set out the visors, a notebook and pen, and one other tool, a special camera with features conducive to night work of a sensitive nature.

I snapped a few frames as a reminder of the table's position then wrote approximate distances and a brief account of events so far. I opened the visors and held them up to see an incredible sight. Just as in Riley's picture, the color green was present. Now a much larger aura spread and pulsed around the table. Seeing it moving, not static as in the photographs, but swirling and dancing before me, took my breath away. Tiny speckles glistened in the eddy. Whether bits of magic or merely dust motes, I couldn't say.

With amazement, I noted the feeling that I was in the presence of a personality, not as in the photos that conveyed residual energy. They had the feel of something left behind, like the faint scent of perfume that lingers in a room after everyone has gone. Here, to my mind, was the source of such an imprint.

Quickly, I jotted down my thoughts while I tried to absorb the reality of them. Not easy, even for one such as I who believed in ghosts. Was it this easy for everyone to see the colored auras? Or was it my "gift" that enabled me to see? I set the notebook aside once again, and took up the visors to sit and ponder. One thing became clear on this viewing, something I hadn't noticed before. Most likely, I was in a small state of shock and unable to take everything in at first. Now in the visors, it was apparent that the green cloud centered on a section of wall where it met the floor, the same spot where I'd placed grandmother's table originally.

I moved the table out of my way and got down on my knees. Yes, this close, the color deepened. On zeroing in, I now could also see a dark vertical line, about three inches long, from top to bottom of the baseboard. I reached out. The line was a cut in the wood. About six inches away was an identical one.

My fingernails weren't long enough to be effective. I grabbed my pen but found it useless as well. I sat a moment and thought. I had plenty of tools downstairs, but what did I have up here? My Leatherman. I kept one, the size of a large pocketknife, in my purse. It is made along the line of a Swiss Army knife, with eight or ten tools that fold into the handle. I unhinged the knife blade and put it to the wall. It worked.

Paint and age made my task perhaps a little harder, but once I traced the vertical cuts with the blade, the baseboard was easily pried away. I imagined jewels stuffed inside, or bundles of old cash. What I found was much more astonishing.

It was a letter. One single, handwritten page. Not so very interesting, you might say? That was my first thought. After reading it, however, I thanked heavens above that I didn't have a prior heart condition and was in stable mental health. There was no doubt whatsoever that what I held in my hand was the most shocking thing I'd seen in a lifetime. It was a letter from a woman long dead. And it was addressed to me.

twenty-seven

Phoebe About Town

Jane was sound asleep when I got back from my dinner date with Bernard. He took me to Muscle Shoals to a real nice restaurant where we had wine served right at our table. I still can't get used to that. All the counties around here were dry for most of my life. No liquor, beer, or wine could be had until a few years ago. I'm not one for drinking, but I sure do like the nice, new restaurants we have now.

The next morning, Jane and I had a lot to do in town. She needed to go to the bank. She said she'd stop by my house to see how things were going later.

I was amazed at how fast they'd been able to get the wall up in my kitchen. I walked through the house to make sure the paint in all the rooms were what I wanted. Not twenty minutes later, I heard Jane's car pull up in the drive.

"That was quick," I said. "I didn't expect you here for another hour."

"I'm quite surprised, too," she said. Her face was flushed pink and she looked like something had upset her.

"What's wrong?"

"I'm not sure. That is, I'm confused really. I've come from the bank. When Mr. Roman came out to meet me in the lobby, he was very nice as always, but he didn't ask me to his office. I was baffled, and he fidgeted and talked nervously. Before I could ask, he told me the bank was experiencing a problem with my loan. When I asked what sort of problem, he practically shoved me out the door saying he'd be in touch."

"The nerve!" I said. Poor Jane. She looked like she was about to cry. I'd be upset too if some little penny-ante nobody did that to me.

"I tried to ask why but he wouldn't give me a chance. He just pushed me through the doors and said good day."

"And you doing him a favor? You don't need him anyway. The little twerp."

Jane had something else on her mind. "Do you think the lawyer's office is open this early? I think I'd like to stop in to see about the document Shelley was preparing. Maybe she could shed some light on the situation. It isn't that I'm anxious, you understand, to take over."

"Oh, I understand perfectly. You just want to know what to expect, right? That's only natural. You want things to be set."

"Yes. Exactly."

We went downtown on the square to the Hannigan and Wade offices. A cool blast of air-conditioning hit us when we stepped into the reception area. It was decorated like George Washington lived there, which is so tacky but sure is popular with rich lawyers and doctors. Nobody was there except the receptionist, a young girl with a bob cut who was new since the last time I'd been in there.

"Good morning. What can I do for you?"

Jane stepped forward. "I hoped to speak with Shelley Barnette if she's available."

"I'm sorry. Shelley is out of town for a few days. Could someone else help?"

"Oh, dear." Jane and I looked at each other. "Did she perhaps leave a document for me to pick up? For Jane Thistle or Cal Prewitt?"

"No, not with me," she said, as she looked through papers on her desk. She went to Shelley's office but didn't find anything there either.

Jane said, "I'm sure Mr. Wade will be very busy today, but if you could leave him a note to call me when it's convenient, I would appreciate it."

As we walked out, I told Jane, "You'd think Shelley would've let you and Cal know she was leaving town. Or brought it out to your house before she left."

As always, Jane made excuses for somebody else. "I'm sure she would have done so if she could," she said. "I imagine it was a family emergency that called her away so suddenly."

"I guess." She dropped me off at my house again. I think old Roman at the bank had made her want to be by herself for a while.

twenty-eight

Jane and the Strange Letter

S o far, the day's events had not been pleasant. I returned home to sort things out in my mind. The mysterious letter I'd found the previous evening lay on my desk. I picked it up and read it again, still finding it hard to believe that a woman I'd never met and who had passed away over a year earlier, long before I even considered moving to this house, had written it to me. This is what Miss Ina Genevieve Hardwick had to say:

"Hello, Jane. Or is it Jean? My hearing isn't what it used to be. Boo will have helped you find this. Forgive the histrionics but I'm afraid someone else will find it and throw it away. I suppose I'm also concerned that if you simply found this note in an ordinary manner, you'd dismiss it and think I was crazy like most folks around here do. It hasn't ever worried me because I knew no one understood.

"You do, otherwise Boo (whose real name is John but he seems to like his nickname better) wouldn't have let you find it. He's a wonderful boy. He won't ever bother you. He's shy and only wants to help. I'm putting the newspaper article about his death in this envelope so you'll know."

I unfolded the yellowed clipping. What Phoebe said had been true. This was the boy who had found the missing girl's doll, the boy who'd been shot in my front room by the fireplace.

"Around here," the letter continued, "they said Boo wasn't right in the head. I'll tell you this, he's right in the heart. There's never been a more loving, gentle person on this earth. You'll think so, too, before long.

"He stays in the dining room mostly, or in the attic. It's full of old family things up there, though who knows if anything will be left for you to find. I hope there's something left, for Boo's sake. He loves being close to the old trunks up there. He also loves flowers so I've always kept something blooming by the bay window where he sits. He appreciates little things like that and will leave a gift for me every now and then.

"He never killed that girl. He couldn't have. He loved children and would rather die himself than see any harm done to anyone, especially a child.

"I hope you'll be happy here. I see very dangerous times ahead, but you're strong and highly qualified. I understand that you're going to take care of everything. That Cal can be stubborn. Good luck and all the best."

I refolded the clipping inside the letter. She knew Cal well.

My resolve hardened. I could let nothing deter me, not even a stubborn old man who still held something back. If he wasn't telling me something vital, and I let him keep his secret to the detriment of himself or his land, I would never be able to forgive myself. Cal must be made to trust me fully. It was time for us to have a serious talk.

$\mathcal{W}$HEN I'D WALKED WITHIN SIGHT OF CAL'S HOUSE, Homer trotted up from the other direction. He'd come through the meadow, for his legs and belly were covered in white dandelion seed fluff.

"Where's Cal, boy? Are the two of you out playing?" Homer looked me straight in the eye, hopped a few steps toward the forest, then made an abrupt turn to see if I followed. "All right, love, I'm coming."

Once past the meadow and across the stream near the spring house, he led me on a trail I had not been on as yet, east into the woods, then north and straight to Cal. He sat in a small clearing on a bed of evergreen straw underneath a pine tree. His back was turned to me as I approached. Across from him was a single boulder about three feet high. Homer and I weren't particularly quiet, yet Cal sat motionless, whether not aware of us or not concerned, I couldn't tell.

Homer went ahead to Cal's left to lie at the foot of another tree. He made himself comfortable on a patch of bare ground. As I got closer, I could hear Cal speaking softly. A small plume of white smoke arose before him. I stopped several feet behind him. He was chanting a native song or poem in Cherokee. The smoke came from a shallow clay bowl about the size of a plate in which sage or some other herbal grass burned.

Still he hadn't noticed me. His eyes remained closed as tears fell down each cheek. He had cleared the pine needles away in front of him and had drawn a circle in the dirt. On either side of the burning sage, Cal had drawn symbols, the meanings of which I couldn't guess. One had a diamond shape, the other had squiggly lines around a circle, like the sun, with other starlike shapes surrounding them.

I was at a loss as to what to do. Should I leave him to what was so obviously private? Another thought came to me: Why would he be here performing a ritual when the great ceremonial hall was so near? It was only then I noticed that the boulder on the other side of the circle also had drawings. I stared, as entranced as Cal, at the ancient carvings of spirals and stick men that dotted the rock's surface. Was there no end to the wonders of this place?

Cal's chanting changed into a more poetic rhythm, slowing between phrases. He whispered the wonderful musical words that mixed with the burning sage in the air. It felt like more than a recitation, almost a creation, for the words seemed to rise and blend with the smoke as if they were something physical that moved into the wisps, as much a part of this place as a leaf floating in its last dance to rest on the forest floor.

His eyes cleared but he said nothing, only stared. Homer got up and walked quietly to us. He lay down at my feet, his paws extended across the circle drawn in the dirt so that he lay half in and half out. Cal's shoulders shook with the wheezing of shallow breaths.

I squatted beside Homer. Cal couldn't be comfortable. "Do you need to stand? What can I do to help you?"

His voice was so weak I could hardly hear. He looked stunned to see me. "It's you. It can't be you. I didn't believe them." He sat staring at me, then at Homer who scooted farther inside the dirt circle so that his front paws touched Cal's leg, his face intent on sending comfort through a steady gaze to his master. "And you, too, friend?" Cal rested a hand on Homer's back as he looked up. More tears followed.

"Did you get the money?" he asked, once he'd composed himself.

"No," I said. His face fell. He covered it with his thin, mottled hands, listening as I told him of the problems with the bank and the bank manager's sudden odd behavior.

Cal shook his head, wiped his eyes. "They've got to him somehow."

"Who, Cal?" He didn't answer. "Someone is threatening you," I said. His look told me I was right. "Someone who might have had these." I reached in my pocket and brought out the shell casings I'd picked up.

"You went to their camp?" he said, his weak voice a mix of pain, a bit of anger, and defeat.

"Whose camp? Cal, tell me what's happening. Let me help you."

"Can't help without the money." I assured him I had it without the bank's assistance and would arrange to get it in cash. This seemed to calm him a bit. "It needs to be quick," he said heavily. "I'm sorry. I'm not used to asking anybody for anything." His voice weakened to a whisper. "I'm sorry."

He pulled himself together, sighed, and told me what happened. "A man came to me. He wanted to use part of my land for a couple of weeks, offered me good money, and promised I wouldn't know he'd ever been there, that he'd clean up good. It was for a training camp, like. What did he call it? Survival skills for yuppie types.

"I said no at first, but then got to thinking I'd need the money for the doctor. He came back with an even better offer so I took it. At the end of the two weeks, I went to see if they were cleaning up right and their equipment was still all over the place. I told the guy he'd have to get his things out quick. He...," Cal choked a little. "He had other ideas."

They wouldn't leave. First, they told Cal they'd like to extend their survival classes for another week. When they didn't pay him, he went armed with his shotgun to run them off. Poor Cal. That had always been enough. This man and three others with him were heavily armed.

They disarmed Cal and surely taunted him, though Cal didn't say so. They knew he was old, sick, and alone, and knew he could do nothing to harm them. Cal was told if he alerted the authorities, they would kill him. To them, that was the ultimate threat. Not so for Cal. He would be more afraid of what would happen to his land if he died before it was safe and in good hands.

"They said they knew I had money. That if I gave them fifty thousand dollars, they'd go."

"I see." Had he no one to help him? Found no one to trust as he trusted me? Not in all these years? I wondered if it were only when he got so sick that the truth of his mortality hit him. "We must call Detective Waters at once."

He protested, insisting that was the wrong thing to do. "Please," he said. "Trust me on this. You can't call him."

The man was exasperating. "All right. You've trusted me and I will trust you, though I do so with much reserve."

"It's going to be all right. See about getting the money. That will put an end to it all. Then they'll go. And I can die in peace."

I agreed to call about a money transfer straightaway, provided he would go home and rest for the remainder of the day.

I left Cal and Homer at the split in the road, they on their way to Cal's house and I to mine. I'd tried again to convince him to let me call the police, but he was even more angry and determined that I should not.

I made him promise to let me accompany him when he gave the militia men his money. Deep down, however, I knew I couldn't let it come to that, not without the help of the police. Cal was desperate and not thinking clearly. I could understand that he wanted things taken care of quickly and easily. I had to think of some other way, or else these criminals would be back again and again. That I couldn't allow.

For the life of me, I couldn't understand why he didn't want Detective Waters involved. Their skirmish at the police station when Cal was questioned surely wasn't enough to make Cal put that nonsense before such a serious threat to himself and his property. The only other thing might be if Cal suspected Waters was somehow involved with the militia men. Being new here, perhaps my instincts were off, but I didn't think so. Whatever the reason, I had to believe Cal knew best so I would respect his wish. For now. In the meantime, perhaps Phoebe's friend, Bernard, could be of help. I might need another able-bodied man, one who was also a trained shooter.

twenty-nine

Phoebe Does a
Stake Out

*A*fter Jane and I got back to my house from the lawyer's office, she had things to do at home. I worked in my closets, about the only place the smoke hadn't gotten in and ruined everything. It was something I'd been meaning to do for a long time anyway. It took me all day to separate out things to give to the church second-hand store. It's not that I'm a packrat but I do have a hard time letting go of clothes. Once I decided what to give and what to keep, I put the giveaways in my car and dropped them off at the laundry. By that time, it was three o'clock and I still had two more things on my to-do list.

First, I went by Jerry Nell Gillispie's to pick up my new rifle. I almost cried when I saw it. I couldn't wait to show Jane. Once I locked it in my trunk, I set out to take care of the next piece of business on my list: Suspect surveillance.

I drove out the 43 Bypass where the new nursing home was being built. Nobody was walking around out front that I could see. I changed lanes and turned left. I circled the block, going as slowly as I could. Not a soul could be seen. Construction people must quit work earlier than other folks.

Just when I thought everyone had already gone home, I saw a curly blond head pop out of the construction office trailer door. I wasn't surprised to watch Treenie Dodd walk out, looking around like she didn't want anyone to see her.

She carried a thick plastic bag but was holding it underneath, not by the handle, like it was heavy. She opened her trunk, put the bag in it, and drove out the dirt road onto the main drag. She was up to something. I knew it before I saw where she was headed.

She went straight to The Pool Cue and parked at the side of the building. It didn't surprise me a bit when she sat there waiting, and guess who came strolling out to meet her. That crew-cut Marine-looking boy, the one I pegged as the leader of those no-account pool players, walked around from the back of the building and up to her car.

I looked at my watch. The second hand was sweeping across the twelve. Exactly five after three. I flipped open my Thomas Kinkade notepad of inspirational cottages and wrote it down. Fifteen hundred and 05 hours. Or was that zero three hundred and 05 hours? I can never remember which is AM and which is PM. On a separate sheet of notepad paper, I jotted, "Buy military watch."

Treenie smiled but he didn't. This was strictly biz. I suddenly remembered I had a throwaway camera in the glove box left over from my last trip to Gulf Shores. I had been meaning to finish up the roll but kept forgetting about it.

I clicked a few shots, scooted way down in my seat, and thought how proud Jane and the police would be when they saw these pictures. Jarhead took the bag out of Treenie's trunk when she popped it open. The bag ripped at the bottom and he almost lost it. The box inside slipped out halfway, enough for me to read "Danger" and a picture of the lit end of a bundle of sticks.

Bingo! I clicked one more picture and felt downright proud of myself. I threw the camera back in my glove box as the two of them walked toward the back door. I hurried inside the front so they would think I was already there.

Inside, the party was in full swing. It wasn't quite as crowded at this time of day, but that didn't seem to keep the ones there from having a good time.

Sure enough, two of his boys were playing pool. I ordered a Coke and had only taken one sip when the leader went to talk to them. They put their cues up. The leader said, "Take the van. Hank, you drive."

I turned to see the leader tossing a set of keys. Hank had pretty blue eyes and a dark beard and moustache. He raised his hand and caught the key ring. Too bad he had a big ugly snake tattoo on his arm. Otherwise he'd have been downright cute.

thirty

Jane Finds Trouble

I made the call to Florida. My savings accounts were still there in the military credit union. They would transfer the money for Cal's land into a new checking account under his name. After Mr. Roman's treatment of me, I didn't relish putting money in the Bank of Tullulah but it would be easiest for Cal. He could withdraw all the cash he wanted whenever he wanted. After we dealt with his intruders.

My mind was a jumble. A cup of hot tea and a few minutes of meditation helped sort things out. However, no ready answers came to me in regard to how to handle the blackmailers without the police.

I went to my desk where I'd set out one of Cal's boxes to look through. He had labeled it "Important" for it was full of legal papers and bill receipts, unlike the others I'd peeked in, which seemed to hold only assortments of rocks and arrowheads, scribbled notes on torn pieces of paper, or odd bits of junk.

An hour later, I'd reached the bottom of the box but was no closer to finding what I'd hoped to find, a copy of an old will. Since it was such a personal thing, I'd not asked Cal what his plans for his land had been before I came along. Still, I wondered. Once the intruders were sorted out, I needed to know he was sure he wanted to go forward with our land deal. In his state of mind, he might not be thinking clearly, just as Dad Burn suggested. I wouldn't take advantage of him. I would help him out of his present difficulties, but then, if Cal decided he wanted someone else to inherit the land so be it. Either way, we needed to talk about it.

I set out once more across the street onto his property. When I reached the bend in the road near his house, I saw his front door was open. "Hello, anyone home?" I called. Homer had not greeted me in the road, as was his custom. When there was no response, I stepped inside and called again. That was when I noticed the broken clay pieces on the floor.

It was the bowl he used in his ritual or one very much like it. Around it lay ashes and shreds of burned sage. "Cal!" I ran through the house worried something terrible had happened. There was no sign of him or of Homer.

I returned to the broken pieces, looked them over as I set them one by one on the coffee table next to a stack of papers. I accidentally brushed the top papers causing several to flutter to the floor. A sheet from a yellow legal pad caught my eye. Instead of words, a series of pictures, sticklike figures, were drawn across it. They were like those I saw on the rock where Cal performed his ritual. I was looking down, absorbed in the diagrams and their possible meanings, when a black boot stepped into my view. Before I could look up, I was pulled to my feet by a strong grip on my arm.

"Looking for something?" A man dressed in a camouflage T-shirt and olive drab pants stood before me. A black handgun gleamed in his hand.

He didn't give me a chance to answer. With unnecessary force, he pushed me out of the room and into the hallway. At the front door, he shoved me into the yard.

"What's wrong?" I said. "What do you want?"

"I want you to shut up and walk until I tell you to stop." He brought the gun barrel to my temple. I walked.

As soon as the cold metal touched my skin, I felt calm and my body relaxed. It was the reaction the Colonel had taught me through many drills and tests.

We walked a few steps. I looked about, surveying my surroundings as best I could. He aimed me toward the woods. Remembering the camp Phoebe and I discovered, I had a feeling I knew where we'd be going.

I knew I had to act quickly. Escaping from one man would be difficult enough. I couldn't risk being taken where more men might wait, men most certainly armed.

My captor gave me another shove. Now he walked behind me. He must have felt I presented no danger, for he no longer kept the gun barrel against me, but close to his body. That made us even. My mistake had been in not being alert, in not hearing his approach. His mistake was in not being smart.

I found early on in my defense training that rhythm of movement led to success. I fell in with my companion's steps, counted two, and on the upbeat of the third, spun around to face him, grabbed his gun hand and twisted it while continuing to walk forward. I pressed the gun against his weak thumb joint until it gave and the gun was mine.

I flipped it round as I turned my body toward him again. Quick kicks to the back of each knee made them give, and an immediate, well-placed knock to the back of the head put him out. It was the oldest trick in the book. I almost felt ashamed of myself for employing such a juvenile tactic.

Just then, a terrible sound came from the forest. A woman's scream.

thirty-one

Phoebe to the Rescue

I meant to just see where they went from The Pool Cue and then go on to Jane's. The funny thing was, it looked like the Jarhead, Hank, and that other no-count lowlife were going to Jane's, too. I stayed back far enough where they wouldn't get suspicious. It didn't matter. There were only three places they could get to down Anisidi Road—Jane's house, the refuge, and Cal's place. I knew they must be going to their camp.

They surprised me though. They split up. The van with Hank and the other redneck took the last turn-off, going left into the Shady Lane apartment complex. The leader's car went straight toward the refuge. I didn't know what to do, follow Hank or follow the brains and stolen dynamite. Since the leader had to be going to the camp, I decided to follow Hank thinking maybe I could see where they went and write down the apartment number. I pulled in a few buildings away where I could see them but they couldn't see me.

I watched the other redneck with Hank talk into a cell phone. He seemed interested when a car drove slowly by. He hung up the phone real fast. He disappeared from the front seat into the back. Hank pulled the van right next to the new car as the driver door opened.

The redneck jumped out the van's sliding door. As soon as the car's door opened, he grabbed the woman in the driver's seat and the next second had thrown her in the van. He held her so close and moved so quick, I didn't get a good look at her. All I caught was a glimpse of her hair, long, straight and red, but that was enough. I gasped. I knew it was Shelley Barnette.

The van didn't squeal out of the parking lot. It went real slow and casual over speed bumps and around the apartment complex until it circled back to the main road. I followed him out and felt around in my purse for my cell phone as we turned onto Anisidi. I held up the phone over the steering wheel so I could dial and keep my eyes on the road at the same time. When I pressed the first button, the phone squealed. I glanced down at the display. It said, "Recharge battery." The stupid thing wouldn't dial. Now what? Flag somebody down? Ram the van from behind?

Then I remembered how a police car had been stationed all the time near the refuge entrance. The van was way ahead of me. When I went around the last bend before Jane's house and the refuge, the van was nowhere in sight. Not only that, but I could also see that the police car usually sitting in the road was, of all times, gone.

My car rocked to a stop in front of Jane's and I ran into her yard calling out "Jane! Jane!" all the way up to the porch and inside. She was gone, too.

I nearly had a fit. I ran to her phone and dialed 911 so hard I nearly broke the numbers. Her phone was dead. All I got was that weird loud static instead of a dial tone. "Dagnabbit, now what do I do?" I hollered.

I ran out the door. Cal didn't have a phone and it would take forever to ride all the way back into town for the police. There was no way I could live with myself if something happened to Shelley before I could get help. I was way out in the yard when the screen door slammed shut behind me. I'd made up my mind what I had to do.

I hurried to the back of my car and opened the trunk. I took a deep breath as I unzipped my new gun carrier, a special fabric one in a green, brown, and black camouflage pattern that Donnie threw in for free.

I lifted out my new AK-46 and a half. Jerry Nell had done a magnificent paint job on it, just like I knew she would. The original black finish, which I loved at first because it was darned scary looking, just didn't fit my personality. Jerry Nell agreed. She knows what I like. She'd made most all the interior decorations in my living room, which is where I planned on displaying my rifle as a wall hanging, so she knew exactly what colors to use so it would match.

I gently stroked the sight now painted in Apricot Blush. The paint job graduated from light at the top to a darker orange at the bottom of the rifle body. Jerry Nell added the two special touches I'd asked for, and she did them just perfect. Up near the barrel, she drew an Indian dream catcher in brown and turquoise, just like the ones she made for me to hang in my windows. Little shadings of gray and black made it stand out real pretty.

The other special touch turned out even better than I imagined. On the big fat end you put against your shoulder, Jerry Nell airbrushed one word in turquoise, the name I'd given my AK-46 and a half for good luck: *Smokahontas*. A little plume of smoke curled and trailed off the end of the last letter. Oh, what I would give for Jerry Nell's artistic genius.

I was nervous and sweating like a hog. It was up to me. Me and the Man Upstairs. With both hands, I raised Smokahontas up toward the woods and said what I could remember of a Cherokee prayer that Jerry Nell had written in calligraphy and framed for me. "Oh, Great Spirit ... Hear me ... I am small and weak ... and I forget the middle part ... but when the sun sets, may I come to You with clean hands, straight eyes, and no shame."

Amen to that. After I set Smokahontas down, I grabbed the box of Israeli bullets and held them up to the sky toward the east. I felt like I needed to say a Jewish prayer, but I only knew one word in Hebrew so it would have to do.

"Shalom," I said, "but not right now." I kissed the box and bowed several times, and then set the box down next to Smokahontas.

Son, I started stuffing bullets into that magazine as fast as I could. While I stuffed, I thought about angels and how so many people believe in them. I do, too, but not the fluffy ones that float around singing all day.

"Dear Lord," I said, "You know that's not the kind I need right now. I need me some warrior angels, preferably of Cherokee or Jewish descent, with tongues of fire flapping off the end of their swords and shooting out of their noses and fingertips and eye sockets.

"But I don't have to tell you what I need," I said, as I clicked in the last bullet. I snapped the magazine up into place. It sounded mean. It felt good. "I have faith You'll protect me and guide me to do the right thing."

I ran to the refuge and turned left onto the walking trail, just like Jane and I had done. When I got to the place where we walked into the woods, I slowed down and stepped as quietly as I could toward the redneck camp, hoping I'd get there in time to save Shelley.

thirty-two

Jane Finds Cal

The cries came from the east, the direction of the refuge. It might not have been Phoebe's voice I heard. However, something in my gut told me it was my dear friend and that she was in grave danger.

I still held my attacker's handgun. I clicked the magazine, checked that it was full, and pulled back the slide to see the edge of a bullet in the chamber, ready to fire.

"Thank you for being so well prepared," I said to my unconscious friend, as I headed toward the forest in the direction of the scream.

I followed the same path Cal and I had taken that first day I'd visited. I made my way toward the stream we'd crossed. A moan of pain came from that direction. My body jumped with terror. It was then I saw smears of blood in the grass and, farther ahead at the water's edge, two forms lying on the ground. They were much too still.

I sprinted across the last of the meadow with horror clutching at my heart. Cal lay near where the spring house spanned the stream. I ran through the thick grass and fell to my knees at his side. I grabbed my stomach on seeing the red stain that covered his shirt and the wound that gaped open in his upper chest. I closed my eyes to pull myself together.

It was a gunshot wound at close range, my guess from a .22 pistol, and not fired by a professional for the shooter had not made certain Cal was dead. He was alive, but he wouldn't be for long unless I could get him immediately to a hospital, and even that thought held no hope whatsoever.

The other prone form broke my heart as well but I couldn't afford to attend to him just then. Homer lay a few feet away. Blood covered the side of his face. He'd been hit hard, I imagined with the butt of the gun that shot Cal. I gently moved my hand under Cal's neck, could feel a faint pulse there. It was weak and erratic. His eyelids fluttered as I cradled his head.

"Cal, can you hear me? It's Jane. I'm here." I lay his head gently in the crook of my arm in what I hoped was a more comfortable position, and also pulled his left arm out of the water to his side. His lips moved but his words were too weak to understand. "Don't talk now. You're going to be fine."

I knew it wasn't the truth. Cal did as well, for he summoned his strength and bored his dark eyes into mine. He knew he was not long for this world. His mouth moved as he tried to speak. "Hank," he said.

Had I heard him correctly? I leaned closer and watched his lips move.

"Hank," he repeated with urgency. "Snake..."

His throat rasped. His eyes opened fully, focused on mine for another few seconds. They spoke volumes, all of good-byes, before fluttering and finally closing for the last time. He breathed out, his spirit released into the forest he loved so much.

Another scream cut through the air. With care, I lowered Cal's head to the grass, brushed my tears away, and gathered my courage as I ran toward the east.

I slowed my pace as I neared the camp area Phoebe and I had discovered. Rather than go straight to it, I remembered the rock ridge that overlooked the clearing and went there for a look. I turned in that direction and was pleased to find a faint trail leading up. Conscious of every step as I drew closer, trying not to make noise, I emerged at the top and lay flat in the trail's head.

A few feet away, another trail led down into the great ceremonial hall where, far down on the right, I could barely see the Maiden. I was nearer the other end of the hall, close to the two great trees I remembered from Cal's map of the canyon, their height stretching for what seemed like miles toward the clouds, their great crowns intermingled. Below and in front of me was the clearing where the survivalists made camp. The log cabin was to the right. I could see no one save the stuffed mannequin target Phoebe and I saw previously, its vacant painted-on eyes staring like those of a dead man in a much too convincing way.

Beyond him was the much-used round archery target. Its red bull's-eye was in tatters with gaping holes where straw showed through. I shuddered. Whoever practiced here shot well, whether with guns or bows. A bowhunter would be a formidable enemy, one accustomed to stealth. I'd been a good shot myself years ago but only in tournaments with nonmoving targets. A hunter would not only be able to shoot moving targets, but would most certainly own a compound bow. Powerful and lethal, this type could kill in an instant and with hardly a sound.

A dreary caste to the air enhanced the feeling of foreboding in my heart as I looked across the empty clearing. I could see the front porch and one side of the cabin where someone moved inside across the window.

I listened intently. The soft sounds of footsteps across a creaking floor and then a man's voice reached my ears just before a loud slapping sound and a woman's cry pierced the quiet.

I descended quickly the way I came and made a circuit of the back half of the clearing, slowing as the cabin came into sight. Loud male voices and another scream quickened my pace. I stepped off the thin trail and veered to the right where the forest was thicker, moving quietly from tree to tree, listening, getting control of my breath. I closed my eyes, inhaled and exhaled deeply and silently, and prayed.

From behind a great hackberry tree, I heard the cabin's floor creaking as heavy shoes walked inside. I moved quickly behind the trees at the back of the cabin where pine needles softened my footsteps and from there, moved to the other side unchallenged. No outside sentries. A long low pine branch partially obscured the window there. I put my back against the cabin, hid as best I could behind the branch, and peeped inside the dirty panes.

The situation was much worse than I could have imagined. Two of the chairs had been brought to the center of the cabin's single room. In them sat Shelley Barnette and Phoebe with their hands bound behind the chairs. Phoebe's mouth was gagged with a white cloth. A man was tying a similar one around Shelley's face. From where I stood, I could see a large red bruise swelling on Phoebe's cheek. Shelley was crying.

I moved slightly as the back of a man moved into view. He crossed and turned as he spoke to the girls. He had a buzz cut and a determined set of jaw. As he turned sideways, I saw a long pale scar on his neck.

This was the man I'd seen on my first day in town in the Piggly Wiggly parking lot talking to Jack Blaylock, Phoebe's gun instructor. Another new worry came to mind, the paper I'd seen on Detective Waters' desk about the ex-military man with a scar. He had a criminal record. And now, he had Phoebe and Shelley as well.

Inside the cabin, a young man with a moustache and beard leaned against a wall. His rifle leaned beside him. Obviously he was unconcerned that his captives would escape. Even so, he was not completely relaxed. It was as if he wished to appear at ease, but his luminous blue eyes looked furtively about. They checked the room as if waiting, calm but alert.

After checking as much of the room as I could, I satisfied myself there were only the two. My opponents were young, well-built men, probably well trained, with access to at least three semiautomatic rifles, which I'd seen inside.

The leader spoke harshly to Phoebe. With slow steps he paced around the chairs. He went to the opposite window to look out. Waiting. Both men waiting. For what, I wondered, or whom? They didn't need more help to handle Shelley and Phoebe. They could be waiting for their friend, the one I knocked out at Cal's house. I didn't think so. He didn't strike me as a decision maker. The leader was here at the cabin yet he waited.

They waited for orders. There must be a higher-ranking member of this band, one expected to arrive soon. Jack Blaylock? According to Phoebe, he was an expert marksman and huntsman. I had to act quickly. Waiting was a luxury I couldn't afford.

I made my plan. I let the tug of anger I'd kept in check sweep through my body like a cleansing fire. One friend was dead. Two more were in great peril. And at my feet, littering the forest floor, were more bullet casings, the metal remnants of vanity, arrogance, destruction. It was a desecration. They would do my friends harm and spoil this sacred place without the least remorse. I gritted my teeth and channeled my anger into a thin stream of thought. *No. Not on my watch.*

I scooped up the casings lying at my feet and waited for a completely quiet moment. When the leader stopped talking inside, I threw a few at the nearest standing target in front of the cabin. The metal clinked on the target's stand and I withdrew, putting my back against the wall around the corner of the porch.

A deeper quiet followed. I knew I would soon have company. I waited, tensed and ready, as the door opened and footsteps tapped quietly down the length of the porch. I saw the nose of the rifle first, edging out from the corner. It moved slowly forward and stopped, then edged left in the direction of the target. The man's head began to turn for a quick glance in my direction. I gripped my pistol tighter and, before he could see me, brought the gun down with a thud at the top of his neck.

It was a good hit. He crumpled without a sound. I grabbed his shoulders as he fell, guiding his weight as best I could toward the cabin wall so he couldn't be seen from the front door or window.

I took his rifle, an AR-15 with an expensive sight, and quickly slipped the shoulder strap over my head. I put the handgun in the back of my waistband. Quickly I checked the rifle's magazine and chamber. Full and ready to go.

I imagined the leader listening at the door, looking out each window. The cabin walls would most likely have muffled the sounds I'd made. Still, the woods were too quiet. I had to assume he heard the dragging of the man's boots, the clicks as I released and replaced the AR-15's cartridge, as well as the scrape of the bolt, though I slid it carefully. He would come and come soon. I went quickly to cover behind a wide tree trunk about ten yards away from the wall.

Since the cabin had no back door, the leader had no option in coming out. A few unlikely scenarios flitted through my mind as I put myself in his shoes. Was there perhaps a way to the roof? Would he exit through a window? No, he must come through the door. The smallest creak from the cabin's front told me my opponent was on his way.

I couldn't hear him. My only warning of his location came when a bird suddenly leapt from a niche in the porch eaves. Its movement caused an almost noiseless reaction from the leader, still out of my view but very close. I could feel him there. I pictured him swinging his gun to the bird in one swift slice, feeling rather than hearing the small rush of wind as his barrel cut through the air.

The leader moved like a shadow, coming slowly into view. He didn't make the same mistake as his predecessor but pied the corner, coming wide around it rather than close to the wall. He snapped his weapon around the corner. With a quick but thorough look about, he took in the sight of the unconscious man and the surrounding area.

His gun was larger than the one I carried. I recognized it instantly. The Colonel was quite fond of Heckler and Koch, a German manufacturer who made the HK-G3 this man carried. An expensive toy with which to play soldier.

This time, a quick knock on the head wasn't going to work. He was too tall, first of all, and to hit him I would have to come out of cover. I would have to take several steps toward him, knowing the possibility of his hearing my approach was great.

He would have the advantage of time. He was surely quicker than me. He was stronger, younger, and male. I had only one advantage. I knew where he was.

I could not allow him to fire. He was surely in better practice than I was, so one shot could be the end of me. This close to the cabin, there was a possibility that stray bullets could kill Shelley and Phoebe. No shootout. Nor could I allow this to become a contest of strength. His biceps bulged out from the arms of his T-shirt and his chest rippled with muscles under the fabric. If he saw me, I'd have no alternative but to shoot and shoot first, and that shot must disable him, if it came to that.

When he made a sweep away from me, I took long, quiet strides from my position behind the tree around the back of the cabin to its other side. From there, a ridge of several large boulders stood quite close to the cabin. My intent was to reach them, but no sooner had I peeked around the corner of the cabin than the leader, suddenly opposite me at the other end of the porch, swung his rifle and put me in its sights. He had backtracked. Too clever, this one. My blood chilled.

I jerked my head back from view. He hadn't fired. The look on his face, changing from severe concentration to utter disbelief, told me he hesitated because of my gray hair, and perhaps my height, and had more than likely ascertained in that split second I was merely a harmless little old lady.

Funny, but I keep forgetting that. I didn't think he could have seen my weapon, only my head. Yet I had noticed something extremely useful about his own gun.

"Oh, dear!" I cried out in a shaky voice and began to sob as loudly as I could. "Oh, my heavens. Please, p-p-please, don't shoot!" Elsa Lancaster would have been proud. I snuggled closer to the cabin wall, took my stance, and readied my gun.

"Come out," he said gruffly, barely disguising his amusement. "Come out with your hands up."

Oh, no, my dear young man. You shall come to me.

I didn't answer him but remained hidden and continued with befuddled whimpering, all the while gauging his steps as they came nearer, counting the rhythm, seeing the moves in my mind.

His boots clopped on the wooden porch slats as he came toward me. I watched the space where his rifle should appear and when it did, I smashed his trigger hand with the hard edge of my rifle butt, smacking his finger away from the trigger, and immediately slammed the rifle again in a quick upward jut to his chin. After another hard strike of the butt's edge to his jaw and nose for good measure, I wrapped my foot around his ankle to ensure his backward fall.

As he fell, I brought my rifle down behind the G-3 he still held loosely and swept it out of his hands to the ground, giving it a kick that sent it off the porch. He'd not taken the time to put the strap over his head, but let it dangle loose to his side. When I'd noticed it earlier, I knew I had a chance to disarm him.

He hit the porch flat on his back. He growled like a wild animal. I could see him struggling to remain conscious, trying to position himself to spring up. I couldn't allow that. When his eyes opened, I had my rifle aimed at his chest.

Several options played out in my head. Even if I had anything with which to tie him, it would be too dangerous to try it with no back up. If I left him there while I untied Shelley and Phoebe, he might then become an unseen threat in the woods. Killing him while I had the chance crossed my mind but was, of course, not an option. Not yet.

"Put your hands on your head," I said. He still lay on his back, his face contorted as if he were in great pain. Something I might do if in his position to gain more time. "Now."

He smirked. He shook his head, willing himself to concentrate. Blood ran from his nose. His smile showed gaps between pearly white teeth as he fully saw me for the first time. "Is that an order?" he said.

I smiled as well, showing all my teeth and softening my eyes in a kind, grandmotherly way. With a quick jerk, I snapped the rifle sight to and fired one shot. It grazed his left earlobe.

His hand moved up in reflex to the small wound, barely a scratch. He stared at the red droplets of blood on his fingertips in disbelief.

"Is that an order, what, private?" I said, imitating the Colonel's familiar bark.

He didn't answer immediately. I do believe the young man had a problem with women in positions of authority. I edged the gun's barrel slowly, slightly to my left toward his other ear.

He swallowed. He gritted his teeth and spoke tightly through them. "Is that an order, ma'am!" he said with great spite.

"Indeed, it is. Don't speak again." I slowly moved the sight of my gun to the center of his forehead. I waited a few moments to let him think about that. "Move your hands to the top of your head. Lace your fingers together. Tightly, please," I said in a calm voice. "Slowly get to your knees."

He did as he was told. I walked around him until my gun pointed at his back. I didn't take a whit of concentration off him for a moment. I checked the back of his belt and his boots. There. I could see the knife he had tucked inside the right one. Possible scenarios went through my head making me come to a very difficult conclusion.

He would try something. Soon, most likely, and he would win somehow—by force, by disarming me, by knifing or shooting me. I didn't care for any of those possibilities. I could not wait for him to make that move. "Now, listen carefully," I said. "I want you to..."

With a quick flip of the rifle, I smashed it down at the base of his skull. Fair and sportsmanlike behavior? No. The only way to ensure the safety of my friends and myself short of committing murder? Yes.

When I was sure he was out cold, I patted him down and found nothing other than the knife. I took it. Keeping my rifle on him, I backed off the porch, retrieved the G-3 and put its strap over my head, then ran inside to Phoebe and removed her gag.

"Jane! That was you out there!"

"Are you all right?" I asked, while using the knife to cut her bonds. I pulled the gag down from Shelley's mouth and cut her free.

Phoebe chattered, apparently trying to relate how they came to be here, but her sentences were disjointed and made no sense. Shelley cried and also spoke in a halting way between sobs. Phoebe managed to say there was still a third man who went to Cal's house.

"I saw him. He won't be bothering us. No more talking now. Listen." I put a hand on each girl's shoulder and gave it a little shake as I gripped. "We must get to safety straightaway. We must put as much distance as possible between us and this place. Hurry."

I helped each to their feet, then took a look around the room to be sure we left no weapons behind. Phoebe moved to the hearth and picked up the third rifle I'd seen through the window, an odd-looking one in a strange color I'd never seen before. Her initiative surprised and pleased me. I would congratulate her later for thinking of taking one of the enemy's guns in spite of the fact she didn't know how to shoot it.

At the door, I checked to be sure my man was still out cold, then listened but only for a second. We had to get away before the other member of their party arrived.

As we walked past the leader, Phoebe gasped. "Did you kill him?"

"No. Now come along," I said. I put an arm around her to hurry her. As we stepped to the side of the cabin, I glanced at the other prone man with the snake tattoo.

"What about Hank?" Phoebe said. "Is he dead?"

"No, of course not." I paused. "His name is Hank?" I said, as I eyed the snake on his arm and thought of Cal's last words.

A sudden rustling of leaves in the near distance caught our attention. Footsteps crackled dried leaves and twigs as someone approached from the forest trail that led to Cal's house. This person wasn't trying to make a surprise visit.

I herded Phoebe and Shelley across the clearing and up the ridge toward the two great trees, stopping behind the nearest boulder. I leaned out just enough to see, my gun raised, as a man came into view. He walked to the edge of the clearing.

Phoebe pushed by me before I knew what was happening. "Oh, my Lord, are we glad to see you!" she said, her arms up in the air, her orange rifle hanging off one shoulder by the strap and bouncing on her hip as she approached Chalmers Wade, who looked quite out of place wearing a three-piece suit in the woods.

"What in the world is going on out here?" the lawyer said on seeing Hank and the leader unconscious. I walked from behind the boulder, stepping slowly, the AR-15 held low.

Chalmers put his hands up in the air quickly when he saw my rifle trained on him. "Whoa there, Miz Thistle! Easy with that thing!" He laughed a little as he spoke, his wide trademark smile lighting up his face, which showed the slightest bit of fright. His expression changed to worry when he fully realized the size of my gun.

When Phoebe reached him, she flung her arms up and around his neck, planting a loud kiss on his cheek. She pointed toward Hank. "That guy abducted Shelley," she said. "I saw the whole thing. He forced her into a van. I followed them." She panted and tried to catch her breath.

"What! Honey," Chalmers said, "bless your heart, you've been through it haven't you? I was coming to see Cal and heard a police dispatch on my scanner that something was going on out here."

Shelley also ran past me into her employer's arms. Phoebe backed away and walked toward me beside the round homemade archery target. She leaned on it as she wiped sweat from her hairline. Her gun hung loosely from her shoulder.

"Shelley, sweetheart," Chalmers said, rocking her back and forth. He held her away from him and brushed a strand of auburn hair gently from her face, then wiped a tear running down her cheek.

With his large hands on her shoulders, he turned her to face us. "Miz Thistle, Miz Twigg," he said, as he reached inside his jacket, brought out a gun, and moved it up to Shelley's temple. "I must ask you ladies to kindly drop your weapons."

Phoebe screamed. When she saw Chalmers' gun, her body shook violently from head to toe, causing her rifle to slide off her shoulder and to the ground.

He was an intelligent coward. All but his face, which he pressed against Shelley's cheek, was hidden behind her tall form. If only a bit more space were between them, I might have risked a shot. I could see no way to take him out without possible harm coming to Shelley. Would he really do it? I hadn't the option of calling his bluff. I reluctantly took each strap from over my head and dropped the AR-15 first, then the G-3.

"Turn around. Let's take a little walk." He motioned in the direction of the two great trees. And the bluffs.

Not good. I did not want to leave those guns. Nor did I want to turn around.

"You don't think the police will find it odd that three women just happened to fall off the cliffs at the same time? That they won't find some sort of evidence against you?"

He laughed. "How could they when I'm not here? I'm at my office at the moment. No reason to suspect me of anything. And it will just be two women. You two."

"I wasn't talking about evidence that you were here. I meant in paperwork. In Cal's handwriting."

A few moments passed. He shook his head. "Nothing suspicious about a man's lawyer looking through his papers. If there's anything to find, I will. You're grasping at straws. You two will fall. The police will assume one of you tried to rescue the other with no success. It could be days, weeks before you're found. Shelley will have a different fate. So far as her travel agent knows, she's on vacation. Or the police will conclude she was abducted and killed by paramilitary extremists. I haven't decided yet."

"A group of which you are the real boss," I said.

He shrugged. "Only in the sense that I hired them. I'm much too well bred to be one of them."

"But they served your purpose, eh? They made a good cover for shooting Cal. You're thinking that will make your takeover of his estate most convenient. Of course, the police will see through that just as I do." He shook his head and laughed. "You killed Cal, didn't you, Mr. Wade?"

Phoebe gasped. "Cal is dead?"

"You're a sharp lady, Miz Thistle. And, by the way, thank you for the loan of your gun."

I paused. Could this be true? "You took one of my guns? To frame me for Cal's murder?"

"They were all so tempting, lying there on your couch after the good detective brought them back to you."

Though I couldn't see his weapon well enough to identify it as my own, I knew he spoke the truth. He was in the house just after my guns were returned. He took one when no one was watching. "And now you wish to kill the only three people who knew Cal wanted to sell his land to me. So you can take it."

"I've worked for it. It should be mine. I've looked after that old man for years when he's had no one else. With you gone, his land will be mine. We need developments here, businesses to bring in jobs. I can do that right here. And if I have to cut down a few trees to put a few million dollars into my pocket, I can do that, too."

"And destroy everything around us. Forest, animals, history. Legally. Or not so legally if you must, eh?"

He moved his gun and held it out straight at shoulder height. It wasn't much of an improvement. He still held Shelly too close. Even if I had time to reach back for the gun in my waistband and fire it, I had no clear shot. I'd have to try something else, something even more risky.

Phoebe looked to me. Tears mingled with sweat that covered her face. She wiped her cheeks, then flung her arms out and embraced me, crying into my shoulder. "Good-bye, Jane. I wanted us to be best friends for a long time. Now we won't get to be."

I had to suppress the urge to laugh out loud. Even in the worst circumstances, Phoebe had a way of lifting my spirits just by being herself. I hugged her and said, "Don't worry, dear. He won't shoot. Bullets would give the police a trail to follow. A multi-million-dollar land deal can't be conducted from prison."

His worried look changed to relief. "When the police find this gun, it will have the dishonorably discharged ex-Marine's fingerprints on it." He nodded toward the man out cold on the porch.

"You killed Cal," Phoebe said, as she gave him a fiery look. "And you're going to kill us? You're a sorry excuse of a man, Chalmers Wade." She still trembled but a bit of fight was now in her voice. "Your good-hearted grandmama is turning over in her grave right now. Why, she would tan your hide."

"Touching, Miz Twigg, but even Granny's disapproval doesn't make me feel a bit worse. By the way, she also disapproved of red-headed floozies like you who can't mind their own business."

Phoebe's infuriated utterances were most unladylike. She suddenly reached to the ground, scooped up a rock and threw it at Chalmers. He started to laugh but never got the chance for I took the small distraction and used it knowing I must act before it was too late.

I rushed him, arms out. He pivoted slightly, took aim, but was too late. I reached across Shelley and grabbed the gun with both my hands pushing it straight up. While close to his body, I delivered several kicks to his legs. He let go of Shelley. When I felt her body move away, I kneed his groin. He dropped his pistol when he doubled over. I kicked it away from us. Before I could reach behind my back for my own gun, he half stood and threw a left hook into my face.

The pain was staggering. I fell backward into the round target knocking it over. I lay over it a moment, stunned, trying to get up, for I could see Chalmers as he lunged for and reached the AR-15 I'd thrown to the ground.

Just then, a shot rang out. Both Chalmers and I froze momentarily. Neither of us had weapons. Neither had been shot.

I looked to my left to see Phoebe falling backward from the kick of the orange rifle she'd retrieved. She was off balance and fell to one knee but she still held the gun loosely, her finger on the trigger. Not a comforting sight.

She righted herself, shouldered the rifle, aimed in Chalmers' general vicinity, and fired again. The bullet hit a boulder about two yards away, ricocheted, and pierced the back of the straw dummy. By this time, I'd managed to scramble to my feet. I stepped to her side as I withdrew the pistol from my waistband and prepared to shoot.

Just then, a rush of cool autumn wind blew between the two great trees from the direction of the ceremonial hall. Scents of pine and turning leaves, sweeter and stronger than before, swept across our faces, and the most amazing, unbelievable event in my sixty-seven years played out before me.

Time and the world ground to an abrupt halt, then moved again in super-slow motion. Everything came into sharp focus. My brain's survival instinct was to sharpen the senses and heighten reality. Why, then, I thought, was my imagination in overdrive as well? For something more was at work here. The air sparkled with a golden yellow tint specked throughout with reflective bits like metallic dust.

A mockingbird swooped down into the breeze. Its slow dip and rise, dip and rise, its haunting melody and repetition, the branches around us swaying in a strange manner like arms of a maestro conducting, all stood out in vivid detail. It was a multi-dimensional symphony, expanded for all senses, as overpowering as the Maiden's Tears in its artistic perfection.

Even Chalmers and the deadly weapon he held, brought up slowly to point at Phoebe, seemed an orchestrated and inevitable part of it. These flights of fancy were not like me, were not in my training. I gave myself a mental shake yet the sparkling air was still there, and looked thicker as I stared at the AR-15's barrel and leveled my own gun at Chalmers.

Out of the corner of my eye, I saw a movement of orange and of Phoebe moving slightly forward. The air pulsed and glittered around her. I stepped toward her meaning to knock her aside out of the AR-15's path as I aimed at Chalmers.

In the heavy golden air, three shots fired simultaneously.

I leaned toward Phoebe but I felt a gentle pressure hold me back, ever so slightly, just enough that the bullet Chalmers fired at Phoebe missed me by no more than an inch.

When Phoebe fired, her rifle once again gave her a good kick. An accumulation of glistening air thickened at her side like a barrier. She tipped in the opposite direction. The bullet Chalmers intended for her missed and embedded itself in one of the two great trees, the huge oak, behind her.

My shot found its target and lodged between Chalmers' upper chest and collarbone making him twist away in pain and fall backward.

Phoebe's shot had an even more dramatic end. I didn't see it hit a boulder but I heard it ping. As Chalmers fell, I looked toward the sound and when I did I saw the air gleaming in golden strands that caught her bullet and whipped it up with the speed and force of a hurricane wind, high into a limb of the other great tree, the maple, just overhead. The limb, long as a car and its branches as wide, snapped and fell heavily on Chalmers covering him completely with red leaves.

Nothing stirred beneath the massive limb. No part of Chalmers could be seen. Only the barrel of the AR-15 stuck out from underneath the mass of leaves. My heart jumped as I hurried to retrieve it. Phoebe came forward to my side. She stood with her weapon trained on the heap should Chalmers emerge. I did likewise with the AR-15.

We spoke at once. "Are you all right?"

We laughed a moment, both still shaking, but sobered quickly as the sound of running feet came nearer through the woods.

"Police! Hold your fire!" Detective Waters yelled as he came into view.

"Don't shoot, detective!" I yelled. "We're putting down our weapons." I let mine drop and put my hands in the air. Phoebe followed suit.

Detective Waters held his handgun straight out as he surveyed the scene. He paused at the two prone militia men as he came toward us. He saw Shelley huddled behind a tree and ordered a female officer over to help the stunned and silent young woman.

"Chalmers tried to kill us!" Phoebe shouted.

"Where is he? Is he armed?"

"Not anymore," Phoebe said. We pointed to the fallen branch, now moving a bit as Chalmers stirred beneath it. Detective Waters motioned for his men to cover it.

"How did you know to come?" I asked.

"The patrol officer I put near your house came back from another call and saw Chalmers' car enter Cal's place. He radioed me. I told him to follow. He found a man unconscious near the house."

Detective Waters looked again at the two men on the ground in the clearing. He looked at Phoebe then at me. He grimaced as he took in the bruises and cuts on our faces then he smiled. I shrugged.

In the distance beyond the detective's head, I saw a man standing in the trees. He was not a policeman. He stared at me with large dark eyes. His black hair fell down over bare shoulders. His skin was a burnished red. One hand with the palm turned toward me came up in greeting. His other arm was disfigured. I wanted to go to him but was stopped by an amazing sight. As he brought down his hand, his body shimmered then became transparent. It morphed into a ball of glittering particles that, in a flash, swooped upward to a pine branch and came to rest as a mockingbird. It trilled, cocking its head as it eyed me. Though able to fly away, it did so with a curious dipping movement, something I attributed to its one damaged wing.

"All right. Everything's okay now, ladies," the detective said, still taking in every detail of the area. He holstered his gun while noting the AR-15. He did a double take when he saw Phoebe's unusual orange rifle.

"Good," Phoebe said. She strode to the mound of leaves, saw it move again, and kicked it viciously. Chalmers grunted.

"Phoebe, don't!" I said, worried she might be charged with assault. She, apparently, was not worried in the least in spite of being surrounded by police officers.

She kicked again resulting in a louder cry of pain. "I'm not hurting him," she said to me. "Hey, Rich Boy." This she addressed to the leaves. "I reckon next time you see a lady with a loaded AK-46 and a half, you won't call her a floozy." She bit her bottom lip and kicked harder than ever. "And that's for your sorry grandmama."

Detective Waters had made his way to Phoebe. He gently put his hands on her shoulders. "Calm down, Miz Twigg. We're going to take good care of him, don't you worry. Now," he said looking all around the clearing and the nearby woods. "Are there any other bad guys around I need to know about? That y'all haven't already knocked out?"

thirty-three

Jane Gets the Scoop

The next morning, Hank came to my house for breakfast. To our surprise, he was a very nice young man. Phoebe sat close to him and kept filling his coffee cup. "So you and Cal knew each other? Why didn't Cal tell us?"

Hank patted his lips with his napkin. He'd had a shave and haircut since we saw him last. He looked quite presentable, which made me regret having knocked him unconscious all the more.

"We talked a few times, yes, but he didn't know I was working undercover. When things got out of hand, he called us at the ATF. He didn't trust the local police."

"Were the others in the survivalist group local as well?" I asked.

"No. Chalmers hired the leader, Trent Smith, an ex-Marine from Indiana. They met on a hunting trip in Montana several months ago. He told him to find a few rednecks who wanted to play soldier. I'd been sent in some months before that since ATF wanted to get someone close to him. Trent's a suspect in several military-base robberies across the country.

"Trent says he was told to lean on Cal hard. We think Chalmers hoped the stress would do Cal in though he hasn't admitted that yet. So, Trent was being paid to harass Cal, and he also saw an opportunity to extort money from him, not something in the original plan."

Phoebe took a sip of coffee and said, "So, Chalmers gave the order and y'all took Shelley. You weren't in on my house bomb, were you?" she said, giving him a stern look.

"No, ma'am. I didn't know anything about it. Trent took that upon himself, too."

"What a relief," Phoebe said. "You sure had me fooled."

"Treenie Dodd had been buying drugs from him," Hank said. "She told him you and Mrs. Thistle found the man he killed and that you knew more about it than you were telling."

Phoebe slapped the table and stood. "Oooh, when I get my hands on that blond-headed little . . ."

I put a hand on her arm. "Try not to get upset, dear. I'm sure the police will take good care of her. Hank, was the poor young man we found also part of the survivalist group?"

"Yes. Trent caught him stealing guns, guns already stolen from a Navy base, and killed him. Chalmers didn't like it when he heard but he used the situation to make things worse for Cal. He told Smith to move the body to Cal's firing range."

I sighed. "That's a horrible way to treat a friend."

"Money does that to you. He needed Cal's land for several major manufacturers who wanted to come to the area. They were about to choose another site in southern Alabama. Chalmers was offered an easy five million just to smooth out the land deal. Today, we're bringing in the manager at the Bank of Tulluluh for questioning. We think he was in on the deal, too; possibly he was promised that some juicy financing would go through his bank."

Phoebe jumped up from her chair. "Chalmers told him to stall Jane! That's why Roman got all funny about loaning her the money for Cal's place! Just wait until my next hair appointment. I'm going to give his sister Eileen a piece of my mind."

"Now, Phoebe," I said.

"Oh, pooh," she said. "I know. It's just so aggravating. Don't worry. I'll get over it before I see Eileen. It's not her fault her brother is a sorry sewer rat."

Hank smiled a moment then looked very sad. "Chalmers was Cal's sole heir for years. He didn't know Cal checked into the rumors of developers buying land in the area. He found out Chalmers had made promises to some influential businessmen to clear most of Cal's land once it became his. He didn't want to believe it at first. But he called Shelley Barnette to make a new will."

"So, that's what they were up to," I said. "I saw Shelley driving onto his property."

"She took a video camera and taped his wishes. Chalmers was furious when he found out in the interrogation room last night."

I got up for more coffee and topped off my friends' cups as well. "We have one final mystery." I told Hank what Cal said at the stream just before he died. "So, you see, Phoebe and I thought Cal meant you were his killer." Hank looked puzzled. "You don't know why he said that?" I asked with a touch of disappointment.

His face lit up. "Wait. Maybe I do. Not the tattoo. I think he wanted me to show you something. Come on."

We clambered into Hank's truck and drove onto Cal's land, past the house and around the woods to a place Cal had not taken me. The stream where I found Cal stayed in view to my right as we rode.

We stopped where it ran wider and moved more slowly across a glen. Large mossy trunks lay about beside the water. Banks on either side had the same type of large flat rocks as the bluff and practicing range. Smooth brown stones covered the stream's bed beneath the cool water.

Hank stepped over to the stream and looked up and down the banks for a moment. "Here!" he said. We looked where he pointed. Phoebe and I walked closer.

"See? I think this is what he meant." A carving was on a large rock at the stream's edge. It had only one undulating line drawn diagonally with a circle attached at the top.

A snake.

"Are you sure this is what he meant?" Phoebe said. "All he wanted to say with his dying breath was, 'Y'all go look at some old rocks'?"

"This has to be it," Hank said. "I'd left camp only a few hours before Cal was killed to tell him I was with ATF and not to worry. This was where I found him. When I saw the rock, he told me he'd carved the snake when he was a boy."

"Surely it is much older than that," I said, as I ran my fingers across the rock's surface just under the water.

"I humored him. He probably was afraid I might come back and steal it. Or tell someone who might. I don't blame him."

Hank walked over and rubbed his palm across the snake carving. "Sorry to disappoint you, but this is all I can think of that Cal might have meant."

Soon after, we headed home and Hank left us. Phoebe and I watched him drive away. She waved to him then put hands on her hips. "So, what was that all about?"

"What, dear?"

"The squiggly snake thing. You'd think Cal would've said 'Chalmers.' What could be more important than fingering your killer when you know you're fixing to die?"

"A very good question."

thirty-four

Jane Finds a Treasure

*L*ater that day, Phoebe returned home. Almost all the work there was finished; only another day or so of paint supervision remained.

Cal's funeral, a small graveside affair, was the following day. Afterward, Shelley presided over the viewing of Cal's short videotaped will with only myself, Phoebe, and Detective Waters present.

Cal explained that he offered to sell his land to me because he discovered Chalmers' plan to destroy the forest. He also explained why he became irate at the police station. Detective Waters had heard rumors of developers buying Cal's land as well. When he questioned Cal about the body found at his shooting range, he asked about the developers' plans since he had heard about them from a reliable source.

From the video, Cal said, "I already knew part of what Chalmers wanted to do but I hadn't really faced it. I couldn't handle the shame of Dan Waters knowing I had about messed up the most important thing on this earth to me. I was ashamed that I hadn't been able to take care of everything myself. Pride got the better of me."

If only Cal had confided in Detective Waters then. He didn't know that Shelley told Chalmers about his proposed land sale to me. She had called him from my kitchen, just before Cal and I signed our agreement, to tell him the police wanted to question Cal. She also mentioned Cal wanted her to draw up our sales document. She couldn't have known that by giving him that information, she gave him a reason to kill Cal.

At the video's end, Cal specified I was to take possession of his land and belongings immediately upon his death. Seeing him that way, so afraid and so very ill, broke my heart.

As much as I loved the land, I hadn't wanted to come into it this way. I'd have preferred buying it. Having Cal for a friend, a companion who like myself enjoyed both privacy and occasional good conversation, would have been a joy. He had many stories to tell about this place. Now, I'd never hear them all.

Homer came home from the veterinarian's office that afternoon. He'd suffered a mild concussion trying to save his master and friend. I kept him inside the rest of the day for a bit more rest. Sitting on the front porch, we grieved together that night. The next morning, we went to the gravesite where Cal lay between his son and his wife. Homer lay down across it, whimpering in the long, high-pitched way dogs cry. I did my best to comfort him, sitting with him for a while, then left him alone. I busied myself in and around Cal's house, not far away, to let Homer know I was still nearby.

After a few hours, he came to find me. I set out a bowl of water for him. He took a drink, then lay down beside my chair in the kitchen, leaning his body against my legs. He goes to the grave every day still but is gradually spending less time there, choosing rather to accompany me during the day as I do my chores and explore the woods. He guards me at night.

I'd been putting off the task of going through the remaining boxes that Cal insisted I bring to my house. They were all covered in dust and they most certainly did not enhance the décor of my cozy book den. I'd finished unpacking my own boxes and had no more excuses to delay taking care of Cal's.

Resolved to remedy the situation, I dragged the box Cal had labeled with a large red "one" over to my desk. I brought a damp cloth from the kitchen to clean off the cobwebs that covered it from top to bottom.

I lifted the cover on which Cal had scrawled, "Start Here." While I absentmindedly wiped the underside and corners, my eyes skimmed a loose piece of ruled paper inside the box, taped to the top of a book. Seeing Cal's handwriting made me smile. So much of his personality came through the shaky loops and jagged lettering. "This here," it read, "is a list of all special treasures and places of interest (that I know of) and that you need to know about, one box per place. The last box is just little things all put together. More books and papers are at the house, you know that, but these here I didn't want anybody else to get a hold of." Below, he'd printed out a list, numbered one through seventeen.

I ran my finger down the entries. "Pirate treasure?"

Homer jumped at the sudden loud exclamation. "Sorry, love. It's just . . . he has listed a pirate's treasure! And has ranked it number four! What in heaven's name could possibly be above that in the top three?"

When I saw what Cal had deemed the number one treasure, I sat silently, staring at the words, wondering what they meant. My hands scrambled into the box. I stopped myself, willing my heart to stop racing and my head to stop spinning.

I flung the paper aside and looked to the boxes stacked against the den wall. All ragged fruit and vegetable crates.

"Clever devil! Homer, your father was a genius." Cal may have merely used the boxes out of convenience or thrift but I didn't think so. He'd hidden what he considered most valuable in plain sight, in boxes of no obvious worth, ones that would not attract the attention of any would-be thieves.

"What's this?" I asked Homer, on pulling out a strange little book, one obviously handmade. Cal had cut thick manila paper into 4 by 4-inch pages, then sewn together two pieces of leather, front and back, at the edge with leather string. Dirty fingers had leafed the pages many times over, the black marks evidence of many years of use.

It was a dictionary of sorts. Most pages contained single words or phrases; some were proper names in Cherokee or Chickasaw with an English translation. Inside the front cover was a pronunciation guide.

The first word was "*Tsalagi*" in large letters and its English translation, "Cherokee." In the margin, Cal had scribbled in parenthesis, "No 'R' in language."

About halfway through the little book, the pages changed from words to drawings and symbols, some with question marks and notes, as if Cal had continued research over a long period of time. Beside each, meanings were given.

He had marked a page in this section with a small piece of torn white paper. I turned there to find six drawings. All the figures were of snakes. Some moved upward, others down. One had a severed head, another was coiled. The explanation next to the drawing that most closely matched the one we'd seen in the stream said, "Follow direction of head to next sign or treasure."

"More treasure!" I said aloud. Homer's ears pricked up as he raised his head. "What have you and Cal been hiding!" He sat up and cocked his head to the side. He rose and stood next to me to see what I was going on about. I put an arm around him and showed him the picture, as if he were a person. He woofed in answer, as if perhaps he was.

Of course, I was excited. Giddy, even. I immediately went outside to the potting shed with Homer following. About halfway there, I stopped. "Should I call Phoebe?" Homer didn't answer but sat in the grass. He held very still and gave me his full attention.

It would be wonderful to have my dear friend with me for such an adventure. Yet, I hesitated. "We'll check it first ourselves," I said, as I bent down and rubbed Homer's ears.

On a nail on the shed's wall hung my old work belt, a leather one I'd used on many a dig. I took it down and, as I strapped it on, a shiver went through me. Silly, I know but it felt as if I were myself again after having been away.

A smile stretched across my face as I chose implements and a pair of old work gloves. We returned to the house for a few more things—a flashlight, my binoculars, a camera, and an assortment of small brushes—then headed out to my car.

"Cal is certainly full of surprises, old boy. What fun we shall have!" Homer barked. His tail wagged in double time while waiting for me to open the back door. I drove on to Cal's place, mine now, I remembered, to the spot Hank showed us.

On the way, I wondered what we might find. Would it be a real treasure or just something interesting Cal had left for me to discover? Like a father creating a game for a child? I smiled, realizing I didn't much care if it was real or not. If it interested him, I would want to see it. Why not have a little fun? When we reached the spot near the stream, Homer went straight to the rocks, barked and sat.

When I joined him, I looked in the direction the snake's head pointed and consulted Cal's dictionary again. "You've been here many times I imagine, haven't you, dear?" He looked up at me, his body still and his tail wagging furiously. "Yes. All right. This way, I think."

I took a step in the direction of the snakehead. Homer jumped up and bounded ahead, as if he only needed the slightest indication to know which path we would take. He touched his nose to the ground once then looked back to me expectantly. "You already know the way," I said and laughed. "Lead on, my friend."

I would swear he smiled at me. He turned his thick body with one jump. I watched in amazement as Homer trotted due northeast, the direction of the snakehead. We traveled another several hundred yards through a lovely section of woods. I longed to stop and have a look through my binoculars at birds that flitted by. Homer forged ahead, however, so I followed, splashing across another shallow stream.

Soon after, I saw we had come from yet another direction to the other end of the ceremonial hall. Homer didn't enter it but made his way around the hall's crown of rocks. He trotted to an open area some twenty yards away from the hall.

He stopped at an unusual boulder about ten feet square jutting up out of the ground. A ledge of sorts stuck out creating an overhang that angled up and outward. It looked very much like a standing stone with a flat rooflike rock on top. Homer trotted up and crept to its edge, looked around a bit, then retraced his steps and sat in the overhang's long shadow.

The ledge was just high enough for me to stand under it comfortably. At first, I saw nothing unusual. Then, as my eyes adjusted to the dim light, another rock carving, small and in a little indentation, came into view.

This one was a dancing figure with sticks for arms and legs and the head, surrounded on one side with straight lines like hair or a headdress, turned to the right. I quickly opened the little book and ran my finger down the pages containing drawings.

I stopped on a similar figure. Its caption read, "Follow direction of head."

I was puzzled. The dancing figure pointed inward toward the

rock. I walked out, circled it twice more. The ledge gave no further clue. "I don't understand."

Homer spoke. It was not a bark or a woof but a soft, muffled sound, the dog equivalent of a whisper. He scooted on his belly a bit and put his front paws up on the rock, a few inches high, and tapped one paw on the rough surface.

I looked closer. There, next to Homer's paw, I finally saw it. An optical illusion made the rock appear to be solid from all angles except this slim space where I now stood. Here, I could see a second sheet of rock had been hewn and placed about three feet away from the boulder, creating a door like opening about six feet high by three wide. From the smell of the air coming from it, it had to lead to an inner cave.

I flicked on my flashlight. A passageway led slightly down. "Astounding. Good work, boy. You know where we are. After you."

I followed him around a corner and into a passageway that sloped steadily downward. We traveled only a few feet before we turned another corner where the passage widened and went another ten yards or so to enter a chamber, one I guessed was enormous from the fresh bursts of air that flowed around us. It felt twenty degrees cooler than at ground level.

I shone my light overhead where the ceiling vaulted fifteen to twenty feet to the ground level above. Although there was the heavy smell of earth, it wasn't musty, for above and ahead of us, roughly fifty yards to the back of the underground room, about a dozen holes in the roof and upper parts of the walls were spaced just so, unquestionably manmade. Other small gaps in the roof revealed leaves and grasses around their edges, with branches and just a bit of sky visible.

Bright specks of dust floated down the light shafts ahead, and the residual light shining down the dark walls made them sparkle with an eerie glow. I moved my light in an arc at our feet. To our left sat an oil lamp with a plastic bottle of commercial oil and a box of matches beside it. I lit the lamp, switched off my flashlight, and carried the lamp by its wire handle.

Homer's eyes glistened in the soft lamplight that outlined his black coat. He turned and loped toward the back wall. "Oh, dear heavens!" I said. I nearly dropped the lamp as I walked faster behind him. There, illuminated by the lamp and the series of track lights, colorful drawings and engravings in the wall took shape. A native man held a spear, another a bow. The artist painted deer and elk beside water. Turtles, snakes, and other small animals were spread out across the smooth surface to the edges of rough rock.

I held the lamp to the wall for a close inspection. The images were done in a black paint with occasional splashes of red, for example, on one deer's side and on a cardinal in flight. I had no knowledge of dating such work. I'd participated in native digs in the Southwest, but none of the sites had anything to match this.

I slowly moved the lamp around, first to the back wall. No drawings there, only the bumpy texture of deep roots coming from above. I continued to the right to the wall opposite the drawings. There sat a stone bench beneath four of the small skylights whose shafts of light dotted the bench seat. I moved closer, the breath leaving my body as I stared.

An object about two feet long and a half foot wide lay centered on the bench. It was made of a dark wood, blackened with paint and highly polished to a brilliant shine, carved in the shape of a reclining man. He wore decorations of shells and feathers, all intricately etched in the wood.

On closer inspection, I saw it was a ceremonial pipe. Its craftsmanship alone might make it a beautiful find, but its most astonishing feature was something much more unusual. Each carved decoration had been traced in gold, making it look more like something from an Egyptian tomb than from a southeastern tribe of North America. With such limited expertise in this field, I knew I'd have much research to do to be sure. My gut instinct, however, was that this was not only a rare artifact, it was most likely singular. I knew of none other like it.

I reached out and caressed its smooth exterior. I began to wonder where the tribe came by this bit of gold and which tribe it might have belonged to; perhaps a Cherokee journeyed here from North Carolina? I seemed to recall mentions of gold finds there and in Arkansas as well.

I'd forgotten Homer, had forgotten the world outside existed in those minutes, and looked behind me to see about him. He lay sprawled out on the floor with his head resting on a flat rock underneath the wall of drawings. I laughed.

"You're taking this rather calmly, old fellow. But then, this isn't new to you, is it, dear?" I set the pipe down and stepped toward him. In his sleek black coat, against the rock that sparkled in the lamplight, he looked very much like the pipe. "Homer, are you imitating the figure?"

I stopped. I think perhaps my heart did as well as I dropped to my knees. I slid or crawled, I'm not entirely sure which, to Homer's side. I gazed at the rock under his head, a rough-edged oblong chunk studded with what looked like fiery, shiny gold.

I held the lamp high and suddenly saw what had been around me the whole time. The room's walls shone for a reason. They were veined with strands of gold. Not a few here and there, but thick and crossed like a gargantuan spider's web, running in all directions. I began to notice some spots in the walls shone differently than the rest, and discovered spots of planed rock. More than gold lay in one such cutaway space. I counted five crosscuts of embedded quartz, large specimens, one in a dim rose, four others in a lustrous purple.

My mind reeled. I felt dizzy. I walked slowly back to Homer who sat up watching me, his front paws out like the Sphinx. I lay down myself, resting my head in the middle of Homer's back. With eyes closed, I let these new revelations spin above my head, so many skeins of what I'd seen and of the stories of these woods I'd heard all tangled and spread above me. My eyes bolted open as the last important strand finally unraveled above me. I stared at it, there above my head, the place where myth, reality, and Cal's vital reason for preserving this place untouched lay.

The ceiling. Through fissures in the ground above me, great twines of roots twisted through the cave's ceiling. In the dim light, the back wall directly before me took on new shapes as the majority of roots stuck out in relief. The roof looked to me about twelve feet high. Roots twisted on the wall from top to bottom and who knows how much further below. By my estimation of the room's length from the hidden cave door where we entered, Homer and I must now lay directly underneath the other end of the ceremonial hall. We lay at the base of the two great trees, whose nest of gnarled roots burrowed into rock speckled with glittering gold.

At last I understood. Dear, wonderful Cal was quite right to rank this his number one priority, above all other treasures. He could never, ever let anyone know, could let no one see. It would be too risky. Even if it were only fool's gold, the dazzling sight of it, the lure of riches would be too great a temptation for someone unattached to its history so intimately as he. This gold could never be mined for it would destroy the sacred ceremonial hall above me.

Even that, however, would be secondary in his mind to disturbing the two great trees, for they made this place all the more sacred where forest and family come together. They were the same.

Tsali and *Tseni*. Charley and Jenny. *Tsali Skatsi* and *Usti Tseni* on the canyon map referred not so much to the place but to the people there, Charlie the Scot and Little Wren, Cal's ancestors, whose bead necklace and small dagger he had cherished above all other possessions. They were not merely a fireside legend of lovers buried with the seeds of trees in their fists, but real people who lived and gave him life not so many generations ago. When I'd first seen *Tsali* written, I didn't realize how it was pronounced. It was only as I lay on the cave floor that I made the connection to *Tsalagi*, which we pronounce as "Cherokee."

I sat up. "What did I do with the notebook?" I asked Homer. I saw it where I had dropped it next to the stone bench. Quickly I scanned the pages for mention of gold.

Cal had begun writing this journal in 1969, according to the date on the first page. On it he had written, "Thomas is gone now so I'm writing this to someone in the future. There's so many things to tell about, I figured I better start at writing it all down." He goes on to tell the story of *Tsali* and *Tseni*, except here it was not a legend, as he told it to me before, but the story of his great-great-great grandparents, with many side notes of Cherokee words, family names, and places.

At last, a reference to gold caught my eye, one noted as copied from a letter sent to Cal's great-grandfather, Zebediah Prewitt, from the U.S. Assay Office in St. Louis, Missouri: "Gold nugget tested 22 karat, July 22, 1884." Another note, taken from a letter from the Assay Office in New Orleans to Ephraim Prewitt dated September 12, 1924, read: "Sample 23 g/tonne." Just under 24 karats. Almost one hundred percent pure gold.

Light from the vent holes had faded somewhat with the moving sun. I'd lost track of the time. I ran my hands once more over the ceremonial pipe, which I decided must be a warrior, resting perhaps before his next call to battle.

With reluctance, I gathered my tools from where I'd left them at the passageway. I held the lamp out for a last look before turning down the wick. I set the lamp beside the entrance, and Homer and I left the secret cave behind.

Once home, I hung my leather work belt on the coat rack just inside the door. There, on the hook beside it, was the canvas bag Phoebe had given me. Its garish orange fabric clashed with the crimson and purple in the kindergarten-style picture of two native children at play.

A wave of happiness washed over me. I started to cry. Homer's paws tapped softly on the wooden floor as he walked closer.

"You must think me very odd," I said to him, dabbing my eyes with a tissue. I bent down and gave him a long hug. "Come. You deserve a very special treat. How about eggs and ham?"

While his snack sizzled in the pan, I looked through the number one box reading snatches of stories. One reminded me of a place Cal showed me in the canyon. The more I thought about it, the more determined I was to see for myself if his story had been true. A plan for the evening began to form. I needed to make a phone call.

"Are you busy tonight?" I wasn't sure how Phoebe would feel about my strange suggestion. I hadn't mentioned my vision of the mysterious golden glow in the woods during our ordeal. To date, she'd not seemed receptive to the idea of any supernatural occurrences at all. However, I thought she might enjoy getting out for a little fun. "Phoebe, there's something important we need to do. The sooner, the better."

"Does it have to do with Indians? Or spirits?"

"Yes, it does. Both." I sighed, knowing she would think me daft, but I told her my plans anyway. To my surprise and delight, she greeted my idea with enthusiasm.

"So, I'll see you around seven o'clock?"

"I'll be there," she said and immediately the dial tone buzzed in my ear.

thirty-five

Jane and Phoebe
Send Evil Packing

nly a small strip of yellow police tape remained in the cabin's clearing. I unstuck it from the porch railing as Phoebe, Homer, and I passed by. Everything else had been taken as evidence, the targets, all bullet casings, even the cigarette butts and other trash. We'd planned on cleaning it all up ourselves. Still, we tidied the area a bit more gathering sticks and stacking them, and straightening inside the cabin.

Phoebe worked cheerfully and was ready to move on to the real reason for our visit. She'd certainly come dressed for the occasion in an eclectic mix of clothing that I can only describe as Native Princess wear. Several necklaces of beads, shells, and one of rawhide and feathers hung over a Navaho print top in dark brown and red with brown leggings underneath. She'd arranged another necklace or bracelet in her hair, teased up and held with French combs in the back, which gave the impression of a tiara. Her earrings matched the rawhide and feather necklace.

"So, how do we do the sage things?" Phoebe asked. We'd stopped by Cal's house on the way to pick up several bundles of sage that hung in his pantry, plus a rock bowl like the one he'd used in his ritual. Phoebe and I took one bundle each.

"I believe they call them smudge sticks. We light them, like so," I said, as I flicked my lighter to one end of each bunch. "Then, I think we wave it in the air and around objects to dispel any evil... ehm... spirits or feelings that might remain."

"Gotcha. Like a hazmat team," she said unfazed, giving her stick a test wave. "To clean up where all that meanness leaked out of those militia dudes' brains and contaminated the trees and rocks, right?"

She was trying to humor me without saying I was loony in so many words. "Yes, well. I know it must sound far-fetched."

"Jane, honey," she said as she put a hand on my shoulder, "if it's important to you, then it's important to me. I'm here for you. Now, show me what to do."

We decided to each take half the clearing, walking with our smudges held before us. Their aroma certainly made me feel better, regardless of its effect on the spirit realm. The cabin was in my half. I watched Phoebe from the door as she spent extra time fanning and fumigating the big limb of red maple leaves that hit Chalmers. She lifted the limb at various points and thrust the sage underneath, her lips moving in an angry way all the while. I doubt she was chanting.

Once done, we walked up the incline to *Tsali* and *Tseni*, set the sage in the rock bowl, and placed it at *Tseni*'s base near where the bullet meant for Phoebe had gone instead. Only about two-thirds of the bullet was buried in the trunk. I managed to pry the slug out with only a little digging. I stared at the small shallow hole and at the bullet, not flattened on impact as it should have been, but, except for the very tip, whole.

"Extraordinary." I considered telling Phoebe then of the cushioning gold light strands I'd seen. She interrupted my thoughts with a long sigh.

"You know what," she said, while she waved smoke over the tree's wound. "I believe things are a little different here. You know, like funny different. Like something or somebody from Up Yonder helped us out."

We looked at each other without speaking for a moment.

"I think you're right," I said.

I decided not to talk about what I'd seen during the shooting. Instead, I told her the story of *Tsali* and *Tseni,* how they lived, loved, and died, and of how Cal had sacrificed so much to keep them and this place safe. "Now it's my responsibility. I wanted to start things off right. That's why I wanted you to come with me." I held out my hand and said, "Here." I dropped the bullet into her palm. "For your memento table."

"Don't you want to keep it?"

"No, dear. It belongs to you."

"But you could start your own table."

I smiled. "Perhaps one day. But not with this. It's rightfully yours."

She giggled like a delighted child. She started to pocket it but on second thought reached down to a sage bundle and thoroughly smoked the bullet all round. "Okay. Now. There's something else I want to do."

She had brought along Smokahontas. I had mixed feelings about the presence of a gun at our little ceremony. She also set out a knife in a leather sheath decorated with a fringe of beads. Just as she'd done with the bullet, she incensed knife, sheath, and Smokahontas with smoke, raised them out over the clearing like a shaman, then out to *Tsali* and *Tseni,* then stepped between the trees and held the weapons out to the ceremonial grounds.

"With these weapons," she said in a solemn tone, "I Thee promise, to have and to hold them, to protect and defend this sacred place, from here on out."

She set Smokahontas and the sheath on a bed of leaves. To my astonishment, she took the knife and scraped a thin, shallow line across her thumb. It wasn't deep enough to bleed much, really, but a few drops of red did appear. She handed me the knife and looked at me expectantly.

"It's all right," she whispered, "I brought Band-aids. The antibiotic kind."

I took a deep breath and followed her example. We clasped hands, holding our thumbs together. Phoebe raised her eyebrows and looked to me, waiting. "Aren't you going to say something too?"

"All right then." I cleared my throat and gathered my thoughts. "I, Jane Thistle, also swear to defend this place, to the best of my ability, by whatever means necessary, for as long as I shall live."

"Amen, Blood Sister." Phoebe nodded her approval. She squinted her eyes and whispered, "By whatever means necessary. I like that. I pity the fool that tries to mess with us now."

A cool breeze blew through our hair as we walked between *Tsali* and *Tseni* and down into the ceremonial hall. Homer, who had been sniffing the bluff area with great interest, trotted around us and led the way.

The sun's last rays moved below the canyon's ridge. "It's almost time," I said, as we walked in the twilight. "We're headed to the benchlike boulders, just there in front of the water." We stepped over rivulets and mossy stones onto the flat rock dancing area, not far upstream from the Maiden's Tears.

I looked up over the rock wall before us to the panorama of open sky. Wisps of clouds moved quickly across the long rectangle of open space between the two high cliffs Cal had shown me. It would be a clear night. Perfect.

Phoebe put her things on a bench and sat. We set the rock bowl between us, letting the sage continue to burn. I took a few candles out of my canvas bag, set them up and, once lit, showed Phoebe the crude map Cal had drawn of the canyon floor.

"Here are the trees," I said, pointing to their drawing. Underneath, Cal had written *"Danitaga,"* a word I looked up earlier that means, "Where the Two Stand Together."

Phoebe's face caught odd shadows and her jewelry sparkled in the candlelight. "We're here," I said. "At the center of the hall."

"What are those weird words?"

"Noquisi Nvya. What the Cherokee called this place. Star Rock." I took out a spiral notebook I'd found in the number one box. "This is the legend handed down to Cal." I paused, holding the book closer to the flames to read his note written in small print. "He says, 'Some tribes believed that at death the people become stars. Like saints. Prayers go up for help. Special nights, they come down to earth.'"

Phoebe leaned closer in the candle's light. "We're not about to get hit by a UFO, are we?"

"No, of course not."

"Because then they might put us on the cover of *The Globe.* 'Alabama Ladies Conked on Head by Native Americans from Outer Space.' Not that I read those magazines. I just see them in the checkout lanes at the Pig."

Our laughter echoed in the canyon while we waited on full darkness. Phoebe gave me an update on the progress of her house. "All done. My new stove and refrigerator are beautiful. You've got to come see my new couch and chairs in the living room. I've had everything smoky either taken out or dry cleaned. Of course, I couldn't take Petey to the cleaners. I'm fumigating him good in a Tupperware bowl filled with a mixture of baking soda and cat litter.

Oh, and Jerry Nell and Donnie are coming over tomorrow night with some kind of special hooks or holder they're making for me. Donnie's going to put it on the wall so I can hang Smokahontas over my memento table. Hey, look. I believe it's fixing to happen."

She was right. I blew out our candles. The darkness deepened around us and a wondrous miracle of nature occurred before our eyes. The rock walls we faced disappeared and became the night sky studded with the glow of thousands of stars.

"Well, I'll say," Phoebe said. Her jaw hung open slightly, and for the first time, her voice held a note of awe on seeing the spectacular in simple nature.

Cal's notes explained the phenomenon. The tiny worms he'd shown me the day we walked through the canyon were known as *Arachnocampa luminosa,* a species rarely found outside of New Zealand. Though he called them glow worms, they were really insects that, in larval stage, glow in the dark. The larvae had a definite blue cast, shining like milky sapphires with a strong and steady light rather than flickering.

"They do look like stars," Phoebe said. She moved about the dance hall, at times leaning out, at others stepping close to the wall and looking straight up the cliff's face. "You can hardly tell the difference from the sky. It's like the stars come all the way down to the ground. Come look right here."

I obeyed. She had me follow her to several other vantage points, being careful not to touch the damp walls or sticky creatures, and to the ponds where we could see the glowing blue dots wavering underwater as well.

"Here. Take my picture," she said. I did so but wasn't optimistic that the glow worms would photograph well, with or without a flash.

"Okay." Phoebe clapped her hands together and rubbed her palms. "We seen it. We done it. Now, let's get back to civilization."

$\mathcal{A}$ LITTLE LATER IN MY KITCHEN, OVER COFFEE AND strawberry sponge cake, Phoebe and I discussed Riley's photos. I'd left them out on the table, meaning to look through them again.

"They're not bad kids," she said. "Just a little off. It's their age. They'll grow out of it." She flipped quickly from one picture to the next, hardly looking at them as she snapped one up, put it down smartly on the table, and picked up another one. "I just can't believe grown people believe in ghosts."

"But in the forest, you said...."

"That's different. Completely different. That was angels. This here," she said, while flapping one of the photographs back and forth between her fingers, "is pure foolishness. Taking pictures of ghosts, my foot. You can't take pictures of what you can't see. Or what's not there in the first place."

I stood to get more coffee. While up, I heard a soft tapping noise from the den.

Phoebe looked up. "What's that?"

"Maybe your squirrel theory needs looking into, particularly after my phone didn't work when you tried to call the police." I poured each of us another cup, set the carafe back in the coffeemaker, and stepped just inside the den to have a look. The tapping continued, though it took me a moment to see its source.

"It's only the wind blowing the rose bushes against the window," I said when I returned.

"I mean, why," Phoebe continued, "would somebody who has already passed over, left this world and is in a better one, want to hang around a nasty old graveyard with nothing there but dirt and weeds? Or a big old house like this one, no offense, when he could be someplace like Las Vegas or Gulf Shores? To get his picture taken by Riley and them girls? I don't think so."

The tapping grew louder and its rhythm increased.

"It just don't make sense to me," Phoebe said. "Because I'd want to be where the action is. Somewhere fun."

"Phoebe, dear, I'm sure that no matter where you are in the afterlife, in heaven or on earth, there will be no shortage of fun."

She smiled. "You think?"

"I'm certain." I reached over to the countertop to a package I'd wrapped earlier. "This is for you." It was just a small gift, a jewelry box in pretty colors I thought she might like.

"What's this for?" She leaned over and gave me a big hug around the shoulders.

"Just a little friendship gift. It's been wonderful having you stay with me. I shall miss you."

As I spoke, a movement in the air behind Phoebe's head caught my eye. Something was floating down behind her. I looked closer at the strange sight, trying to understand the impossibility of it, wrestling with it and finally comprehending.

"I think these are for you," I said. "Another farewell gift." We stared at the floor behind her where a little mound of red rose petals had softly fallen and come to rest.

Phoebe left hurriedly. I hardly had time to scoop up the petals and put them in her new jewelry box. Her only comment was, "Jane, you need to check your screens, hon. All kinds of stuff is blowing in here."

I followed her quick steps out the front to the porch, refraining from pointing out that all windows and doors were shut tight. Homer and I watched her car back out of the drive, and I waved goodnight as her headlights swept across the lilac bushes, the porch, and away down the road.

A STRAY RED PETAL LAY ON THE PORCH NEXT TO HOMER. I picked it up and touched the silky leaf to Homer's nose. As the chair beside him rocked slowly, I became aware of the smell of cigarettes and whiskey in the air. Homer snuggled closer to the chair. I knelt and rubbed behind his ears.

I rose and walked to the small table and chair I'd set up at the end of the porch, similar to the way Phoebe arranged hers with a lamp and a potted geranium. The lamp's light wasn't very bright, but strong enough to read by if I chose to. I'd set a sketchpad on the table for when I felt like drawing plants or birds I'd sighted.

"Cal," I said to the creaking chair, "I want you to know that everything is okay now. The land is safe. Rest easy, my friend." I looked again at the rose petal.

"Boo," I said into the night air, "I'm very happy you're here. I hope you don't mind that I'm your new . . . house person." I sat quietly, turning the petal in my fingers. "It was a lovely gift. Phoebe will cherish it, as I cherish the gifts you gave me. Perhaps I will make my own memento table after all," I said, thinking of the acorn and red maple leaf.

The evening sounds of crickets and night birds comforted me. I sat there until late in the night, sketching things from the last few days, pondering all the new, odd, wonderful images in my mind. Star Rock. Phoebe in her princess wear. Homer, whom I'd come to regard as the most beautiful and noble of beasts.

I was right to come here. My lifetime fascination with history, nature, and archaeology had all led me to this place. The surreptitious training of the Colonel's sneak attacks, shooting practice, my childhood ability in seeing ghosts, and the secret government work were all only practice for my real mission as caretaker of this forest. With a glance at my pad, I saw I'd drawn the carved reclining warrior, eyes half open, hand beside his knife.

After sketching a while longer, I looked up from my work. Homer had moved and now lay between the two rockers. And there, in the creaking chair, sat Cal. His head rested on the chair's back, his eyes were closed. He sensed that I was looking at him and turned toward me. With a wave and a smile, he let me know he was fine, just as he had in our first encounter.

I had another guest as well. In the other rocker sat a young man perhaps in his late teens with short brown hair. His round face and the spray of freckles across his nose added to the look of perpetual innocence. He wore denim overalls with a blue shirt underneath. He was bending down to Homer to give him a back rub.

The boy looked suddenly to me, as if caught doing something wrong. "It's all right, dear," I said in a soft voice. "Very nice to see you. And thank you for helping me find Mrs. Hardwick's note." With a shy smile, he looked at the floor. "She was absolutely right. You are a beautiful boy."

His cheeks flushed bright pink. He smiled and looked away again in embarrassment as his body shimmered, became shiny particles, and diffused into a rose tinted gold, like the evening sun sparkling on a lake, as he became transparent and vanished from sight.

Cal smiled in his bourbon-induced way, closing his eyes as his head leaned back again, and he disappeared as well. Both chairs continued to rock in a slow, steady motion. I wondered who else might stop by for an evening visit in the coming weeks and years.

"Homer, we shall have to invest in more rockers."

He raised his head, blinked his eyes, and set his chin on his paws with a sigh of contentment.

It is mine. I closed my eyes and breathed in the clean, fragrant air of the forest. Soon I would have many questions to ask and many decisions to make. Who will help me keep it safe? Dare I confide in anyone? How can I reconcile its need to be kept secret with the joy it would bring to others, just as it had done for me?

Will I be remiss if I don't allow any scientific studies or archaeological digs? Or was Cal right, that all should remain untouched and undiscovered? And most importantly, how can I ensure its future after my death? All must be carefully considered.

But not tonight. Tonight, I would smile as the mysteries on Cal's list of treasures danced like sugarplums over my head. Tonight, I would revel in the forest's quiet beauty. I would pray that peaceful dreams come to every creature, large and small, within its arms. And I would give thanks for the creation of all things, visible and invisible, in heaven and on earth, most especially this place, where the visible and invisible reside together, where my heart has found its home.

acknowledgments

Though there is no real Tullulah, many aspects of Jane's magical forest are based on a real place, Dismals Canyon, in the wilds of northwestern Alabama. You can compare my fantasy with the reality at their Web site, dismalscanyon.com, which tells all about the canyon's history and natural wonders. My sincere thanks to all who have played a part in preserving it through the years.

Certainly all characters herein are entirely fictional, and any likenesses to parents, aunts, uncles, sisters, brothers, cousins, nieces, nephews, in-laws, friends, dogs, acquaintances, or complete strangers whom I may have passed on the street in Alabama or elsewhere in the South is coincidental and, thank goodness, downright impossible, considering. The ghosts are real.

Phoebe's gun is named after a lady I used to work with. My thanks to Ron Harris for coming up with such a great nickname, to the rest of the Bellevue gang for perpetuating it, and to Lynette Jennings for being such a good sport, with a nod of sympathy going out to all exiled smokers.

Thanks to Brian Green for listening to my crazy ideas and for making weapon and tactical suggestions. Also thanks to Joe Collins and Mark Pfeiffer on the Weapons Info list for sharing their gun expertise.

Special thanks to Marian Young and Kelley Ragland for making Jane and Phoebe's foray into the world possible.

compas